THE

RULES OF
MATRIMONY

THE
RULES OF
MATRIMONY

A
MATCHMAKING
MAMAS ROMANCE

ANNEKA R. WALKER

PROPER ROMANCE

SHADOW
MOUNTAIN
PUBLISHING

To Amy Clawson

Your love, light, and influence still reach those who knew you.

Library of Congress Cataloging-in-Publication Data
Names: Walker, Anneka R., author.
Title: The rules of matrimony / Anneka R. Walker.
Description: Salt Lake City : Shadow Mountain Publishing 2025. | Series: Matchmaking mamas series ; 4 | Summary: "Lord Ian Reynolds, determined to avoid marriage after his father's betrayal, becomes entangled in a fake engagement with Miss Amie Tyler. Forced into a calculated union, Ian, with his political ambitions, and Amie, with her desire for independence, clash. Yet their affection grows. As love blossoms, they must decide whether risking their independence is worth pursuing a future together."— Provided by publisher.
Identifiers: LCCN 2024046122 (print) | LCCN 2024046123 (ebook) | ISBN 9781639933983 (trade paperback) | ISBN 9781649333636 (ebook)
Subjects: LCGFT: Romance fiction. | Novels.
Classification: LCC PS3623.A4343 R85 2025 (print) | LCC PS3623.A4343 (ebook) | DDC 813/.6—dc23/eng/20241004
LC record available at https://lccn.loc.gov/2024046122
LC ebook record available at https://lccn.loc.gov/2024046123

Printed in the United States of America
PubLitho

10 9 8 7 6 5 4 3 2 1

CHAPTER 1

London, England—April 1823

Ian met his father's glare with a fiery one of his own, showing the man less respect than he had probably ever received in his life, and set his hand down firmly on the black-walnut desk between them. "I repeat: I will not marry."

With the battle lines drawn between them, Ian's father leaned forward in an attack position. "Her name is Miss Margaret Foster. Call on her tomorrow and every day for the next fortnight. I want the banns posted and an announcement in the Society papers by the end of the month."

Ian usually faced his fears, met his challenges head on, and always confronted his foes, but the word *marriage* thoroughly rattled him. Especially when paired with his own name. Regardless, he refused to cower to his father like some vulnerable prey. "I'm already acquainted with Miss Foster. Her father is Lord Halbert, an idiot politician who never took the time to check his silly daughter. She is the last person on earth I will ever tie myself to."

Red was not his father's color, but it was better than the purple climbing up his neck and into his cheeks. "Do you question my authority? Ask anyone and they will tell you that I, Lord Kellen, am an earl whose vote in Parliament sways the majority of the House of Lords. Indeed, my decisions affect the state of this nation. I will not have my son's whims and fancies overriding my position in this family. You *will* marry Miss Foster. Discussion over."

Ian straightened and flat-out laughed. Did his father really try throwing the weight of his title at him? As though he could rule his family the way he did his so-called friends? "I do not question your authority, Father, but you must question mine. Ask anyone, and they will tell you that I, Lord Reynolds, am a viscount whose vote matters the most in respect to his own person. And, might I add, this decision affects the state of my entire life. My whims and fancies, as you call them, may differ from your own, but they are *perfectly* valid." Finally, the discussion could be over. He turned to leave, took several purposeful strides, and had his hand on the door handle, when his father threw out a warning that stopped him cold.

"You will marry, or the consequences will be great indeed." The deep, rumbling threat shook the ground under Ian's conscience. His father had been angry with him before, but this tone superseded them all. "Don't put anything past me, son." Fury punctuated each word. "I've had enough of your impertinence over the years, and I will not tolerate such insolence any further."

Ian knew what his father's derisive words meant.

Disinheritance.

Possibly disowning him altogether.

Ian had pushed his father hard this time, but was this what he had hoped to accomplish? A life without his father, certainly, but not a life without his home in Brookeside or one without his mother and the friends they kept. Right now, Ian would give up a great deal to avoid being a puppet under his father's control. Money meant little to him, but that his father would use it against him burned. His grip tightened on the door handle. With a hard yank, he threw it open. Biting down every last spiteful word he could think of, he marched away, appreciating the echoing slam of wood behind him.

He didn't stop his staccato march through the tiled corridors until he'd snatched his favorite D'Orsay hat from the butler's extended hands and stormed from the house. A liveried groom held Ian's horse at the ready. He accepted the reins and jammed his hat on his head, not caring if he ruined its shape.

Ride. He needed to ride. He was glad he had the foresight and had planned for it. Like all conversations with his father, this one invariably required fresh air afterward to cool his temper.

His black thoroughbred tossed his head, sensing Ian's agitation.

"Don't worry, Moses," Ian soothed. "You'll get your exercise."

An hour later, Ian slowed his bruising pace just outside of London as he neared a small country churchyard. He hadn't realized this was his destination, his primary thought to put distance between himself and his frustrations, but for better or worse, he was here now. Moss crept up between the cracks of the narrow church building, casting it with a green hue, and a crooked tree in front greeted him with its bent branches. He sighed, releasing some of his pent-up emotions in the elongated breath. It had been some years since he'd been this way, but it hadn't changed at all.

Tying up his horse, he entered the white picket gate and strolled around the side of the church to the graveyard. His feet moved without thinking until he reached the familiar marker of the late Lord Reynolds, who hadn't lived long enough to inherit the title of earl, as Ian's father had.

"Hello, Grandfather," Ian whispered. Exhaustion hit him like a brick wall, making every inch of him sag with defeat. He wasn't just tired in spirit; he'd not slept well since his father had begun harassing him day and night to marry. He'd always thought he'd have to fight off his mother, the queen bee of the Matchmaking Mamas, but his father? Ian preferred it when his father was too busy to remember his only child existed.

Without another thought, Ian dropped beside his grandfather's headstone and sprawled out on the crabgrass. He covered his face with his hat and attempted to forget all about his responsibilities as Lord Reynolds—particularly, his father's selfish edict.

Utterly infuriating.

Ian would never marry Miss Foster. Garish on the outside and insipid throughout.

He sighed again, this time without a specific cause. He needed a nap. Some nightmares were worse when awake. Fortunately, he'd unknowingly sought out the peace and quiet of a graveyard.

He shifted, the sun not quite warm enough to keep the dampness from soaking through his trousers. The peace was worth the sacrifice. Here he could enjoy the company of those who did not lecture incessantly about his duty and how he was failing the next generation. Only the dead could appreciate the beauty of solitude these days. Grandfather beside him, for example, made an excellent *silent* companion.

Ian reached over and studied the ground next to him. While he could never overlook the man's infidelity, he'd heard enough stories to know his grandfather had done good with his life too. He'd rallied investors for a volunteer-run hospital, a center for training physicians, and a needed dispensary for medicine, donating a tidy sum of his own money in the process. And all this was done before his death at five and thirty. Ian hoped to change the world, too, but he would not fall into the same pitfalls as the other men in his family. He would be wise enough to avoid the complication of love or marriage. He forced himself to relax. The faint chirping of birds and the slight breeze were the perfect combination to soothe his nerves.

This. This was what he needed.

"Good morning." A singsong voice filtered through the silence.

For heaven's sake, could a man not have three minutes strung together to himself? He lifted the brim of his hat and spotted a woman facing away from him. She was several feet away and speaking to a headstone, not him. He relaxed again, determined to fall asleep if it killed him.

"I know I came yesterday, but as you are the only one who ever misses me, you cannot be surprised that I came again."

Ian cringed. Did she mean to have an entire conversation out loud? The dead were far more popular than he had anticipated. He prayed she would not stay long. If she was a regular patron, as she claimed, she should respect that someone else had come here first.

"Mama is driving Uncle mad," the woman continued, her articulation notably genteel. "We've been here a fortnight, and already she is determined that we will be homeless. Oh, I know; she means well. I suppose I am not being charitable. My mind is all but consumed with our situation." The woman produced a heavy sigh, deep enough to match the ones he'd exerted. "*Cousin Robert* is back from his trip. I wouldn't admit this to anyone else, but Uncle still indulges Robert's every whim, and I'm afraid Robert is quite spoiled." Her voice turned desperate. "I'm even more afraid Cousin Robert sees me as his next prize to collect. What if Uncle gives *me* to him? Oh, Papa, what am I to do?"

A sympathetic chord struck in Ian's chest. He tipped his hat back, leaned forward on his elbows, and took a longer glance—this one with actual interest. The woman had hunched down but was not quite kneeling. The angle made it difficult to discern more than a few details about her. She was of marriageable age, with unruly, curly brown hair and wore a dark-brown dress covered by a rather ugly knitted shawl.

Many women found themselves in similar, pitiful situations, where their very future depended upon their relatives. It irked Ian to no end to hear of a young lady being abused. Blasted people. If the plight of the human race weren't his greatest weakness, he would despise more humans.

He massaged his brow. It was better not to know their problems because then he felt obligated to do something about them. It was the calling of the Rebels, he and his friends liked to say, to fight against the injustices of Society. But such battles were not without their drawbacks. No one could help everyone. It was impossible, if not exhausting. And this morning, Ian needed to help himself before he lost his mind over his father's controlling, aggravating ways.

Collapsing back against the prickly grass, he set his hat over his eyes once more. He would pay the young lady no mind. He was sleeping—the single, sure way to escape the weight on his shoulders.

More voices sounded in the distance. They were only passing by. Nothing he couldn't ignore too.

"Oh, fiddlesticks!" the young lady mumbled in low frustration. He heard a rustle of fabric, but he chose to ignore whatever had her flustered. Maybe she would finally leave and give him the peace and quiet he had come for. Her footfalls brought her closer to him. A gasp sounded a moment later, far too close for comfort.

"Sir? Sir?"

He squeezed his eyes shut. If he didn't respond, she would cease speaking to him. An *oof* sounded beside him, and he sensed more than felt that she had sat down.

This wasn't happening. Why must he forever be surrounded by people?

Make her go away!

This prayer, among other silent frustrations directed toward heaven, was not answered.

A weight hit his chest, and arms circled about him. His hat flopped off his face, and his eyes flew wide. What madness was this? She—a perfect *stranger*—was hugging him. And her blasted head was resting on his chest!

This wasn't the first time a woman had tried to place him in a compromising situation in the hopes of a good marriage, but there was no way this woman even knew who he was.

How desperate was she?

"Miss, please release me," Ian said.

The young lady's head swung up, and her piercing brown eyes, framed by thick lashes, dazed him. For a moment, he didn't react—didn't know how to. He blinked away what was surely a rush from raising his head so quickly and not because of her startling gaze.

Thankfully, his senses returned. "Miss, I must insist."

She seemed caught in the same daze. "I thought you were dead! I—I was listening to your heart." She sat up quickly, dropping her arms from his chest and taking with them a warmth he immediately missed.

Because his clothing was damp from the dew on the ground, obviously, and not because he missed her nearness. He shook his head. Honestly. Of all the ways to meet a person.

He really could have used that nap.

"As you can see," he said, sitting up, "I am far from dead." His heart, on the other hand, now that was negotiable. Although, at the moment, it was beating an erratic rhythm, as though he'd run a foot race . . . or had had a woman lay on his chest. It couldn't possibly be from those luminous eyes. No, his fatigue was confusing him.

She drew back a few more inches and visibly gulped. "Well, you never know. Someone could have dumped your body here. It is a graveyard." There was nothing fanciful about her voice. It was sure and resolute.

"Your imagination is impressive, but—"

"Shh!" The young lady pressed her finger up to his mouth. The voices from the road were growing louder. Anxiety flooded her eyes. Her response was intense enough that he allowed her to leave her finger poised on his lips.

It smelled like vanilla.

He loved vanilla.

But no one was allowed to touch his mouth, he reminded himself, and he snatched her finger away. "No one shushes me." He wasn't angry but astonished. He didn't know how to respond to her boldness. *He* was usually the bold one, and most were too intimidated to order him to do anything—except his father, of course. At least she hadn't been trying to trap him, as he'd first thought.

She frantically shook her head. "Oh, please don't speak. They'll hear you."

"Who are *they*?" he obediently whispered.

"My neighbors."

He supposed no one should see them like this together—alone—but this was clearly something more since she had reacted to their voices before she had even seen him. He drew a few quick conclusions based on his observations. She was in a desperate situation with her mother, lived with a volatile uncle, and was being forced to marry her cousin. In addition, her neighbors were some kind of scary creatures she hid from inside a graveyard.

Had she nothing good in her life to recommend her? Besides her enthralling eyes. Those were by far her best quality.

He humored her and remained quiet for several long minutes, in far too close proximity with her just beside him. Her head was angled so she could watch the road. His own eyes weren't on the road at all but on her. Since he couldn't see around Grandfather's headstone with her in the way, there was nothing else to look at.

Slight freckles dotted her otherwise fair skin just below each eye. Above her right brow was the slightest pull of a scar. Her slender, button nose led to well-shaped lips—the bottom slightly fuller than the top. He did not believe he had ever examined someone so closely before. She was pretty in a quiet way—except for those soul-filled eyes—which suddenly turned on him again.

"I believe they are gone," she said.

"Mmm—good." He sounded like an idiot who couldn't speak properly. But admittedly, he was a little taken back by her. Her clothes and thoughtless manner did not hide that she was well-bred. Did she not realize how unseemly it was to hide behind a headstone with a man? No, that thought likely didn't pass through many people's minds. Even so, he found her innocence appealing. She was not so obsessively tied to tradition that she could not think for herself. But the nonsense was over, and he had business to see to. Urgent business. "If you'll excuse me, I would like to finish my nap." He laid back down on the grass and fixed his hat over his face for the third time.

There. No more sad, brown eyes tricking his senses.

"You really shouldn't sleep here," she hedged, her gown rustling the grass as she *hopefully* stood to leave.

"There is no sign preventing me from doing so." He squeezed his eyes shut, annoyed that he could still see two pools of brown and their accompanying long lashes behind his closed lids. The memory was an astonishing thing and equally vexing.

She huffed from somewhere beside him. "Perhaps not, but this is an extension of the church."

"And?" His family paid for the upkeep of this particular parish. The least they could do was allow him a few minutes of peace.

"And you really shouldn't drink so much."

He frowned. "Who said anything about drinking?"

"Are you so far gone, you do not remember?"

His irritation grew. He was not the type to drink himself into a stupor. He valued his control too much. "The only matter I remember is my intention to sleep."

"You need more than sleep," she said. "You need to abstain from—" Another voice sounded in the distance. "Oh, fiddlesticks," she growled again, though this time it did not hold any fear. "I have to go."

"Good." He didn't mean to sound rude, but nor did he know what else to say. It wasn't exactly a proper place to converse alone with a woman, and despite his feelings on Society's silly constraints, he did believe in protecting a woman's reputation.

He peeked once more when he did not hear the sound of her footfalls. Surprisingly, she hadn't left yet. She danced back and forth, torn about something. He quickly lowered his hat again and pretended to breathe deeply. It was the kindest way he could think to hint at a dismissal.

The next thing he knew, he had grass stuffed into his mouth.

He sat up like a wind-up toy, sputtering. "For all that is good and holy!"

But the young lady was already running away. "You'll thank me later," she called over her shoulder. "Be careful not to overindulge in the drink next time."

Overindulge? Incredible nonsense. And why on earth had she shoved grass in his mouth? Was she trying to suffocate him? Was she so angry about her cousin that she thought to get rid of the male gender altogether? She was mad! He wiped at his tongue and spat on the ground.

This was yet another reason why he wouldn't marry. Never would his mother convince him that a woman could bring him happiness. Nor could his father convince him that one would benefit his position in Society. Ian was better off alone. No single pair of brown eyes would induce him to change his mind. Women were deceivingly pretty but unpredictably dangerous.

Who else would think grass was an appropriate weapon? There was a lingering sweet-and-cool sensation on his tongue now—an odd aftertaste for grass. He focused on his ire instead, because that woman was not sweet or cooling for his temper. His nap—or lack thereof—was permanently ruined. There was no way he could relax enough to sleep now.

This trip had solidified his plans. He was determined to refuse his father at all costs. Women were a nuisance and not worth the gamble of becoming emotionally involved with. His father had shown him how marriage was nothing more than a means to an end, and Ian would be more creative than that and think of a better alternative.

"Unbelievable," he muttered, glancing in the direction Miss Brown Eyes had fled. And to think, he'd actually felt sorry for her. He glanced at his grandfather's headstone, wishing someone had witnessed this insufferable moment. But the headstone prompted thoughts of his grandfather's marriage—riddled with problems. Of all his notable accomplishments, why could Grandfather not have been faithful to his wife? And how could he set his own son up for the same future?

The answers eluded Ian, but what he knew of the past was enough to confirm his choice. Heartbreak ran thick in their family's blood. Marriage was not for him.

CHAPTER 2

Amie Tyler had one goal in life: keep a roof over her head. Couldn't Mama try a little harder to cooperate? Telling Aunt last night that her hair was ugly was *not* trying. That sort of behavior was exactly why Amie had to insist Mama join her on a morning stroll, because leaving her at home, unsupervised, was no longer an option. Mama's penchant for trouble was threatening to undo their future—again.

"Must we walk so early?" Mama complained, fidgeting with her rather plain bonnet.

Plain was a word they had both become very familiar with. "Most of the gentry are still abed, so yes."

Mama's lips formed a pout. "What do you mean by that? Isn't the point of a walk to be seen?"

This sort of mindset had always led to trouble in the past. "Uncle Nelson doesn't like us to be seen, remember?" He had a standard to uphold in Chestervale and maintained strict rules for them. If they did not conduct themselves with the utmost decorum, he would abandon them too. After living with six different relatives, she and Mama were out of family who would willingly take them in.

Mama sniffed. "I never liked my husband's cousins."

Amie linked arms with her. "Liking something is a luxury we cannot afford."

Mama's pretty face turned more sullen. Amie bit back an exasperated reply that would surely canker a growing hurt. If Mama would learn to handle her emotions better, they wouldn't be so desperate. When they'd first left Chestervale after Papa's death and moved in with family in Reading, Mama had disliked a decorative side table and had donated it without permission. That had been the beginning of many offenses. She said and did the most absurd things when flustered. If they intended to keep appearances for the Nelsons' sake, Amie had to keep her mother away from Society. Hence their early morning walk.

Amie stole a glance at Mama as they maneuvered around a lower-hanging branch in need of trimming and felt an ounce of regret at her harsh thoughts. She *was* a good mother—sweet and always attentive. As a daughter of a baronet, it wasn't her fault she had been raised with far more privilege than she could possibly expect to ever have again. She had married a gentleman, but not one who could support her in death. This, too, was not her fault, nor that Amie had been born a daughter and not a son who could inherit. But even so, sometimes Amie wondered if Mama was sabotaging their situations on purpose.

"Are you certain we shouldn't return home and walk a little later?" Mama asked. "Not a soul is out, and at your age, you should be paraded about during a sociable hour to catch a man's eye."

Amie suppressed a laugh since Mama was being completely serious. A walk wouldn't suddenly make a man interested in her after all these years of figurative famine. To keep her smile hidden, Amie pretended to adjust the simple bouquet of poppies in her arms that she had purchased the day before. "Today's walk is to visit Papa, remember? The graveyard was rather crowded yesterday, and I prefer to visit with some semblance of privacy today."

Crowded was a bit of an exaggeration. There had been one man. A drunk lying around midmorning *in a churchyard*, of all places. She hoped the mint leaves had helped him settle any upset stomach known to follow a drink. It was a good thing she had had some on hand to give to her neighbor. The last thing she wanted was to find the contents of his stomach dirtying up one of her favorite places. She did not recall Chestervale being the sort of town where drunks were allowed to sleep in respectable places. London was growing too big and spilling over its lack of morals onto their streets.

"I wish you wouldn't go to the graveyard every day," Mama said. "I do not think it proper for a young lady to be seen there so often."

Perhaps not, but they hadn't lived close to Papa's grave in years, and Amie was making up for lost time. "It is a good thing everyone is asleep, then. In any case, we cannot miss it this time. It's been eleven years today since Papa died."

They rounded the corner to the churchyard, and Amie barely withheld her groan. For there stood the Peterson sisters—the worst of the worst gossip mongers. They were hardly older than Mama and even more troublesome.

"Fiddlesticks." They excelled at provoking just about everyone with their cynicism and hypocrisy. Life did like to laugh at her. "What are they doing awake at this hour?"

"What are any of us doing awake?" Mama asked in return.

The sisters stood beside a grand carriage Amie did not recognize and were on their toes, peering through the windows into a cab that must have stood empty. There appeared to be a seal on the door, signifying the owner as a significant person, which had no doubt lured the two women from their beds. The driver sat tight-lipped and resolute and would not converse with them. Smart man.

Tugging on her mother's too-thin arm, Amie made a desperate attempt to pass by the sisters unnoticed. Mama did not care for them either since they made her extremely nervous, and she gave a nod of agreement. Fortune smiled upon Amie and Mama—a rare occurrence—and they made it to the gate of the churchyard without being spotted. Amie shut the gate behind them, not a creak sounding even though she knew such an effort would not keep anyone out who had the mind to follow.

The churchyard was not grand in size. It was a simple, grassy garden with one path that led to the church and a second that led to the graves on the side of the building. When they rounded the church, a woman Amie did not recognize stood in front of a headstone, her face lined with sadness. She was neither old nor young, but rather, her appearance was timeless and her clothes nothing short of exquisite. Amie's heart constricted. Loss touched everyone—rich or poor. She had never been very good at seeing anyone grieving or depressed.

At least it was not the drunk man again. She had been unable to stop thinking of *him*. What had sent him into such a sorry state? It must have been an awful matter for him to end up asleep beside the dead.

Amie pulled her mother to a stop at Papa's grave and sneaked another glance at the stranger. "Excuse me for a moment, Mama." Unable to restrain herself, she set one flower out of her bouquet on Papa's grave before leaving Mama's side and walking toward the grieving woman.

Mama's eyes followed Amie, but Mama remained behind.

"Pardon my interruption." Amie stepped up beside the stranger. "Would you take my flowers to set on the grave you are visiting?"

The woman blinked her watery eyes. "What a sweet offering, but I mustn't take them when you clearly brought them to decorate a grave of your own."

Amie would not be dissuaded. "I know it cannot erase the hurt, but I find the act of leaving something brings me comfort." She extended the flowers and set her hand on the woman's arm. Touching a stranger was frowned upon, but grief was a universal language and eased the gap of introduction and manner. "My father is just over there, and he receives flowers often enough that he won't mind."

The woman glanced at Amie's hand with a look of surprise, but an appreciative smile bloomed on her face. She reached to accept the flowers. "Thank you."

Amie gave a slow nod. "I hope happy memories find you."

The woman's eyes tightened, and her lips gave an almost imperceptible tremble. "You are very kind."

Amie shook her head. "It's nothing. Just a few flowers."

"It's not nothing. I am hesitant to admit it, but I had a sudden yearning to not be alone just now. Your presence brought me comfort."

"I am pleased I could be of assistance, then."

The woman's expression grew thoughtful. "I meet a great deal of young ladies, but I imagine very few of them approaching me with such guileless intentions. Truly, I must thank you again."

Amie produced a small, humble smile and retreated back a step.

"Wait," the older woman put out her hand. "I want to return the favor, if I can. Is that your mother there?"

Amie nodded.

The woman wiped away the traces of moisture from her eyes. "I should like to meet her."

Amie hesitated. But she loved Mama and shouldn't be ashamed to introduce her to this fine woman. So long as nothing made Mama nervous or made her feel lesser in any way, surely she would not have cause to say anything untoward. Amie stepped away to collect her mother.

"What is it, Amie?" Mama hissed, looking around her shoulder at the stranger. "Who is that woman? You cannot know her."

"I don't know her, but she requested to meet you."

"She did?" Mama's brows rose, measuring the woman from top to bottom. "Her person is rather fine." Mama straightened with an air of self-importance that Amie supposed came from being raised in the upper classes of the gentry. Such airs were often found offensive by others who knew Mama to be naught but a penniless widow living off the charity of her relatives. "Of course she wants to meet me," Mama said. "Lead the way, Amie."

Amie grimaced inwardly, but she led Mama past the few headstones between them and the woman without saying a word to the contrary.

Amie motioned to Mama beside her. "May I present my mother, Mrs. Tyler, and . . . Forgive me, I do not know your name."

"Lady Kellen."

"A lady?" Her mother's voice pitched high, clearly impressed. She patted Amie's shoulder a few times too many and hissed loudly in her ear, "She's a *lady*, Amie." As Mama was once a respected matron in the community, status was extremely important to her.

"It is a pleasure to make your acquaintance, Mrs. Tyler." Lady Kellen smiled with amusement. "And you must be Miss Tyler?"

"Miss Amie Tyler." Amie dipped a curtsy.

"Deeper," her mother chided under her breath but loud enough for their present company to overhear.

Amie lowered herself farther, her cheeks warming.

Lady Kellen did not withdraw in disapproval but let her smile widen. "I insisted on meeting you, Mrs. Tyler. I am so touched by your daughter's kindness toward a perfect stranger. It is a rare sight."

"She is a good girl." Mama beamed. "Some say she is a wallflower, but I do not believe it. She has everything to recommend herself." No one could say Mama wasn't proud of her, though Amie had done nothing to deserve it outside the bonds of blood. She had no real talent for anything. And she *was* a wallflower.

Lady Kellen complimented Mama's bonnet—a difficult task since there was little beauty in it—and the two of them began chatting away about ribbons and fabrics. Nothing in Mama's behavior now left anything for an onlooker to criticize. They turned toward the grave Lady Kellen had just been standing in front of, with Amie trailing behind in awe.

"Might I introduce you to my deceased family?" Lady Kellen pointed to the headstone she stood in front of. It read *Lord Reynolds*. "He died before I met him. You might think it strange that I mourn his death, and rightly so, but his influence has played a great role in my life. I wish I could have known him. Perhaps if I would have, I might have understood so much more about my present situation."

Mama gave a distinguished curtsy to the lifeless stone. Amie did not know how to respond. She did think it strange that Lady Kellen would mourn a man she didn't know, but Amie also understood how a single death could affect so much of one's life. She, too, dipped her head out of respect.

Lady Kellen set Amie's flowers on Lord Reynold's grave. "Family is everything, is it not? Your daughter is a credit to you, Mrs. Tyler. If

I should have had a daughter, I would have hoped for her to display such genuine goodwill toward others as yours has."

Mama smiled. A real smile—one Amie had not seen for years. "Amie is my treasure."

"We will leave you to have a moment of privacy." Amie had simply done what her conscience bid her to do and was uncomfortable with such high praise. "Come, Mama, we should get back."

Lady Kellen lifted a hand in parting. "Good day to you both. I will not forget your kindness." She flipped a pretty dark-blue veil over her face, one no doubt employed for privacy and to hide her emotions. Amie smiled back at her before she and Mama took the path to the gate.

"What a gracious woman, did you not think?" Mama unlatched the gate for them.

An affirmative was on the tip of Amie's tongue when the Peterson sisters pounced.

Drat. Amie had forgotten about them.

The older spinster, Miss Peterson, was the worst of the two, a pencil of a woman, with her gray hair pulled back tight on her scalp. "Mrs. Tyler, Miss Tyler, what are you two doing up at this ghastly hour?" she asked.

Another famous Peterson statement, recognizable by its hypocrisy.

"On our way home," Amie said at the same time her mother answered, "Visiting the graves." Amie did not correct their mismatched statements but tugged her mother a few steps farther.

Miss Peterson stepped in front of them with a scowl. "Visiting your dead father? That man was useless, and you should be glad he is gone. He left you with nothing, and you were forced from your home like common beggars."

Amie tugged her mother again, but it was no use. She would not budge.

"Common? Amie, did she say common?" her mother asked.

Gritting her teeth, Amie pasted on a fake smile. It seemed a conversation—or should she say, an exercise of patience—must occur, but she would do her best to keep it short. "Regardless of our misfortunes, we are happily situated, Miss Peterson, but thank you for your concern."

Miss Peterson harrumphed and looked down her long nose at Amie. "Happy, indeed. You have finally returned only to be a burden to your relatives." She turned her sharp gaze back to Mama. "You should have had a son. He could have provided for you."

Amie felt Mama's back straighten beside her and quickly inserted a response before Mama could. "Thank you again for another insightful observation, Miss Peterson. We shall be on our way now."

Another tug and no movement from Mama.

"Sister, if either of us had a daughter, she would be married by the time she was eighteen."

The younger, Miss Matilda Peterson, nodded. "Indeed, sister. How old is Miss Tyler again?"

"I am four and twenty," Amie said, her careful patience waning. She had felt young just yesterday. She was aging by the moment. "Come, Mama, Aunt will be missing us."

"If—" Mama's reply was cut off by Miss Matilda's gasp.

"Four and twenty?" Miss Matilda said.

Miss Peterson clucked her tongue. "Why, she is firmly on the shelf."

The hurtful words stung, no matter their truthfulness.

Mama trembled beside her, and this time Amie was not quick enough to speak first. "It takes a spinster to recognize another spinster, does it not?"

Amie barely withheld her groan. No matter their impertinence, the Peterson sisters had money and a position in Chestervale, and Mama shouldn't offend them. It would get back to their Aunt and Uncle, and then what?

Miss Peterson's nostrils flared. "Why, I have never heard anything so rude."

Mama opened her mouth to deliver another setdown, but Lady Kellen's timely appearance made for a welcome distraction. She slipped through the gate and crossed over to them. She took Mrs. Tyler's arm, leaned over and whispered something to her—no doubt an embarrassed goodbye . . . and a particularly long one at that.

Amie thought she caught the word *favor*. And something about *family name*. Lady Kellen caught Amie watching her, and with a twinkle in her eye, delivered a promising smile her way. The driver alighted from his seat and swung the carriage door ajar. Lady Kellen hurried toward him, and with a strong hand, he whisked her inside.

As soon as the carriage door shut, Miss Peterson's shrewd eyes pinned Mama in place. "*Who* was that?" she hissed. "A woman of consequence, no doubt, but I cannot abide veils. Only the guilty should want to hide their face."

Mama did not answer her question. Instead, she asked one of her own. "What were you saying about my daughter being on the shelf? Upon my honor, she is not." Mama's voice was oddly firm.

"Mama, please," Amie begged. They needed to hurry home so they could begin writing letters of apology, not stay here and make matters worse.

Miss Peterson batted a hand in the air, unfazed. "We have already established that Miss Tyler has reached the age where it is obvious she is unwanted by any men. Now who was that strange woman? I must know."

Mama cleared her throat and spoke louder. "My daughter is not an old maid, because . . . because she is engaged to be married."

Silence.

Utter silence.

And perhaps a little choking on Amie's end. She needed air and fast!

"Engaged?" The Peterson sisters said at once.

"Mama!" Amie finally sputtered, clutching her throat. Shock reverberated through her ears down to her scuffed half boots. "What are you saying?"

"Not now, Amie." Mama shushed her, then as if she were announcing to the entire street, declared loudly, "My daughter is *engaged* to Lord Reynolds."

W-who was Lord Reynolds?

Amie's eyes widened past their conceivable size. Oh, no. No, no, no. That was the name etched on the headstone Lady Kellen had pointed to! The world tilted underneath Amie's feet. She could faint. Mama had announced Amie's engagement to a dead man!

"Lord Reynolds?" Miss Peterson repeated, her voice as incredulous as if the apparition of Amie's dead betrothed had appeared directly in front of her.

Mama's mouth opened and closed several times like a fish before she settled on a nod.

"Mama!" Amie scolded, begging with her eyes for her mother to confess the truth.

Lady Kellen's carriage rolled forward, ignorant of the scandal erupting behind it. What would the kind woman say to having her family's name abused? And worse, tied so shamefully to Amie?

"Why are we just hearing of this? It's all rather shocking," Miss Peterson said, and Miss Matilda nodded.

"It was a secret," Mama answered succinctly. "And now it is not." She justified her lie as calmly as one would describe the weather.

Amie covered her face with her hand, the world spinning behind her closed lids. It had happened again. Her mother's pride and nerves had gotten the better of her. But this! This was by far her worst mistake yet!

Miss Peterson beckoned Miss Matilda to follow her. "We must tell everyone. No one will believe it." The Peterson sisters rushed away in the opposite direction the carriage had gone.

Amie's heart pounded, fear tightening around her ribs and threatening to burst. "Mama, how could you have done something so foolish?" She was too upset to even produce tears.

"Forgive me, Amie, but whatever you do, do not correct them. Your reputation depends on everyone believing us."

"So does our living situation!" Amie did not get angry easily, but her fears added to her mounting frustration. "What will Uncle think of this?"

"He will congratulate you the same as everyone else." Her mother had the gall to look satisfied with herself. "You might think me foolish, but I think it is the best day of our lives. What good news to have you engaged!"

Amie would laugh if she could, but she found absolutely no humor in the situation. "But it's all a lie. Eventually, people will wonder why a suitor never visits and why I never wed."

Her mother tilted her head as though a glimpse of reality passed in front of her for a brief moment. "We will find a different suitor before that happens. You are a special daughter, remember? Try not to worry, and trust your mama."

Trust Mama? What Amie needed was not trust but a miracle. Once her aunt and uncle learned of her mother's deceit—and they would—nothing would stop them from sending Amie and Mama away. With no money or connections left, there was nowhere else to go.

They would be homeless.

CHAPTER 3

ANOTHER DAY, ANOTHER ARGUMENT. IAN stalked away from Father's office. This time he didn't have his horse at the ready for a quick escape. This particular attack had been an ambush.

His mother stood at the end of the corridor, fussing over another bouquet guilt-purchased by Father to make himself feel better for his transgressions. The bright blooms overflowing from the top of the French-style console were an antithesis to the giver's personality.

When Mother looked up, her calm facade did not quite hide the tension Ian knew lay just beneath the surface. She normally did not come to London for the Season, not with the regular rumors of Father's mistresses circling about, but she had made an exception to keep the peace between him and Father. She was single-handedly the greatest reason Ian had no desire to marry. Father had neglected both of them for the majority of Ian's life, and Ian would never ruin a family like his father had.

Mother picked up a pile of letters from the edge of the table, but her attention was wholly on him. "Ian . . ."

"Don't you dare tell me that you agree with Father." He rooted himself in front of her, refusing to budge on the matter. "I cannot relent, even for you."

Mama's rigid posture did not even flinch at his harsh tone, and she employed a firm but gentle one in return. "Your father hopes this marriage will secure your future. He wants the best for you."

"He wants the best for himself." How was it not obvious to her?

"You have only seen the worst in him for years now, Ian. He's trying so hard to connect with you, and I do wish you would make an effort in return." She clutched the letters to her chest in a pleading motion.

"If this is his attempt to forge a relationship with his only son, he should have done better than to try to force Miss Foster on me."

Mother sighed. "Miss Foster is a spoiled child, but she will certainly provide the needed political alliance your father seeks for you."

"Exactly my point." How his mother could love that man, Ian would never know. "I will not marry her."

Mama nodded. "I should hope not. I had higher expectations for my only daughter-in-law."

Ian rocked back on his feet, the shock of Mama's words effectively cooling his temper. "Does Father know you object?"

She reached out and fingered a rose petal. "He does so much for me, I can hardly make a fuss."

Ian ground his teeth together. A woman shouldn't have to live off a pile of letters every Season. Father didn't do enough of what mattered. Ian's hand slid to his waist and forced his anger to a simmer. "Then, you must know that Father intends to cut me off."

"I thought as much." She dropped her gaze, revealing a glimmer of hurt. "There is one alternative."

Ian folded his arms across his chest. "Anything is better than a union with Miss Foster."

"I hope you mean that, because the only solution is to marry someone else first."

His jaw dropped. He should have known his mother would turn to her matchmaking methods to conceive a solution. Of course it made sense to her to solve a problem of an arranged marriage with a second arranged marriage. "Utterly ridiculous. I have no intention of marrying. The house and title can fall to Cousin Edwin. I will commandeer the Dome as my home and live out my life in peace." The one-roomed Grecian temple on their Brookside property would be his castle—and he its bachelor king. He maneuvered around his mother and attempted to stalk away, but Lady Kellen followed after him, two of her soft footfalls sounding to every one of his.

"Cousin Edwin has recently been declared mad. The house and title will go to Mr. Balister, your second cousin."

Ian stopped so suddenly, he had to steady himself with the wall, narrowly missing a portrait of the late Lord Kellen's dog. "Mr. *Howard* Balister? The idiot who burned down his last house in a drunken rage and is now living with his mistress? I heard his wife and children fled to Scotland." Ian had tried to find the family in order to send funds, but they were yet to be located. Seven. The man had seven children. "Why has no one declared *him* mad?"

"What can I say? We have a family history of madness."

Ian pursed his lips. "After this morning, I feel the same lunacy threatening to take me over." He massaged his eyes with his thumb and two fingers. "I'm not giving our lands and titles to Balister." He growled under his breath. "I am not agreeing to anything, and I cannot even believe I'm considering this, but tell me who you have selected as a candidate to rival Miss. Foster."

She shrugged. "I have no one in mind at present—at least not someone who could contend against Miss Foster."

Ian opened his eyes and stared at his mother. "You have no one in mind? You've planned the marriages of all my friends and not even spared a thought for your own son? I cannot decide if this pleases me or distresses me."

"I adore you, son. You are my entire world. But I must say, you are not the easiest person to find a match for."

"How can you say that?" He gave a short laugh. She was right. He couldn't disagree.

"You are a good man, extremely generous and loyal."

"But?"

"But you lack a certain softness that would make for an ideal companion."

"Softness?" He chuckled. "Isn't that for the weak?"

"I think you mean meek, Ian. The women might chase after you at the balls, but marriage is far more than a dance. You are all passion and no restraint when it comes to your words—a great attribute for politics but not for a husband. And . . ." She waved her hand like the rest didn't matter.

"And?" He wasn't trying to make his day worse, but something made him press.

Mama shrugged. "And except for your closest friends, you are rather intimidating. But you are a good, valiant son to me, and that is all a mother can ask for."

Ian blinked at the stark list of his faults set so efficiently before him. No matter how she tried to disguise it with interspersed compliments, it was a mite humbling. He placed a hand on his hip and quipped, "Could you say it any plainer?"

She shook her head. "I would rather not waste time with specifics. Your father is taking me in the barouche to Hyde Park."

If this was a political move for his father, a few carriage rides wouldn't convince the public of his devotion to his wife. How could Mama not resent his piddling efforts, as Ian did?

"If you agree to this alternative," Mama continued, "we will have a great deal to do and not a lot of time to accomplish it. You will have to trust me. I will find you someone sweet and good-natured, someone who will complement your life goals."

Could he really marry someone? No, he hadn't the taste for it— nor, clearly, the aptitude. His friends had been a lucky few to have found love, but the odds were against him. He'd incur misery. "Never mind, Mama. I will think of another way to get back into Father's graces. You will be relieved to know, it will not consist of ruining some poor debutante's life by an engagement to the hopeless Lord Reynolds. And it certainly won't include Miss Foster."

"But, Ian—"

Ian cut her off by reaching over and patting her arm. "There, there. Distract yourself by matching up another unsuspecting fool." He shivered. He had almost been foolish enough to leg-shackle himself. He was in a real dilemma, no doubt. How could he make a difference in Society without his inheritance and position of influence? His father might not care a whit about Ian's ideas, but after Father died, Ian would take his place in Parliament. Ian couldn't let his pride ruin his opportunities to make a wave of change in the world. It was his dream. His passion. People—good people—needed their voices heard. There had to be another way out.

He just couldn't think of it.

Mama held out one of her letters before he could step away. "Read this before you decide on anything."

He frowned and accepted the missive. The familiar seal of Lord Felcroft was already broken from his mother's previous reading. Their good family friend could have nothing to say that would sway him on the subject. He scanned the letter with little patience. "Congratulations on the upcoming nuptials of your son, Lord Reynolds." Anger seethed from his chest, and he shoved the paper back into his mother's hands. "How did Father get this out already?"

"I think you ought to keep reading."

He eyed her sideways and reluctantly took the paper back. "The name *Miss Amie Tyler* is on everyone's lips. We look forward to an introduction!" It was signed by Lady Felcroft—a woman he had known all his life to be upstanding and sincere. She was not in the business of passing on random gossip. "Who is Amie Tyler?"

"Don't you know?"

"I have never heard the name in my life. Why would Lady Felcroft think I am marrying a Miss Amie Tyler?"

"That is a question you need to find out for yourself." His mother handed him a second letter. One from his best friend, Paul. "The messenger brought it here when they discovered you were not at your townhome. It must be urgent."

He took it and tore into the letter.

I heard the most outlandish rumor of your engagement. I knew at once it could not be true. Let me know if you need my assistance in rectifying it.

Paul was the best barrister Ian knew, and Paul's skills had been useful on more than one occasion. Surely Ian did not need his help absolving a mere rumor.

"Of all the ridiculous notions," Ian said. "Maybe if we ignore it, it'll go away."

Mama shook her head. "You cannot have gossip spreading like this. If you don't put an end to it straight away, you will have to do right by her."

He coughed. "Marry a stranger? This is worse than one of *your* matches."

"The sooner you fix this, the better. These things have a way of getting out of hand. Hire an investigator and find her. You and your father could use a few days apart. Just be back by next Friday when you are to meet with Miss Foster for dinner."

"Heaven forbid I miss it," he grumbled.

"Do not make light of your father's stubbornness," Mama reminded him. "He means well, bless his soul, but he *will* follow through."

"Don't I know it. Try not to worry overmuch. I will think of something." He leaned over and kissed his mother on the cheek. "But you may pray for my sanity. It might not be intact upon my return."

Not a half hour later, Ian was riding toward the Western side of London to the office of a private investigator he had used a time or two before by the name of Harry Boyles. He wasn't much to look at, with his wrinkled clothes and poor hygiene, but he was a thorough worker. His office was just up from Fleet Street. Ian turned his horse to cut through a side block and nearly cursed under his breath. A sizable crowd filled the road, preventing him from riding any farther.

He should have turned around, but a woman's scream stopped him. A wave of curiosity mixed with urgency persuaded him to direct his horse closer. A grizzly man outside the butcher's shop gripped a young woman roughly by her arms. She fought against him, but by her gaunt figure and young age, no more than sixteen or seventeen, there was no way she would win against the much larger man.

"Someone find a constable!" the rough man shouted. By his blood-stained canvas apron, Ian judged him to be the owner of the meat establishment. "I've caught a thief!"

More shopkeepers piled onto the street, and bystanders edged closer to the scene.

"What did she take, Mr. Allen?" an older woman demanded from the back.

Mr. Allen dragged the woman forward. "Why, she tried to take off with me cart of meat. It's worth fifty pounds and not a farthing less!"

"Fifty—!" Ian sputtered under his breath. That was enough to serve as a death sentence. He brought his horse to a stop, quickly swinging his leg over the side. This wasn't his day.

"He's wrong!" the young thief cried. "I was 'ardly takin' enough for me and my family. I swear it!"

"A liar and a thief," Mr. Allen said. "I'll see you hang for this!"

"The noose is the only way," another shopkeeper said. "We don't need more scum on the streets robbin' our wares."

It was a regular mob of store owners against a starving girl. Ian had one chance to do something about it, and he needed to do it right. "Sir," Ian shouted to the butcher, hoping to be heard over the arguing and scuffle in front of him. "Sir, you have my servant." His words were lost in the chaos.

"Drag her to the Old Bailey!" the older woman cried.

"Dirty thief ought to learn a lesson right proper," growled another.

Ian shoved his way through the onlookers, urgency sweeping over him. "Release her!"

His strong voice caused the butcher and the thief to momentarily still.

"Unless you're the constable, you'd better shove off." The butcher growled.

"This woman is my servant." Ian pointed to the unkempt young lady, her scraggly blonde hair strewn half across her face.

The butler seethed, his cheeks turning purple. "This woman is a no-good thief. Didn't I tell you to shove off?"

Ian folded his arms across his chest and narrowed his eyes to match the man's attempt to intimidate him. In his sternest voice, Ian demanded, "If you don't release my servant, you will be the one who pays the consequence. This meat was meant for me, but I forgot to educate the newest member of my staff on the correct way to purchase it." He faced the poor girl, her pallor the familiar chalky nature of the half-starved. "You must give the shopkeeper the correct address and payment before you take the meat next time."

A man behind him laughed high and sharp.

Ian didn't exactly have time to finesse his rescue, so his bumbling efforts would have to do. Ignoring the onlookers, Ian's gaze moved to the furious butcher, who was not at all amused. "She was never trained properly," Ian explained. "I accept full responsibility." Ian pulled out his coin purse and unrolled several banknotes and overpaid the man—mostly to shut him up. He did not believe for a minute that the young woman was attempting to steal an entire cart of meat in broad daylight. It was a good thing his father hadn't cut him off financially yet, because this was a costly little rescue.

The butcher spat on Ian several times with his incessant tendency to speak through his crooked, gritted teeth as he spouted his indignations, and then the man finally released the young lady into Ian's custody.

Relief soared through Ian. Not once did the startled woman object, although there were plenty of others about them who cursed and complained how the rich controlled the world. They were both right and wrong. Money couldn't buy everything, but today it *had* been essential.

He set the young lady on his horse and walked to the end of the street and around the corner, leading his horse by the reins. Then he stopped abruptly and looked up at the woman. All this time, she'd said nothing.

"What's your name?" Ian asked.

"Edna."

"Do you work hard?"

She glowered at him as if he'd just insulted her. "I do."

"Are you prepared to make an honest woman of yourself?"

Her face marginally softened. "Ye're not going to sell me to the brothels?"

Maybe his mother was right, and he did look mean. "No, I am not going to sell you."

Her eyes widened, and she smiled with relief. "Thank ye, sir. Oh, thank ye."

"Well, can I trust you?" It seemed like a silly question to ask a woman who had been caught thieving.

"I am an 'onest woman, I swear it. I used to be a lady's maid and good one, too, until my parents died of the fever. But 'ard times can turn even the 'onest into the desp'rate."

That he was well aware of. Every time he ventured out of Mayfair, another sobering image engraved itself into his mind. "Do you realize you would have hung for the amount of meat Mr. Allen accused you of stealing?" The criminal law of England had a harsh system, and hanging was the consequence for far too many crimes—hence the infamous nickname "the Bloody Code."

"I had to do it, sir." Edna's face crumpled. "I would 'ave died without it. Me and my sisters."

There was a whole family of them, was there? Did they all look as hungry and war-torn from surviving life on the streets as this one? He ran his hand down the smooth leather reins of his horse and gave a nod. "The job is yours, then. As my servant." He would have his housekeeper decide the best place for her and her sisters. He was fortunate to have control of his staff at his townhome and hunting box, because his father would probably see this as another of his many weaknesses. He pointed a stern finger at Edna. "If I so much as see you pocket a spoon, you're out of luck. I can be generous, but I won't be a fool."

Her eyes widened further, disbelief etched onto her every feature. "Bless you, sir."

He waved off her thanks and led his horse to a stall selling meat pies and bought some for her and her family. She ate hungrily, thanking him profusely.

Instead of pride in his heroic effort, he felt undeserving of her gratitude. She was one of many who needed help. How many innocents had lost their lives at the Old Bailey only blocks away? At least today, Justice, whom Ian generally respected, hadn't taken Edna. The Bloody Code had enough people swinging in the gallows; it had no need to take the life of a young woman doing everything to save her family.

But what was one person to hundreds of others who would not be so fortunate? Most weren't murderers or hard criminals. They were starving people who deserved a prison sentence or deportation for their petty crimes before the loss of their life. One humbling glance at Edna and his soul twisted inside him. Maybe it was his longing to take control of something when everything in his life seemed on the brink of falling apart, but never had he wanted to cry out for reform like he did in this moment. He yearned with everything in him to undo centuries of tradition and give England a better system. What little influence he had outside of Parliament, he would wield. Others would be spared too. He would make it his duty.

God help him, Justice would meet his sister, Mercy.

CHAPTER 4

IF THERE WAS ANYTHING WORSE than being engaged to a dead man, it was living in the same house with Robert Nelson. He sat across from Amie at breakfast, his blond hair fluffed several inches above his already high forehead and his beady eyes watching her eat her piece of toast, as though she were fattening herself up to be his next meal.

Uncle and Aunt had engaged Mama in a talk about wedding plans. How easily she lied about the details. Mama seemed quite content living in her dream world. But this wasn't the real Mama. This was what she had become after years of grief.

Amie glanced at Robert again, and his weaselly smile appeared. "Aren't you going to eat?" she asked just loud enough for him to hear.

"Your engagement has caused me to lose my appetite."

His dramatics might work on his parents, but they would not work on her. Still, she couldn't be angry with him. He didn't know any better. He was used to having everything he wanted. Soon he would put this childishness behind him. Barely withholding her exasperation, she said, "Go on, try your breakfast. You need your nourishment."

"I haven't the will, but I am helpless when you command me." He picked up his spoon and took a bite, all without taking his eyes off her.

Now that he was occupied in eating something, it was the perfect time to excuse herself. Mama and Aunt Nelson finished at the same time and stood as well. Aunt went straight to the drawing room to do her morning sewing like clockwork, and Mama took to the music room. The strains of the pianoforte soon filled the house. Music was Mama's greatest solace in the world, and her playing generally put Aunt straight to sleep.

Amie went to the corner of the drawing room and waited. Soon enough, Aunt had her head tipped back, and a soft snore purred through her nose. Amazing, since she had been awake for a mere hour or two yet, but Amie would not complain. She was eager to escape the house. Despite having already taken her walk to the grave-yard, she needed to be free from Robert's presence.

She turned to find Uncle striding toward her from the breakfast room.

"Do you know, Amie," Uncle said, stopping before her. "I am still put out that your betrothed did not seek my permission before secretly engaging himself to you."

She forced a smile. "It wouldn't have been a secret if he had sought your approval." It was wrong to play along, but she wasn't left with much alternative. She needed time to find another living arrangement before the truth came out.

"Exactly my point. And does he mean to?"

"I shall ask him when I next see him." Which would be never since he was long from this earth.

"And when shall that be?" Uncle had asked Mama this question a dozen times.

"I haven't the faintest notion. Men do as they please." She had done her best not to lie directly and tried to strictly omit the truth. There was nothing like stalling before the inevitable happened.

"I do not like it. Not one bit," he said. "Robert would have you as his wife, and he is quite determined."

The blood seeped from her face. She had seen this coming, but it still rattled her. She had been in denial thinking Robert would let it go. "But I—"

"I know, I know, you are spoken for. But these things can change. A woman has been known to alter her course before."

Her fingers shook, and she clasped them tightly in front of her. "My reputation, sir."

"Robert is a good man. You will have our family's protection."

"Forgive me, but I cannot." She spoke firmly, hoping to avoid any further pressing.

Uncle Nelson nodded and mumbled something about telling Aunt that he and Robert would be at his pub. By the time he left, not just her hands but her entire body, too, was shaking. She was not used to speaking back to her elders, but the idea of marrying Robert scared her more than all Mama's lies put together.

Amie waited by the drawing room window until she could see the men leave, then she slipped quietly past her sleeping Aunt and moved toward the front of the house. Amie took an apron off a hook by the servants' entrance and, with trembling fingers, tied it to her waist before pushing outside into the front garden. But she could not even look at the flowers to tend to them. When the fresh air did not bring a solution to mind, her breathing came faster, and she wrung her hands together. What was she to do?

"Oh, Miss Tyler!" Mrs. Jensen called, waving from her carriage.

Amie swallowed her problems long enough to greet her neighbor. "Mrs. Jensen, good day. How is your cold?"

"Better, thanks to your poultice recipe. I wanted to wish you congratulations on your upcoming nuptials!"

Amie brought her arm up to wave back, her smile weakening. Within an hour of Mama's announcement, the Peterson sisters had spread the news of the engagement throughout the entire town. It had been a single week, and if she were anyone important at all, all of England would have known by now. Being a nobody never had a more useful purpose.

But even a nobody had to take care of herself. With Mrs. Jensen out of sight, Amie started pacing in front of the flowerbeds. She needed a house and distance from her cousin. And fast! Her hands went to her hair, no longer safe since she had neglected her bonnet. "What to do? What to do?" she said to herself as frustration curled out from her fingertips and she pulled at her hair.

A giant of a horse rode up, a handsome stranger sitting regally atop it. He pulled the black beast to a quick stop in front of the walk, the horse rearing up just enough to make her reflexively step back, although she was a safe distance from the road.

His eyes set on her, and his mouth turned down into a frown.

Wait, this was no stranger. She had seen him before. It was none other than the drunk from the graveyard. The last time she had seen him, he hadn't been too happy with her. She ducked her head before he could get a good look at her and pretended to fuss with the roses. She had been invisible to Society her entire life. Was it wrong to suddenly wish for five more minutes of the same bad luck?

CHAPTER 5

REINING IN HIS HORSE, IAN took his first glimpse of the Tylers' unremarkable brick home. There was nothing significant about the small, simple estate, even down to the plain door. He had nearly passed it by. But it was the third house on the lane, just as Boyles, his investigator, had explained. Since Miss Tyler's family had been affluent before being forced on the mercy of their relatives, and resided a stone's throw from London, Boyles been able to locate her in less than three days. He had also reported a brief explanation of her situation, with the promise of more should it be required.

Ian scanned the house front. Inside this typical neoclassical box of a house was a woman who had caused him a great deal of trouble. He needed to resolve this . . . this inconvenience straightaway. He had pressing matters to attend to—a plan to satiate his father's agenda and a plan to execute his latest Rebel project: reforming the Bloody Code.

After dismounting, he searched for someone to hold his animal. No one was about but a woman dressed in a serviceable gray, her hair sticking out at all ends—a maid of all work, no doubt, tending to the garden.

Well, he didn't care to waste time by taking his horse to the town mews. Only a moment was required to straighten Miss Tyler out and return to London. He swung his leg over his saddle and dismounted, calling out as he did. "Miss?"

The maid turned but did not raise her head. "Would you be so kind as to hold my reins? I have business in this house and will be but a moment."

"Of course, I would be happy to." She ducked lower and hurried to him.

Her words and tone were soft and vaguely familiar. Perhaps she had worked as a servant in his townhome before. He dismissed the thought at once. He hadn't come to study a strange maid but to break a woman's heart. He couldn't wait to set this Miss Tyler straight—the upstart who coveted his title and spread lies to attain her wishes.

He muttered a thank-you and marched toward the door.

"If you are here to see Mr. Nelson or his son," the maid called out, "they are at the pub in town."

Ian shook his head without turning around. Boyles had mentioned the Tylers lived with the Nelsons, but it was not the Nelsons he sought. "I am here to see Miss Tyler and no one else." He rapped on the door, and almost immediately, the butler let him in. Perfect. An obliging staff member. He handed over his hat. They might be terrible, dishonest people, but their servants seemed quite decent.

He gave the butler his card and requested an audience with Miss Tyler. A melancholy tune from a pianoforte sang from some distant room. Was his feigned fiancée musical? The funeral march she had selected was the right tune for the occasion.

The butler was leading him to the drawing room when a woman behind him yelled, "Wait!"

He turned to see the maid rush through the front door. "What? Who has my horse?" He valued his mount a great deal.

"A trustworthy boy." The maid stumbled to a halt, her eyes this time brazenly met his gaze.

He opened his mouth again but recognition cut off all his words, for this was no maid. He hadn't forgotten those stark brown eyes edged in gold. "You!"

She nodded. "Me."

"The grass!"

"The grass?"

He pointed at her. "You put a handful in my mouth."

She gave a small laugh and reached for the paneling on the wall of the vestibule to steady herself. Probably because he was glowering at her. He had a tendency to do that.

"It wasn't grass, sir. It was mint leaves. Can you not tell the difference?"

So, that was what the sweet-and-cool sensation had been from. "I didn't keep it in my mouth long enough to dwell on it. And you still shoved it in my mouth."

"It was for your stomach. I was trying to help you."

He blinked. How was trying to kill him helpful? Maybe it was the tufts of hair sticking out, but she wasn't making a good case for herself. "I'm afraid I am at a loss."

She leaned forward and in a low whisper added, "From the usual sick stomach that accompanies drinking all night."

He reached up and pinched the bridge of his nose. "Miss, I know my limits. I have never been in such a state. For the record, I was napping." He sighed. "Never mind, it is not worth the explanation. If you will excuse me, I have business in this house." This maid—no, she was no maid. This woman before him—was she a neighbor? He hoped her uncle or cousin or whomever it was, was not the cause of her haphazard state. He would spare her a prayer tonight, despite the grass or mint leaves, but that was really all he could offer her. He dipped his head to bid her goodbye.

"But you requested to speak to Miss Tyler."

She remembered. "Yes . . . Do you know her?"

"*I* am Miss Tyler."

He blinked. Then blinked again. "You? You are *the* Miss Amie Tyler?"

Her brow furrowed with what appeared to be confusion. Why was she confused about her own identity?

"I have never had anyone add an emphasis to my name." Her tone held a touch of wonder and an equal amount of self-deprecation.

"I am simply Miss Amie Tyler. No frills or implication of anything more."

There it was again. So much innocence. She was not at all who he'd expected to find here. Her humility stunned him.

"Forgive me," she said, untying her apron, "you must have traveled from somewhere since I have not seen you around town since that day. You must be weary. May I offer you some tea?"

She did not strike him as the kind to make up an engagement of marriage, no matter how strange she was. He could not make sense of it. "Tea would be nice." They had a lot to converse about and might as well sit down for it.

She wiped her hands on her apron before handing it to the butler. "Mr. Goodman, have the kitchen send up the tea things. We will be in the library since my aunt is napping in the drawing room."

He found her instructions strange. Not that she approved of napping in a drawing room as opposed to a graveyard but that she did not desire to awaken her aunt, who should be their chaperone. Was Mrs. Nelson as terrible as her husband and son? Is this what prompted Miss Tyler's ghastly falsehood about their engagement? He carefully thought over his conclusion as they weaved through the house to the small library. It was a square room with one large window, a small fireplace, and a single wall of books. They were not heavy readers by the looks of it.

Miss Tyler ensured the door remained wide open and instructed Ian to sit in one of two chairs by the cold fireplace. A small table with a chessboard sat between them.

She took her own seat with far more grace than he expected and asked, "How can I be of assistance to you, Mr.—Forgive me, I don't believe I caught your name."

"No, I have yet to reveal myself. I am *Lord Reynolds*." He waited for the moment of recognition.

She smiled cordially. "It's good to officially make your acquaintance." Her smile froze on her face. She tilted her head and squinted her eyes. "Did you say Lord . . . Reynolds?"

He gave a firm nod.

"This is silly. Remarkably silly. But any relation to the Lord Reynolds on the headstone in our parish's graveyard?"

He nodded once. "My grandfather."

Her eyes went as wide as the saucers on the table, and her skin paled. "Oh, fiddlesticks!" That word seemed a favorite of hers. "I thought you were dead." She squeezed her eyes shut. "I mean, *he* was dead. He *is* dead."

Then, all at once, Ian realized what she had done. "You engaged yourself to a *dead* man?" He gave a sharp laugh. And then laughed again. How perfectly absurd. But a dead man? Really? Tears stung his eyes. He couldn't remember anything more humorous.

"Sir?"

He tried to collect himself. "I'm sorry. I shouldn't be surprised. Everything about you, Miss Tyler, is wholly unexpected."

She blew out her breath and crossed her arms over her chest. "I will have you know that I did not engage myself, as you say. My mother did."

"Your mother?" He sobered. He vaguely recalled, when speaking to the headstone that day, her saying that her mother was making her uncle angry. "So, she is responsible for this mess?"

Miss Tyler put a fingernail between her teeth. "It is a mess, isn't it? I've been sick about it for days. And now you're alive—or in existence—and it is so much worse. I had no idea, I swear. I would've been more insistent with Mama otherwise."

Ian gave a nod. "But you let her lie, didn't you?"

"She can be difficult to manage."

"Must you manage her?"

"I can only attempt to. As you can see, I do not always succeed." Her hand went to her hair, mussing it further. He could safely assume it was this lie that had caused her appearance to be in such disarray. "I knew the truth would come out soon enough when no suitor came for me, but I hoped to prolong it long enough to find another place for my mother and me to live. Once I am unengaged, we can no longer stay here."

He rubbed the cleft in his chin. He had thought the engagement was to take advantage of his name but had not imagined her situation or the level of despair that came with it. Instead of the firm tone he'd imagined he would use with her, he kept his voice gentle. "Unfortunately, the charade cannot continue any longer."

The tea things arrived, and Miss Tyler set the chessboard on the floor, knocking over several pieces in the process. It felt symbolic to the apparent state of her life. He felt sorry for her. But he would speak to her uncle about the misunderstanding or help her find a friend or relative to live with if no forgiveness could be found. He was a Rebel, after all, and pledged to help those in need. He had turned a blind eye to her plight before, but he felt a sort of kinship with Miss Tyler after their two unique meetings.

As soon as the maid left again and the chess pieces were sorted, Amie sat rigidly still. "I'm sorry, your lordship. Of course, we cannot be engaged."

"I am glad you see things my way."

"I will tell everyone I made it up. Your reputation will be protected at all costs."

His reputation was never truly in any harm. It was a hindrance, to be sure, and the circulating rumors would enrage his already furious father, but no real damage had been done. Not to him. It was her reputation that would be slaughtered. Women always suffered in this sort of situation. Society would shun her. She would lose all her chances to ever marry. And her own family would suffer the shame right along with her.

But the truth had to be told.

He swallowed, his throat suddenly dry.

She asked him how he took his tea, and he muttered his answer. She fixed him a cup, and they both sipped silently. The liquid burned instead of satisfied.

He was not one to pry, but he found himself asking the question before he could stop himself. "You said you were looking for other living arrangements. Have you other family who could take you in?"

"No," she said decisively. "No other family will take us. My mother has made sure of that. But I have long desired my independence and have no shame in seeking work."

"I see." He lowered his gaze to her hands. Gone was any trace of her time in the garden. Indeed, they appeared too soft to work. She had an air of maturity to her but lacked confidence and the obvious experience. Would she be able to care for her mother and herself? Many would take advantage of her innocence, maybe even abuse her physically. He swallowed. Guilt held him to his seat. Minutes passed, and the tension inside him mounted. He had no reason to linger. They weren't even speaking any longer. When his cup was drained, he set it aside and forced himself to stand before he said or did something foolish.

"I thank you for the refreshment," he managed to get out, "but I must return to Town."

"To London?" she asked.

He nodded, stalling for what more to say, for there was little comfort he could offer at his parting. "If there is any problem—"

"There won't be," she said, cutting him off. She clasped her hands in front of her, those perfectly almond-shaped eyes full of sincerity.

Or denial. How could there not be problems?

She lowered her chin. "I never meant to slander your name, and I beg your forgiveness."

"I do not hold a grudge." He was surprised he meant it.

She stared at him, her expression full of awe. "I do not deserve it, but I thank you."

She shouldn't be thanking him. He wasn't doing her any favors. He dipped his head anyway.

"I will walk you out," she insisted.

He motioned for her to leave first. They walked down the corridor side by side. He stole a look at her the same time she glanced at him. This was by far the most awkward meeting of his life. He was ruining her. Or better yet, letting her ruin herself. Either way, he was a cad.

They reached the vestibule at the same time the front door swung open and in stepped two men: one older with a round face and heavy jowls and one younger with a prominent forehead and a flame of bright-yellow hair. Their beady eyes, however, were identical.

"Lord Reynolds?" inquired the older one. "It's you!" He dipped into a floppy bow just before coming right for Ian and grabbing his hand. He pumped it up and down several times before dropping it. "So, we are acquainted at last. I told my butler to call for me immediately if you ever visited. I am out of breath for my rush home. You must know, I am most unhappy about this arrangement. You should have come to me to request my permission. But as she has no dowry, you must not have been too particular. You are a viscount, or so I've heard from some friends."

More guilt piled on, and the tea swirled in his stomach. But this wasn't his problem anymore.

"Lord Reynolds," Miss Tyler said. "May I present my uncle, Mr. Nelson?"

Ian tipped his head just as Mr. Nelson's son bounded up beside him.

"Father, why are you not putting a stop to this madness?" He grabbed his father's arm much too roughly, looking angry enough to hit someone. "You know this marriage would be the worst thing for Miss Tyler. For me. If he is not man enough to ask decently, he has no right to marry her."

Miss Tyler cleared her throat, taking a half step back. Her voice came out far more timid than before. "And this is my cousin, Mr. Robert Nelson."

Ian needed no explanation. The spoiled cousin who wanted Miss Tyler for himself, as though she were an item to possess and not a person with feelings.

"What happened to your hair?" the cousin asked her, his eyes darting to Ian. "Did he touch you?"

Her hands flew to her head and patted around until she located the misplaced tufts. She squeezed her eyes shut momentarily. "I must've snagged it on a branch when I was in the garden." She did something with the pins in her hair, which smoothed back some of her curls. "Please, do not disparage Lord Reynolds," Miss Tyler said quickly. She seemed on the verge of tears. "He had no part in this—in any of it." She seemed to steel herself. "In truth, the whole matter is a mistake. I—"

"I should have asked properly," Ian said, cutting her off. His heart pounded like an executioner's drum. The weight of what he was about to say cost him dearly. But it was the right thing to do, and heaven help him, he had to do it. "I take complete blame."

"What?" Miss Tyler said, her voice small beside him. "No."

He turned to her. "May I call again tomorrow? I should like to take you on a ride in my curricle." He gave her a pointed look. "We have a great deal to discuss."

Her whole coloring was off, but she gave a tremulous nod.

He turned to Mr. Nelson. "Is that acceptable to you?" Ian stood straighter and took on what his friends called his intimidating stance. Ian had used it to the Rebels' advantage on more than one mission, and it had worked fair enough for the butcher in Town recently.

Mr. Nelson looked from Ian to his son, who shook his head furtively. "I suppose I cannot refuse, but I would like to go over the particulars of the marriage agreement."

Ian waited for the bile to form in his throat, but surprisingly, his stomach now felt oddly calm. "That can be arranged."

He turned and bowed to Miss Tyler—his *intended*. "Until tomorrow." He strolled from the house, his boots clicking on the tiled floor until they met the gravel path just outside.

What had he done? He scoffed. No one would believe him.

He did not even believe himself.

CHAPTER 6

AMIE DID NOT OWN ANYTHING fine enough to wear on a ride with a viscount, or better yet, masquerade as his intended. She and Mama had lived off the charity of relatives for so long that her wardrobe was worn and depleted. Aunt was not one to converse greatly, unlike her husband and son, but she did insist Amie take one of her better shawls. She also instructed Mama to make an appointment with her modiste before Amie embarrassed the family.

Amie appreciated the generosity. With so many other concerns, her poor wardrobe was the least of her worries, and her need to understand this new situation she found herself in superseded her fears and hopes for the future. She wrapped her aunt's floral silk shawl tightly around her shoulders as Lord Reynolds spoke to Mama just beside his sleek, black curricle. Thankfully, her relatives were otherwise engaged and not hovering during an already awkward meeting.

"There is a slight breeze, so do not keep her long," Mama instructed Lord Reynolds.

Amie withheld her sigh. The breeze was but a trifle. Honestly.

Lord Reynolds took her mother's hand. "I shall shield her from whatever wind until I can return her to your side."

Mama's eyelashes began to flutter, and a faint blush crept into her thin cheeks. "Forgive me, my lord. I have no doubt you will do right by her in every way."

Lord Reynolds stole a glance at Amie, his face stern, before returning his eyes to meet Mama's. "I shall endeavor to try."

Amie swallowed. He was kind enough to Mama, but Amie was not certain yet what to make of this Lord Reynold's character. Whether he was good or not, he didn't seem to hold a very high opinion of her. This engagement was growing stranger by the minute.

"Do enjoy yourselves, then," Mama preened. She hadn't shown an ounce of guilt when learning Lord Reynolds was alive. And by the looks of Lord Reynolds today, he was *more* than alive. He was quite robust in his dapper attire tailored to fit his broad shoulders and trim middle to perfection.

Lord Reynolds dipped his head with more patience than a saint.

Mama gave a little wave with her handkerchief, her grin full of silent congratulations—congratulations all directed at herself and the masterful marriage she had arranged for her daughter.

A hand appeared in Amie's periphery. Lord Reynolds intended to assist her up. She accepted it but wasn't prepared for a second hand to meet her waist. Before she could even gasp in surprise, strong arms propelled her into her seat. Amie slid to the opposite side of the single bench, leaving as much room as possible for Lord Reynolds to climb up beside her. She grazed her hand on the partial roof folded back behind her, and her eyes drew to the skyline. The weather could not have been better for an open ride, especially after the terrible rain the night before. There'd been thunder too. The very thought of it sent a chill down her spine.

She hated thunder. Despised it, rather. So, at least something was going in her favor this morning. Sunshine was a balm to her soul, whereas the opposite wreaked havoc on her anxiety.

Lord Reynolds settled in beside her with his tall, intimidating form and gave a final parting nod to Mama. Amie stole a glance up at him, all thoughts of the weather fled. Why, she was riding with a man drawn straight from a magazine. Aunt had enough fashion papers around that Amie should have made the connection before.

It was more than his clothes. Lord Reynold's hair was cropped short in a Titus fashion, and his face was worthy of an artist with his serious brow, angular jaw, and prominent cleft chin. No one would have thought to take down *her* physical description and memorialize it anywhere. She was his opposite in every aspect, not just in appearances and social position but in personality too. It made the whole act of sitting as a couple seem all the more pretend. Except the game they were playing came with dire consequences if she lost. Or, should she say, *when* she lost.

Lord Reynolds took the reins in his hands and flicked them just enough to send his handsome pair of geldings into a trot. Despite all Amie's misgivings, for once, she almost wished the Peterson sisters would see her. A moment as grand as this was not likely to be repeated.

"I hope I did not complicate matters yesterday," Lord Reynolds said, interrupting her thoughts. He expertly steered the cart toward the edge of town before straightening in his seat. "The circumstance seemed rather desperate, and I was merely trying to help."

If he did not mince words, neither would she. "I was taken aback when you insisted on taking the blame." No one besides her parents had ever spoken up for her before, and Lord Reynolds was a complete stranger. "Why did you do it?"

He glanced over at her for a long moment and then swung his eyes back to the road. They were just passing a neighbor's orchard on the outskirts of Chestervale, and he directed his horses to the side and guided them to a stop. It was the perfect spot for a romantic rendezvous, both lovely and private, but this was anything but romantic.

Lord Reynolds turned his head again to face her, and his mouth pulled into a grim line. "If you could have one thing in this world, what would it be?"

His question threw her. "I couldn't say."

"It is important you answer truthfully. I will explain everything afterward."

She played with the end of her shawl while she thought about her greatest desires. A new gown or two would be nice but not essential. Not like a roof over one's head. As for marriage and family, they were luxuries for women who could afford to have a Season and possessed dowries to attract a man. She had always been forced to think more practically. "I suppose I should like my independence." To not depend on her relatives for her and Mama's every need sounded a little like heaven.

He frowned and rubbed the cleft in his chin. "I see. You mentioned the idea yesterday, but I was not certain if you were being optimistic. If this is honestly your desire, then I have a proposal for you. It is not ideal for your wishes, nor mine really, but I believe we can find a mutual agreement that ought to suit us both. What I propose is a marriage of convenience."

Had he been drinking again? A viscount could have whomever he wanted. She had learned yesterday from her uncle that Lord Reynolds's father was an *earl*. Imagine her connected to a viscount, let alone any esteemed earl. He deserved far better than her as his wife. There was only one answer she could give him. "No, thank you."

He tilted his head to the side. "No, thank you?"

Oh, she had forgotten his title. "No, thank you, *your lordship*."

He gave a short laugh. "I'm not asking if you would like gravy on your roast and potatoes; it's a proposal of marriage."

"An obligatory proposal," she corrected boldly. "You do not have to humor me, Lord Reynolds. I am not afraid of the consequences should we tell the truth." In all actuality, she was terrified, but he need not know that.

"I am being earnest in my asking."

She shook her head. "You cannot be."

"I do not make such an offer lightly. I have reasons why this will benefit me. Namely, I have chosen to devote myself to the betterment of my country. A family will distract me from my purpose, which is why this suggested partnership suits me best. In turn, I can arrange for you to have as much independence in your future as possible."

"I see." Clearly, he was a driven man, and his passion was at least admirable.

Lord Reynolds met her gaze head on. "Can you specify what an independent life looks like to you? I will not presume to guess your desires."

She stared blankly at him, not exactly ready to share her greatest hopes with him. She would keep her answer as simple as his. "I will humor you, your lordship, even though I find this whole idea of yours completely nonsensical. I want security and freedom from my relatives. And I suppose, it would be nice to be the matron of my own house." She currently had no hope for achieving any of these and felt foolish stating them.

He gave a decisive nod. "I believe I can adequately fulfill these wishes once we are wed."

She did not take him too seriously, though she had a strong feeling he was entirely so. "What would you possibly gain from such an arrangement with a person like myself?"

"I would not have to marry Miss Foster, a selfish woman my father has selected for me."

"Surely she is better suited to your position than I am."

His face was impassive, and she could not tell if he agreed or not. "I have never desired to wed, Miss Tyler. I have specific goals for my future, as I mentioned, and I haven't the motivation to invest my time or energy into courting and wooing the perfect candidate. My hand is being forced, so I would much rather have a situation of my choosing and on my own terms."

"So, in a way, you desire independence as well?"

He nodded again. "Very much so. Not to mention, the unusual arrangement feels justified, knowing I am helping you in the process."

He was outwardly austere, but in this, he appeared generous too. She didn't like the alternative thought of him never marrying. She had come to terms with it for herself, but it sounded so lonely for anyone else. The man was an anomaly. He did not show much emotion, besides the glimpses of frustration or even briefer moments of gentleness, but she sensed he needed people more than he allowed them in. If he were to finally do so, it shouldn't be to her.

"Perhaps you should get to know me better before you agree to something foolish," she hedged. "You've hardly spent a moment with my mother just now, but she clearly is dishonest. And look at me, I am hardly a refined lady suitable for your circles."

He rubbed one hand down the leather arm of the bench. "When I was searching for you, I hired a private investigator. I do know a little of you, besides the fact that our two encounters so far have been rather *enlightening*. If this were the usual type of courtship, then yes, I would think more time was necessary. However, a marriage like ours will be more of a formality that will secure your future and require very little of you otherwise."

She clasped her hands together. "But I hardly know *you*. Besides, of course, that you are prone to drinking and sleeping in strange places."

His brow jumped. "Not that again. Let me clear this up once and for all. Do you recall smelling any alcohol on my waistcoat when you brazenly pressed your head to it?"

Brazen? That was a bit thick. "I wasn't sniffing, I was listening for your heart."

"Must I produce witnesses of my whereabouts from that morning or previous evening for you to trust me?"

She had met one of his relatives in the graveyard, and that woman had been kind. Amie couldn't recall her name or her familial connection, but she had been a lady. An aunt perhaps? Too much had happened between then and now, and Amie had all but forgotten. Besides, she had never been tutored in the peerage and dared not admit to more failings. Maybe she could discover the relative another way and seek her opinion about Lord Reynolds. "I suppose I can trust your story, but can I trust you to keep your word on every other matter for the rest of my life?" Any other woman would've jumped at the opportunity to marry a viscount, but such a leap would be foolish if this new situation proved worse than her current one.

He eyed her like he could not believe she was questioning his character. "You can be assured, I follow the honor code of a gentleman."

"That is something, I suppose." He at least *claimed* to be honorable. If she dared believe him.

"Except," he continued, "when a rule in Society bothers me."

"Oh." She drew back. "What sort of rules bother you?"

"Most of them."

She scoffed. "I cannot put my trust in that, Lord Reynolds. It is too vague."

"I suppose it will come down to your desires. Do you want security?"

Amie nodded.

"Then, I shall provide it. You will have little reason to interact with me otherwise. Rule breaking or not. We must be together long enough to meet my parents and have a wedding, but beyond that is negotiable. I have a hunting lodge in my name that I rarely visit, and you can make your own. Though you might enjoy living with my mother, I will not subject you to my father."

"And where will you live?"

"As it is clear by now that I do not get along with my father, not with him. He will have no reason to force me to London for the Season after I am wed. So, I suppose I will live in York until Parliament is out of session and then return to my hunting box or my London townhome. Once father dies, which won't be for some time, I shall inherit an additional two estates, and you can move to either, should you wish to."

She stared at the trees, not really seeing them. What choice did she have? Face ruination, or live an astonishingly comfortable life? The answer was simple. "Very well."

"Good. Except . . ."

"Except?"

Lord Reynolds straightened his jacket. "My father. He has to believe we are married in every sense of the word. A little playacting will be required when he is around. I believe we ought to make an effort to be together and take a trip or two a year to see my family. If you cannot agree to that end, the arrangement is off."

"It is a small request, I suppose. If the same can be applied to my mother. I am her sole child, and she would take to her bed if she heard I'd married for independence."

"A fair agreement." He tapped his hand on the arm of the bench. "Now that we have both consented to this much, I thought to add a few rules for us to conduct ourselves by. Nothing overmuch, just three simple points to ensure this contractual marriage does not lead to anything more."

"More?"

"Like falling in love."

It was hardly perceptible, but she swore she saw the faintest hint of pink in his cheeks.

Well, she needed no rules. Who would dare fall in love with him? He did not seem the kind to even allow the thought of it.

"Number one," he began, "no touching beyond being escorted into dinner or the like. I borrowed that idea from a good friend. It worked well for him for a time. Until it didn't." Lord Reynolds coughed into his hand.

"Why did it stop working?"

Lord Reynolds met her gaze head on. "He decided he liked to touch his wife."

Her eyes widened, despite her attempt to temper her reaction. She gave a slow nod. "I see." Yes, falling in love with Lord Reynolds would be completely out of the question. Even now, she felt herself inching away from him in fear of accidentally touching him.

"Number two," he said, oblivious to her concern, "no growing attached to the other's family. I took that from another good friend. We cannot be too careful when it comes to emotional attachment."

She nodded again. "I don't see that being a problem for you, but I like most people. I will do my best to respect your rules and not grow attached."

"Good. Number three, no reading, researching, or acquiring lessons on romance. I took that—

"From another good friend?"

He nodded.

She did wonder if he actually did have any friends at all, with his intimidating glower, or if he'd picked up these oddities on the street.

It would be rude to question him on that matter, so she attempted another route. "These rules are a bit strange."

He leaned his forearm on his leg and rotated more toward her. "I am preparing you for whatever may come. If you agree to this match, you must know you will be taking on a few enemies. They look rather innocent next to my father and your uncle, but they are people who cannot be ignored."

She didn't like the sound of this. "Who are they?"

"A renegade of mothers. The deceptive, conniving kind who do not take no for an answer. They have the uncanny ability to predict your next move before you even think it. The next thing you know, you'll be in love with me and I you."

She wondered if she dared lean forward to see if he smelled of the drink like he'd suggested earlier. What a curious man he was. "Surely you exaggerate."

"I wish I were. They will not go easy on us. We will be a challenge to them, and they cannot resist such a thing."

He was a viscount and she an invisible wallflower, so perhaps he knew more about matchmaking mamas than she did. "What do we do?"

"We beat them at their own game."

She gave a slow nod. "By following the rules you listed?"

"And by avoiding my friends since they are all a little addlebrained at the moment."

"Then, you do have friends?" She'd blurted the question before she realized it.

He smiled. Actually smiled. He hadn't done that since she'd admitted that her mother had engaged her to a dead man. "I should be affronted you sound so shocked. Impossible as it sounds, I do possess a few true friends, although many will profess to be close to me when they are not."

She forced a smile of her own. "Then, it shouldn't be too hard to avoid them."

"That's the spirit."

She gave the smallest shake of her head. "This is a lot to take in."

He nodded. "I have no desire to pressure you to make such a life-changing decision with me hovering over you. I will return on the morrow to receive your answer and speak with your uncle. The specifics of our contract will remain between us alone as a mutual understanding, while your marriage settlement will be arranged with Mr. Nelson."

She opened her mouth to answer, but a barking noise caught her attention. She looked just beyond Lord Reynolds to see a large, white cat chasing a little Yorkshire Terrier. "That's terrible."

"It is?"

She waved her hands. "Not you. That." She pointed to the cat-and-dog chase. "Doesn't the dog have any shame, running from a cat?"

"That cat is bigger and probably protecting its home."

But what if the terrier didn't have a home? She felt a sudden kinship with the helpless creature. It felt like watching her problems chasing her down, why she tried unsuccessfully to flee from them. It was suffocating. "I have nothing against the cat or the dog, not really, but we have to do something."

"We do?"

"One of them is liable to get hurt." Just as she was liable to get hurt no matter what path she chose. Everything in her life was out of her control—she was considering marrying a stranger, for heaven's sake—but couldn't she do this small thing? She set aside her shawl. "Help me down."

"Miss Tyler, I don't think—"

She was already standing, waiting for Lord Reynolds to move. He reluctantly climbed out of the carriage and assisted her.

"Let me take care of this," he begged.

She shook her head, charging forward. She couldn't save herself, but she would help this dog. "The ground is damp. I would not want you to dirty your boots."

The terrier came racing back around toward her, and she lunged to snag it from harm's way. Her boot caught on the hem of her dress, and her knees slapped the ground. She managed to get her arms around the squirming, shaking dog, but when she righted herself, she was covered in mud.

Fiddlesticks. She had managed to save the unfortunate creature, but she'd ruined her best dress. She returned to Lord Reynolds with uneasy steps, her nerves rattling like the terrier in her arms. Was this God's way of telling her that she was better off relying on others than barging forward on her own? But for heaven's sake, if something was meant to go wrong, why did it have to be with this man watching? His wide, uncertain stare matched all the other times he'd looked at her.

"I will consider your offer carefully, your lordship," she said once she reached his side. She clutched the terrier tighter to her chest. "But perhaps you had better consider it yourself."

He stared at her for a long moment before pulling his handkerchief out to hand to her. The small square would not suffice, and they both knew it.

With reluctance, she accepted it. "And while we are conversing about difficult decisions, how hard would it be to convince you to help me find the owner of this dog?"

CHAPTER 7

IT WAS NO SURPRISE WHEN Paul Sheldon stopped by Ian's London townhome demanding answers.

He took one look at the dog in Ian's hand, folded his arms across his chest, and eyed him with a mixture of suspicion and concern. It was the look best friends gave when they knew something was completely and utterly wrong. "You did not respond to my letter, but you will not be able to avoid me any longer. Tell me truly. Are you engaged?"

Paul's barrister tone amused Ian. Paul rarely employed it on Ian, and Ian was almost touched.

"Will you believe me if I say yes?" Ian asked.

"No."

Ian chuckled, leading Paul into the drawing room. "I don't blame you. I am still coming to terms with it myself." After a little explaining, Paul would understand. It was common knowledge among Ian's friends that he had always shunned the idea of marriage, but his conscience wouldn't allow him to see an innocent woman ruined. He'd been backed into a corner from every foreseeable direction.

His drawing room was sparse compared to most of his station, but he didn't have a need to impress anyone, especially since he rarely hosted anyone but his friends. He waved to the lone sofa—a muted gray floral with scrolled arms. "Take a seat, please."

Paul stared at him, unmoving. "How are you not even angry about this? I knew your parents would force an arrangement on you sooner or later, what with your mother being the head of the Match-making Mamas and your father always griping about your lack of heir, but I thought you would move to the Canadian colonies before you would agree to it."

Ian went to the fireplace and straightened a small picture frame containing a watercolor of Brookeside. "My parents did not arrange it. I did. That's the difference." He couldn't believe he was taking the blame in front of his own best friend, but he'd made his decision, and he would not speak ill of Miss Tyler.

"You're starting to scare me."

He was scaring himself. "What do you think of my new pet?" Ian crossed back to Paul and handed the immaculately clean York-shire Terrier to him. "Miss Tyler named him Tiny."

Paul gingerly accepted the black-and-tan terrier no bigger than both his hands put together. "Your betrothed gave you a pet?"

Ian had known Paul since childhood, and Paul deserved a direct explanation—about the dog, at least. "After she rescued him, Miss Tyler insisted we inquire around the entire town for his owner. If anyone missed our rumored engagement, they couldn't miss us yes-terday. Tiny was unclaimed, and he, of course, must be cared for by someone."

"And that someone is you?"

Ian shrugged. "The local farmer explained that people often drop animals off in the country when they do not suit. It quite upset Miss Tyler. She has a soft spot for, well, just about everyone. I know be-cause at every stop we made in search of Tiny's owner, someone had to tell me a story about how Miss Tyler helped them. She hasn't lived in Chestervale long either."

"Interesting. And she persuaded *you* to keep the dog?" Paul shook his head in wonder. "I must meet her. This is not like you at all."

"What do you mean? I like dogs."

"Not lap dogs."

"It wouldn't be my first choice . . . or my second."

Paul scoffed. "And you never do something just because some-one asked you. There has to be a good reason for it. Why do I feel as though you are ill or have recently been struck in the head?"

"Why would I make up something like this? I am more likely to pretend such an engagement doesn't exist." Ian collapsed back on his favorite Pocock-original reclining chair. It was a good decade old and worn in just the right places. And he needed to relax before he drove out to see Miss Tyler again this afternoon. Every meeting with her was more unpredictable than the last.

Paul hovered over him. The very man who respected personal space above all else. "What happened, Ian? The Rebels can help you if you're in a bind."

Ian gripped the arms of the chair. "The Rebels have more impor-tant causes to fight. Indeed, we have yet to discuss my latest passion to rid this country of the Bloody Code. By the way, did you read the letter I wrote you about the criminal law? I sent one to each of the Rebels, requesting their help."

Paul pinched the bridge of his nose. "Yes, it was brilliant. But what about your engagement?"

Ian waved his hand to dismiss whatever concern was eating at his friend. "It's nothing in comparison. A trifle. My plan is simple. It is a standard, unspectacular marriage of convenience."

Paul's frown deepened. "You're right. I'm unimpressed. But I will not let my personal opinion get in the way if you are determined. Do you require my assistance in drawing up a contract?"

Ian shook his head. "We have a verbal agreement. I can trust her."

Paul groaned, holding Tiny up to his eye level. "This is worse than I thought."

Ian balked. "What do you mean? I have everything well in hand."

Lowering Tiny, Paul said in a rather plain and strict tone, "You told me exactly how you felt when the matchmakers presented Louisa to me, and I will do the same with you because that is what good friends do for each other." Paul took a deep breath. "Ian, you're being an idiot."

Ian lurched forward in his seat. No one called him an idiot. "A little harsh, Sheldon."

"Quiet. I need to think." Paul paced to the marbled fireplace, stopping once or twice to shake his head. He pivoted abruptly and came straight back to Ian's side. "If you care for this Miss Tyler at all, you will call this off or marry her properly."

Ian had never liked being told what to do, and his amusement was gone. "You sound like my father, and you know exactly what I think of him."

Paul nodded. "I do. But I also know anything else is unfair to Miss Tyler. She deserves a chance at happiness, and marriage solely in name alone will do neither of you any favors."

Ian pulled himself from his chair, his time relaxing far too short-lived. "Miss Tyler has had a difficult upbringing and has found herself in an uncomfortable situation. I might not be the ideal husband, but her alternative, I assure you, is much worse. I swear, I will not force anything upon her, but I would ask for your support should we continue. It might not be the kind of marriage you and Louisa have, or those of the other Rebels, but it is what I choose and that has to matter for something." His jaw was set when he finished, his resolve firmer than ever.

By some miracle, Paul's features softened, and he blew out a long breath. "Why didn't you say so in the first place?"

Ian forced himself to sit again. "This isn't easy for me."

"No, it cannot be. I know you better than anyone, and you would not do this unless it were dire." Paul stared at him for a moment before handing him Tiny. "I suppose I can support you. A good cause is always worth rallying around."

Those words were not lightly given. Ian knew him better than that. Paul's russet hair had darkened with age and his face and body lengthened, but he was still the same loyal friend Ian had depended upon since childhood. Ian gave a somber nod. "Thank you. I'm going to need it."

And when this wedding was through, Ian hoped Paul would rally around a different cause with him. Ian had already written a handful of letters and made appearances at every club he had membership in, but what he'd learned about the attitude toward the Bloody Code had not been favorable. He felt as though he were a lone man against a sea of united opinions. For now, his focus would be on his bride-to-be, and he would save dissecting a centuries-old law until after the wedding.

A few hours after speaking with Paul, Ian stood in front of Miss Tyler's home. His friend's warning about doing right by Miss Tyler rang fresh in his ears. His solicitor had drawn up a few papers to go over with Mr. Nelson. Next would be introducing her to his family and performing the actual ceremony. This was entirely too real. Was he doing the right thing? All his confidence in front of Paul was waning. Perhaps there was another alternative he and Miss Tyler hadn't considered.

He'd gone over Boyle's file on Miss Tyler again before he'd left. The information dated back to before her father's death and had strung together several living situations since then. Miss Tyler had had a hard life. Was his own involvement in it going to better her future or worsen it? He'd like to think his offer of a home and security was sufficient, but what about the parts Paul mentioned—family and happiness? Ian couldn't give her those outside his name. Not to mention that even with a marriage of convenience, their position in Society would require certain obligations from Miss Tyler that he hadn't prepared her for. She would be a viscountess. Would she be up to the task?

Uncertainty plagued him as he tied his horse to the fence post, not daring to ask any passing maids to hold his reins for him. When he proceeded up the short walk, no strange-haired woman stopped him, attempted to shove mint leaves in his mouth, or offered him a muddy dog. It was almost disappointing. He put his fist to his mouth

to smother a sudden smile of amusement. Not many things entertained him, and he had to force control into his expression. He lifted
his hand to knock, but just before it connected, he hesitated. Did
he hear voices coming from the side of the house? One sounded dis-
tinctly like Miss Tyler's.

Dropping his hand, he jogged through the garden to investigate.
He rounded the corner of the cottage and drew up short. Mr. Robert
Nelson had his grimy hand on Miss Tyler's elbow, his words low and
indiscernible.

Hot anger coursed through Ian. No wonder Miss Tyler was desperate. Her cousin was a contemptible blackguard.

"Am I interrupting something?" Ian asked loudly, striding toward them.

Mr. Nelson did not withdraw his hand and seemed to tighten his
hold instead. "This is a family conversation," Mr. Nelson said with a
deep scowl.

Ian gave a swift nod. "As I will soon be family, perhaps you might
enlighten me." His reservations flew to the back of his mind, and his
displeasure lent him full confidence. He didn't care one bit for the pos-
sessive way Mr. Nelson clung to Miss Tyler or the fearful look in her
eyes. When Ian reached them, he put his hand on Miss Tyler's other
elbow, gentle but firm enough to send a message to the obnoxious
man across from him.

Mr. Nelson sneered. "*If* you become family."

Ian tightened his fist by his side. He was no pugilist, but he had
the strength and size to do the necessary damage if a situation required
it. And no one deserved a setdown as much as a man who dared harm
a woman.

Mr. Nelson took notice of Ian's fist, and a wariness flashed over
him. "So, that's how you will play it," Mr. Nelson said. "Very well.
We were just finishing here anyway." He finally dropped his hold of
Miss Tyler and gave her one last hard glare, then marched away to
the back of the house.

Ian watched him go but did not release his own hold on Miss Tyler. His protective instincts had never been so ignited. His hand seemed glued to her arm, as if needing to assure himself that Miss Tyler was well and safe. "Are you hurt? Is anything wrong?"

"No, and nothing that cannot be remedied." She visibly swallowed. "I have made my decision. I am prepared to marry you forthwith." She held up her chin, her determination palpable. For a fleeting moment, with her petite jaw set and her shoulders back, he could actually picture her as not just a viscountess but a future countess as well.

The image rocked him.

Perhaps she was far more prepared for this arrangement than he was. He took a glance to the back of the house following the path Mr. Nelson had taken. Whatever vile thing he had said or done had driven Miss Tyler in the opposite direction. The direction Ian had been vacillating about moments ago while tying up his horse. It was time to solidify his own mindset once and for all. There was one certain way to do this for him. He cleared his throat. "Then, are you prepared to meet my family for dinner next week?"

This would be the ultimate test, a personal show of commitment, and Miss Tyler's last chance to cry off.

Miss Tyler visibly swallowed. "I am ready to do whatever is required of me."

An answer to a proposal of marriage had never sounded less romantic. Which meant everything was going exactly as planned. "I will send my carriage for you Friday at seven. Dinner will be at eight."

She squared her shoulders. "I will be ready."

Brave as she may be, he would do everything he could to protect her. "Very good. Let's find your uncle."

CHAPTER 8

LORD REYNOLDS HAD KINDLY SENT his carriage to collect Amie and Mama for dinner with the earl and the countess. A constant stream of her mother's nervous chatter bounced in Amie's ears more than the constant rumble of the carriage. Both the conversation and the conveyance stopped at the same time in front of an elegant house three stories high. Two stone lions flanked the stark, black door. Beside them sat two ornamental potted trees. Amie had been to London a time or two, but her excursions were limited to the shops in Cheapside. The respectable suburb was nothing to the rich opulence here.

"Oh, dear me." Mama gasped. "I knew I was underdressed."

Mama had borrowed a nicer cast-off gown from Aunt. No one would know, as it had been taken in to fit her narrow frame perfectly. "You look very well tonight, Mama. Truly."

Amie smoothed her own gown. A new one. She hadn't had anything new in a very long time. The style was simple since the modiste had needed to work quickly to finish it in time, but the fabric was fine, the deep burgundy color a welcome change from the drab colors of the rest of her wardrobe. Aunt's maid had spent a good hour taming Amie's hair into submission, too, adding pomade to smooth out the wild tangles.

A footman assisted them from the carriage and the great black door to the house opened for them. Lord Reynolds stood waiting just inside the vestibule. If his appearance had been pleasing before, it was uncommonly so tonight. Indeed, her intended came from an elite class in looks as well as position. He was unnervingly handsome. Besides his appearance, he was doing an admirable job at pretending to be a dutiful suitor. Bless him for meeting her at the door. She had been anxious about the possibility of making introductions before his own arrival. He dipped his head, and she and Mama curtsied.

"Good evening. You look well, Mrs. Tyler. And, Miss Tyler, you look"—he paused, appraising her. She waited on bated breath for his approval or, worse, his disapproval—"different," he finally said.

Her brow creased. Different? Was that a good different or bad different?

He dragged his gaze away from her before his eyes could give her any clues.

Before she could overthink his words any further, he spoke again. "How was your ride?"

Her ride? Well, her ears were ringing from Mama's incessant talking, and her hands were shaking, but she forced a smile and said what was expected of her. "Comfortable, thank you."

Mama inserted herself into the conversation. "Not merely comfortable, your lordship. The seats were softer than pillows, the ride as smooth as butter, and the anticipation of the dinner positively thrilling."

Lord Reynolds's opened his mouth to respond to Mama, but he closed it again.

Mama had that effect on people.

"How is Tiny?" Amie asked quickly.

Lord Reynolds's jaw flinched. "He chewed up one of my favorite boots."

Her hand flew to her mouth. "I am so sorry."

"I gifted the second to him, so I hope he is generous and spares the others in my closet." He motioned to the corridor with his head. "My parents are waiting in the drawing room with our other guests. May I?" He extended his arm to her.

She set her trembling hand on his. He noticed it and glanced at her, a flicker of concern passing over his features.

She averted her gaze, and he said nothing. He pulled her down a corridor on the right, her mother trailing behind.

"At dinner, I would request you call me Ian." His whisper in her ear startled her and tickled her neck.

"I could never."

"I must insist."

She withheld her argument. He knew more about how things were done than she did. "I suppose you must call me Amie." When she looked up at him, his nearness sent her heart pounding. He was more man than any she had ever met. Every woman who came near him was likely as affected as she. Could she really call him Ian? It was so intimate.

"Amie," he uttered, drawing out the short syllables like long drips of syrup. It was likely a mere exercise of his tongue, but the feather-soft word sent a shiver of pleasure down her back. Never had a man outside her family said her given name, and never with a voice such as his. How could one word, one name, send her imagination whirling? If this was what being engaged did to her, she was entirely unprepared for marriage.

Thank heavens for Lord Reynolds's rules. Er, Ian's rules.

Her awareness of the rest of her surroundings sharpened suddenly as Ian led her into the drawing room. Soft blues accented the room, two tan sofas sat parallel to each other, and a stunning whitestone fireplace crowned the room. Her eyes glossed over the elegance, drawing quickly to the five people whose chatter abruptly stopped.

Why, it was the woman from the graveyard! Lady Kellen—was that her name? What was she doing here?

At once, everyone stood.

The man next to Lady Kellen cleared his throat. "These are the guests you insisted on inviting tonight?"

Was this Ian's father? His brows were set low over a pair of stern eyes. Did . . . did he not know about Amie and Ian's engagement?

She wanted to ask Ian, but this man's commanding gaze silenced any desire to speak. Ian had warned her, saying he wanted to keep her away from his father. She should have asked more questions. The man resembled Ian in height and breadth of shoulders, but his coloring was darker. Their frowns, however, were extremely similar.

She looked up at Ian, whose own brows and the set of his mouth stayed remarkably steady. He wasn't intimidated, but *she* certainly was. It was quite clear that her presence was not desired.

"Yes, these are the special guests I told you about." Ian turned to her. "May I present my parents, Lord and Lady Kellen, and our guests, Lord and Lady Halbert and their daughter, Miss Foster?" He motioned to Amie next. "This is Miss Tyler and her mother, Mrs. Tyler."

Amie dipped into a hasty curtsy. Out of the corner of her eye, she noticed Mama dip into a much more careful curtsy, one that impressed and surprised Amie. Should Amie have lowered herself more? Kept her head bent? She felt completely out of her element, especially with her antithesis, Miss Foster, standing ten feet away. Miss Foster's flawlessly molded white-blonde hair was an extension of her utterly gorgeous gown. She was an exemplary model of the prime of Society, where Amie was the neglected, overlooked sort. How Amie must pale in comparison to everyone here. Ian had chosen wrong for himself. No matter his excuses, he should be engaged to Miss Foster.

"It is an honor to meet you," Mama said, her hand curled in a half circle at her chest, and her other hand flared out to the side. Anywhere else, Amie would have called her silly, but here it seemed appropriately dramatic.

This was not the kind of world Amie was prepared to live in.

"It is wonderful to see you again," Lady Kellen said, stepping forward.

"You know them?" Ian's father asked.

"We've met briefly," Lady Kellen answered.

Ian's brow rose. "I had no idea."

"It must have been fate. We encountered each other by chance, you see," Lady Kellen clarified, coming to stand by Mama. "Do you remember?"

Mama preened. "Indeed. You were partial to my bonnet." The way Mama said it was as though she were the lady and Lady Kellen her lesser.

"I was." Lady Kellen grinned. "It is so good to see you both again, and on the arm of my son."

"I did not guess at your close relation," Amie said, finding her voice.

"Titles can be confusing," Lady Kellen explained. "The late Lord Reynolds was my husband's father. By the hand of fate, he never lived to be the Earl of Kellen. My husband, however, took on the role fairly young in life. We do not always choose our path, do we?"

Amie ducked her head, knowing this answer all too well. "No, we do not."

Lady Kellen reached for her hand. "How happy I am that you can be our guests tonight."

"It is I who am happy," Ian said quickly. "I have news to share. Miss Tyler and I are engaged to be married." For someone who claimed he was happy, he sounded a lot like he was pronouncing someone's death.

Indeed, the room reacted as if he had. Lady Halbert gasped, while Miss Foster paled.

"What did you say?" Lord Kellen stepped away from the sofa toward them.

Amie unintentionally gripped Ian's arm, though she had no idea if he would do anything to protect her. The shock in his father's eyes and the perplexed look in Lady Kellen's confirmed her earlier suspicions. They did not know about the engagement.

"Lord Kellen, what is this?" Lord Halbert said, full of bluster.

"That is what I would like to know," Lord Kellen answered.

"We are engaged," Ian repeated, "to be married."

"You already said that," Lord Kellen barked. "I'm waiting for you to say something sensible." He turned to the Fosters. "Please excuse me. I must speak with my son privately."

"Indeed," Lady Halbert agreed.

Ian held his ground. "We can discuss the particulars another time, Father. We have guests who deserve our attention. Dinner will be announced at any moment."

Lady Kellen remained remarkably quiet through the tense exchange, but at this, she gave her husband the barest hint of a nod. This was worse than a run-in with the Peterson sisters. Amie did not care for contention. In fact, she hated it. When Ian's father's face turned a shade of purple, she winced.

"Very well," Lord Kellen said. "We will discuss this tonight after everyone has left."

They were informed of dinner being ready a moment later, and they filed into the dining room. Ian did not let go of Amie's arm until they reached her chair. He pulled it out for her, and she reluctantly relinquished the safety of his nearness. She found herself seated next to Mama on one side and, thankfully, Ian on the other. However, her position gave her a rather uncomfortable view of Miss Foster, who sat directly across from her. Lady Kellen, a supposed ally, was at the upper end of the table and too far away to offer any ready comfort from her agitated husband, who took the seat beside her. Without looking, Amie could feel Lord Kellen's glare searing her cheeks.

Footmen carried in the first course. A cream mushroom soup, buttered asparagus, salmon baked in pastries, pudding, and several dishes she could not identify were presented like works of art. Unfortunately for her, she'd rather lost her appetite.

Miss Foster broke the awkward silence after Amie forced a second bite of soup. At least it was not Mama who spoke.

"Miss Tyler, pray tell, why is it we have never heard of you before?"

Amie set her spoon down so she could concentrate and not embarrass herself. "Likely for the same reason I have never heard of you." She hadn't expected another gasp from Lady Halbert, who suddenly clutched the pearls that matched the white streaks in her hair. Amie glanced at Ian, who had his fist to his mouth and the hint of mirth in his features.

She rethought her answer and realized it did sound off-putting, though that had not been her intention. She tried to remedy her response. "I meant, I have not come to Town for the Season. You would not have seen me at any of the assemblies here."

Mama nodded. "I would never presume to parade my daughter about as so many others do."

Amie cringed, wishing the floor would open beneath their chairs like a behemoth mouth and swallow them up. But they were not so fortunate. Could they make a worst first impression?

"She is my best kept secret," Ian said, raising his glass to her before taking a long drink.

Amie gaped at his flirtatious tone and words.

He returned her gaze, holding it and not letting go. Perhaps she did not want to be swallowed by any floor monster after all—not if it meant Ian wouldn't hold her in his gaze ever again. He didn't smile, but she found she wanted him to. Because if he wasn't joking, she had no idea what to do about it. He could hardly expect her to flirt back. She didn't know how.

"Have you discussed dates?" Lady Kellen asked. If she was jumping in to steer the conversation to safer grounds, this was probably not the way.

"*Amie* and I hope to be wed as soon as arrangements can be made." He set his hand on the back of her chair. He wasn't touching her, but he might as well have, for her back heated just the same.

What was Ian doing? Even a dunderhead like herself knew that his leading statements would rile Satan himself. Dropping her given name was the finishing touch. She dared a glance at Lord Kellen. Sure enough, his color darkened, and he appeared on the verge of an apoplexy.

It was one thing to convince *her* family of an engagement, but there would be no coming back from this. She fumbled with the napkin in her lap. If she had to marry into this family, she did not want them to hate her. Except rule number two forbade familial connections of any sort.

Cursing rule number two, she did her best to muster her agreement to Ian's bold statement of marriage by lifting the corners of her mouth as high as she dared.

Fortunately, or unfortunately, Mama had plenty to say that was far less subtle. "I do hope it is a grand wedding with plenty of flowers. I do not care for weddings without enough flowers. We cannot have guests thinking it is another day at church and not a special occasion. I will invite all my family, of course. And surely the elite of the *ton* will come. My future son-in-law is a viscount, after all. We couldn't have anything less."

"Lord Reynolds doesn't care for grand parties," Miss Foster said. Her smile resembled that of a cat. "Everyone who knows him at all would realize that."

Amie didn't know. In fact, she knew very little about the man next to her. She was a fake. A pretender. And wished she could disappear until the dinner was over.

Ian bent over her to address Mama. "But I cannot disagree about the flowers. Would you be willing to make a list of your favorites?"

Mama was not put out in the slightest by Miss Foster, and she beamed under Ian's attention. "I should be glad to."

Lord Kellen's voice cut through the room. "I will not have another word breathed about this wedding." He let the cold words seep in before he adjusted his tone and, in a tight but calmer voice, added, "It is hardly good dinner conversation. Lord Halbert, tell us about the men on your land committee. Are they well informed?"

Ah, politics. Another matter Amie knew nothing about. Not surprisingly, this potentially volatile topic carried less tension than that of weddings. Hallelujah for safer waters to tread.

Lord Kellen dished his wife's plate, wordlessly fussing over her while he exchanged a sophisticated conversation with Lord Halbert that Amie could barely follow. She did not know what to make of the man. He treated his wife well, but there was a sharp intelligence to his words that created an image of intimidating authority.

Amie listened with painstaking exactness to every word passing between the men, hoping to educate herself, lest she act the fool again. They discussed landowners and property rights and something about the disparity of taxes. They dropped names and chuckled over a line she did not realize was a joke. She leaned forward, trying to follow the complicated turns of phrases.

"Amie," Ian whispered in her ear.

Gooseflesh erupted down her arms. She would never get used to hearing her name on his lips. "Yes?"

"Is there something wrong with your appetite?"

She glanced down and discovered her soup missing. She had hardly touched it and had not realized a second course had been brought in.

Ian did not wait for her to answer and dished her some braised beefsteak and a side of roasted potatoes. "Don't let the present company keep you from seeing to your health." His whispered words were so genuine and thoughtful, she forgot all about her efforts to listen to the discussion of politics.

"Eat," he said.

She nodded and took up her fork. As soon as she finished her last bite, Lady Kellen urged the women into the drawing room.

Ian stood too. "I will pass on the port. I do not want my guests to be without me on their first visit."

His father was none too pleased that Ian chose the women's company over the men's, but Ian seemed to not care one whit what his father wanted. Despite all her objections to too much drink, she wished he would at least humor his father a little so there was not such dissonance hovering between them. She withheld her sigh and followed the others to the sitting room. Without a knowledge of the history between them, any judgments on her part were unjust and purely ignorant. Indeed, her ignorance seemed the theme of the night.

Lady Kellen sat beside Mama, but Miss Foster took up the opposite sofa.

Amie wondered where Ian would direct her to be, but he led her past the sofas to an outside door leading to the veranda. "You must see this view." His words were loud enough for the others to hear, and they were well in sight of them even after they stepped outside. The night was warm enough that her long gloves kept her adequately comfortable.

Ian dropped her arm and leaned his forearms on the balustrade. "That went well."

"It did?" She fidgeted with the skirt of her gown, unable to be as at ease as he was. "Your father is going to have your head tonight."

Ian chuckled. "Don't worry, you will not be widowed before we are wed. I can hold my own where he is concerned."

"Perhaps, but should you?" She could not help prying.

He gave her a sideways glance. "It is hard to explain a lifetime to a person you've just met. My father is an important man to everyone but me. He has never attempted to remedy the fact, so I don't put a lot of stock into maintaining a relationship that is undesired on both sides."

She nodded, even though she did not fully understand. She stole a glance behind her to make certain no one could hear them. Lady Kellen was deep in a conversation with Mama, and thankfully, Lady Kellen was the one speaking. Lady Halbert was listening with a sort of curious disapproval.

Amie couldn't watch. "Will your father let us marry? Miss Foster—"

"Miss Foster is nothing to me," Ian said decisively. "And my father is getting what he wants in the end—a wife for his son."

She realized with sudden intuitiveness that a wife was not what his father wanted at all. "You mean, he expects an heir." Such a thing didn't exactly fit with Ian's first rule about no touching.

"There will be no heir." Ian straightened his shoulders and leaned his hip against the stone. "Of course, I need time to convince my family and the courts that my cousin Mr. Balister is inept for the job. My cousin Edwin Harris will inherit instead. Some claim he is mad, but I have dug around a bit, and he is terribly awkward, but I have my doubts about the diagnosis. He has always been a morally upright man, and there are plenty of eccentric women who would marry him. I have no doubt he'll sire a child or two in good time. I'll do my best to put in a good word to the Matchmaking Mamas. They cannot resist a project."

"You have thought this through, haven't you?"

Ian crossed his arms. "If you recall, I mentioned my goals for the future. I have never wanted to marry because I desire to use my time and resources for aiding the less fortunate and, someday, by making changes in Parliament. Family life will divide my attention. So yes, I have thought about the consequences of my choice."

Her throat constricted. Had *she* thought about the consequences? No children? No real family? Everything was moving so quickly, she hadn't thought past the engagement and the gift of a house and her independence. But after Cousin Robert had delivered his own forceful proposal, his grubby hands pawing her arms like he was a spoiled child who had never been denied anything, she had caved to Ian. Especially upon comparing Robert's touch to Ian's firm but gentle hold when he'd hurried to protect her. Regardless of her future sacrifices, she knew she was picking the best choice she had.

"What comes next, then?"

"With your permission," Ian said, carefully, "I begin to dominate your social calendar. I'm afraid it is imperative to our plans. We must be seen together if an engagement is to be believable."

"Of course. It makes perfect sense." She wouldn't have dared say no anyway.

"I think at least two public outings are acceptable enough before I obtain a special license. Having connections is one benefit of being my father's son. We are family friends with the archbishop, and he will understand when I tell him that I want a quiet ceremony without the *ton* flocking to gawk at us."

Special licenses were not common and were terribly expensive. It was yet another reminder that she was a weed trying to hide in a well-cultivated garden. "What sort of outings did you have in mind?"

And what would she wear?

"If you consent, I shall take you to a musical where we might attract the attention of a number of witnesses. And how about the theater on Saturday?"

A sudden thrill at the opportunities before her overtook any concerns of wardrobe. "I love music, and I have always wanted to attend the theater."

He frowned. "You've never attended the theater?"

"I haven't had the opportunity."

He playfully shook his head. "I am marrying Miss Unfortunate."

She scoffed. "I have been quite content with my life—minus the lack of stability. And what about you? Perhaps you are the unfortunate one, *Lord Grumpy*."

Ian straightened fully, his lower lip pulling down on the corners. "And what if I am?"

She took a step back, not sure why she had thought it a good idea to tease him back. "I . . . don't know."

He smirked and took a step back toward the drawing room. "The theater will be a priority. Everyone ought to experience it at least once." He gave a little flourish with his arm. "Lord Grumpy will send his carriage."

CHAPTER 9

SITTING BESIDE AMIE AT THE theater was entirely distracting. No matter how Ian tried, he couldn't focus on the play. His gaze kept straying to her. She was not at all what he had expected. It was as true now as it had been from the beginning, but he thought he would be able to predict her a little bit more by now.

For starters, her clothing had changed. Her gowns were now fitted in just the right places, the colors warm and inviting. Her hair had changed too. Where were the tufts of curls spilling out at strange angles? And her wide smile that she so freely bore while watching the play below them gave contest to her dewy eyes.

The truth was she was a far prettier woman than he felt comfortable marrying. Blast. It was a little too late to realize that, wasn't it?

Matters were progressing in other realms as well. Father had thrown a royal tantrum and kept Ian up the entire night after their dinner party, but Ian had won out in the end only because his father had called his bluff. He did not think his son would go through with the marriage.

But all the eyes of the audience had wandered their way at least once already tonight. Word had traveled past Chestervale and through all of London. So no matter how pretty Amie was, he wasn't backing down. He was getting married.

At least the musical had gone without exception. Minus Amie's humming along. Ian coughed into his hand to hide his laugh. She was rather naive. It was charming. *Almost.* He squashed the thought before he became carried away.

His parents' gazes suddenly seared the back of his neck. Father and Mother had joined them in the family box, and it was a good reminder that he did not want a relationship like they had. A one-sided love was undesirable and heartbreaking. His mother deserved better. His father deserved nothing. They had had an arranged marriage, too, but supposedly had come to love each other in the beginning. A lot of good it had done them. Just as Ian's grandfather hadn't stayed faithful to his wife, neither had his father or his father's brother, for that matter. The men in Ian's family were glowing examples of a lack of familial bonding. He had no plans to perpetuate the pattern for future generations.

In fact, he hoped that after his marriage, he wouldn't have a reason to see his father again.

Amie laughed at the antics on stage. It was not a quiet laugh but a full laugh. Ian couldn't help smiling at her reaction. Seeing life through her eyes had to be an enchanting experience. But he was Lord Grumpy, as she had so plainly and correctly dubbed him, and he was content just the way he was. He defied anyone—especially his father—to try to change him.

When intermission came, his parents took a walk to stretch their legs. He'd thought he and Amie would never be free of them. It was the perfect opportunity to speak privately with her.

"Are you enjoying the play?" he asked.

Her eyes lit up. "I adore it!"

"Good. I will have to arrange for you to see another after the wedding." By herself, of course, since they would not be meshing their lives together. He cleared his throat. "Everything is in order for the ceremony day after tomorrow. Will you be ready by then?"

Her unguarded expression suddenly closed. "Yes. My aunt has generously seen to my wedding clothes."

Ah, so her aunt and uncle were providing her new wardrobe. He had left them money for wedding arrangements, but he still wondered why they hadn't *generously* seen to caring for her before their engagement. "Is there anything you need? No trouble with your cousin?"

"I thank you for asking. He is moping about the house and refusing to speak with anyone, including me."

"I am glad to see he has given up. Will you tell me if there is anything else you require? If you say the word, I shall see to it."

She lowered her gaze to her hands, where she started absently pulling at the tips of her gloves. "About the wedding . . ."

"Yes?"

"Rule number one . . ." Her voice drifted, and she looked up at him expectantly.

He finished the rule in his head: *no touching.* "What about it?"

"The ceremony."

Ah, she was referring to the marriage kiss. The Anglican church preferred a more solemn ceremony, without displays of affection, but it was not unheard of for couples in love to do so anyway. "We'll keep to the contract. No need to put on a show for anyone."

Amie nodded but didn't look at him. He hoped he had brought her a measure of relief. He would speak with the rector performing the ceremony and make certain there wasn't a mention of anything of the sort. He did not want anyone to be confused, especially his wife. She deserved to be treated with utmost respect.

This was part of the reason he'd planned a secret wedding, not even inviting his closest friends, with the exception of Paul, who had agreed to act as a witness. There was enough gossip bubbling through the *ton* over his engagement, and he did not care for random spectators to join the wedding party or crowd the streets to gawk at them. This would be an extremely private affair. The perfect beginning to their marriage of convenience.

Perfect, in the loosest sense. An air of awkwardness hovered between him and Amie, and he had no doubt that it would worsen by the time they were wed.

He cleared his throat. "I will send my carriage for you and your trunks in the morning. The ceremony will begin at half past nine."

She gave the smallest nod. "I won't be late."

"Excellent," he said, satisfied with his plans. He had been thorough, and he had no intention of anything going wrong. Getting married at all was trouble enough.

CHAPTER 10

AMIE WORE A SOFT-PINK GOWN with puffed sleeves. It bore a pretty flounce on the hem and a stylish lower waistline. Aunt had insisted she wear a pearl band in her hair, a gold chain at her neck, and new slippers—pink, to match her gown. Amie had not relished her time with the Nelsons, but she would forever be grateful that their pride had led to a more updated wardrobe. It did not give her full confidence in marrying a viscount, but it did give her a little. If only she could gather her courage to walk into the church. Mama was already inside.

"Are you ready?" The stern male voice made her look up. Lord Kellen met her with Lady Kellen on his arm. "I have never escorted anyone down the aisle before, but I have no intention of dallying and dragging it out."

She forced a smile. "Thank you for responding to my note. I could have easily asked my Uncle Nelson to escort me in place of my father, but it seemed more appropriate to ask you."

His cheeks flinched, as if the thought occurred to him to smile, but he changed his mind. "If my son did not object, then I have no reason to."

"I don't see why he would. After all, weddings are intimate occasions and generally for the closest family and friends." And her relationship with her uncle was not close at all, despite their sudden gifts thrown her way.

"I shall be waiting inside." Lady Kellen released her husband and kissed Amie's cheek. "You look radiant. Ian will not be able to take his eyes off you."

Heat bloomed from Amie's cheeks to her toes. "Oh, he won't be—"

"He will," Lady Kellen said, cutting Amie off. "It's going to be a lovely ceremony." She turned and left Amie alone with Lord Kellen.

The man arched his back, the tight muscles likely circumstantial. Then he cleared his throat not once but twice. "Shall we?"

Amie set her hand on his and before she knew it, Lord Kellen had led her through the church doors. This was really happening. She was getting married—with strict parameters—but married all the same.

She had never fainted before, but when she saw Ian standing like a regal prince, with his fine-tailored suit emphasizing his long, angular figure, and his exquisite profile fit for a marble statue of a Greek god, she went weak in the knees. Would she be able to make it to him without fainting?

His gaze swung to meet hers, his keen blue eyes drawing wide. She did not dare believe it, but she swore his cheeks colored too. Ian—the stoic Lord Reynolds—Lord Grumpy himself—had actually reacted to seeing her. Did he think her beautiful? The impossible thought did something to her nerves. It steadied her, allowing her to put one foot in front of the other.

However, the flattering thought did not mean she could continue to stare at him and soak in his commanding presence. Her eyes darted to either side of the aisle at their guests. There were more people in attendance than she had expected.

Mama dabbed a handkerchief to her wet eyes, and beside her, Uncle and Aunt sat rigidly in their seats. Cousin Robert was nowhere to be seen. His absence was a fortunate one.

On the groom's side, Lady Kellen sat beside a young woman lavishly dressed, with a feather in her hair and stunning features. At least she was not Miss Foster. Perhaps a cousin? Ian couldn't have many friends, despite his earlier assurances that he did. He did not have the personality for it.

But then again, Ian had not mentioned any other guests coming. There were three other couples in attendance. All about her or Ian's age. A man with a wide grin leaned over the arm of his bench and winked at her. Her brow jumped up her forehead. What a shocking thing to do. Why would any of Ian's relations wink at her? His wife, or Amie supposed her to be his wife, leaned forward, too, and gave a little wave. Their knowing looks did not sit quite right, as they were perfect strangers to her.

She and Lord Kellen were mere feet away from Ian now, and she caught him whispering something to the vicar—a handsome young man with short, perfectly coiled dark-brown curls. He smiled at Ian, causing dimples to appear, and motioned for him to look forward.

When Ian did, his gaze met hers again, just as Lord Kellen brought her the rest of the way to him. Lord Kellen took her hand and lifted it for Ian to take.

Ian scowled at his father, making Amie tense all over. But when he took her hand, it was with the utmost gentle touch. Lord Kellen stepped back and found his seat beside his wife.

It was time.

"It is a pleasure to unite you both in marriage today," the vicar said, his calm voice not quite consistent with his almost mischievous smile. He lifted both his hands, one holding the Book of Common Prayer, and raised his voice for the others to hear. "Dearly beloved, we are gathered together here in the sight of God . . ."

Amie did her best to listen, momentarily caught with guilt when he mentioned marriage being primarily for the procreation of children. For the rest of the vicar's speech, Ian arrested her attention. His blue eyes were bright in the church's dim light. His high cheekbones, sharp jaw, and cleft chin were such perfectly sculpted masculine features. She followed the straight line of his nose down to his mouth and stopped.

She had never been married before, but she had been to a few family weddings. The groom had always kissed the bride at the end. But she had agreed to the contract and wouldn't question the matter further. Still, it seemed a little embarrassing to not kiss, as though emphasizing that they did not truly care for each other despite trying to pretend that they did.

But Ian knew best. He was the viscount.

They joined right hands, and Ian repeated his vow, sending a flutter to her stomach. Those words, with Ian's eyes so intent on hers, wove a spell over her heart. It was her turn next, and with miraculous clarity, she repeated her own vow. Apart from the contract and all the silly rules, she believed her oath. She was promising to be Ian's wife—in every way. God and the angels were her witnesses.

"The ring?" the vicar asked.

Ian withdrew a ring from his waistcoat pocket and gave it to the vicar. With due reverence, the gold band was blessed before Ian retrieved it again. She lifted her shaking left hand, and Ian slid the ring around her fourth finger.

Her stomach fluttered at the barely existent touch and the slight weight now resting on her finger. Ian covered it with his hand and repeated, "With this ring, I thee wed; with my body, I thee worship; and with all my worldly goods, I thee endow: in the name of the Father and of the Son and of the Holy Ghost. Amen."

The vicar said a prayer followed by these sacred words, "Those whom God hath joined together, let no man put asunder." The vicar cleared his throat. "You may now kiss your bride."

Ian's face whipped to the vicar's, his scowl deepening at the words he had sworn would not be said.

The vicar only grinned, clearly overjoyed for them. To him, this was an unofficial but cherished part of the ceremony. It was likely that everyone thought the same. Amie easily recalled Cousin Harriet's kiss with her new husband last spring in the church in Bath. They had been a love match, but weren't Amie and Ian supposed to be pretending to be one as well? Hadn't their outings fueled such rumors all week?

The truth belonged to them alone. And a wedding kiss was off the table.

She had promised to keep all his rules, embarrassment or not.

When Ian faced her again, his eyes were glacier blue, and his cold expression was not that of a happily, newly married man. But happiness had never been part of his plans, had it? Their well-thought-out future suddenly looked rather bleak. For them both.

Well, hang his rules. This was his wedding day, but it was her wedding day too. The only wedding she would get. Shouldn't they finish it properly?

Was she or wasn't she his wife?

She had certainly vowed to love and cherish him only moments ago.

She had no idea what possessed her next action. She grabbed the lapels of his jacket and pulled him down at the same time she launched herself up on her toes. Then she did the most audacious thing she had ever done in her life: She kissed Ian.

Their lips touched with a jolt, his mouth softer than she'd imagined. But a peck wouldn't do for a wedding. She closed her eyes and moved her lips against his, as her cousin had done with her husband. If Amie was only going to do this once, she was going to do it right. The connection, however, did something to her that she hadn't witnessed last spring or ever . . .

A wave of heat poured through her, awakening all her senses. She leaned into it, letting the feeling consume her. Somewhere, a voice screamed for her to stop, while another insisted she make the kiss look as real as possible. The third voice was the loudest and the strongest, and it declared kissing to be the most wonderful experience of her life.

She listened to voice number three, savoring every sweet second. Her hands went up around Ian's neck, wanting—needing—to be closer, and the weight of his hands fell naturally to her waist. She had never been held like this before, and gooseflesh erupted down her back and legs. Ian's mouth began to move against hers, responding and answering an unspoken need. Was it the church, or were all kisses this heavenly?

Someone cleared their throat beside her.

The vicar!

Amie broke their kiss, stepping back too quickly and stumbling. Ian tightened his grip on her. She looked up into his turbulent gaze. She had broken his most important rule and even put on a show—just as he had said not to do—and heaven help her, she did not regret a moment of it.

But her husband . . . He clearly had not decided whether he would forgive her yet.

She pushed down a trace of fear threatening to steal away the sweetness of the moment they'd just shared. Kissing Ian was the scariest, most terrifying thing she had ever done.

And she wanted to do it again.

CHAPTER 11

FOLLOWING TRADITION, THERE WAS NO clapping or cacophony of cheers echoing through the church. The solemnity of the marriage rites penetrated Ian's mind, but something else utterly transfixed the rest of him.

Amie.

She looked the part of an angel—no, a goddess. Her divine vanilla essence hung between them like a euphoric cloud. And that kiss. She was something of a heathen for launching herself at him in a church, no less. His heart was still quaking in his chest from the effects of it. *Impossible.* That particular organ was meant to be dead, and he refused to believe Amie had woken it.

She gave him a nervous, dazed smile. She was too naive to understand what she had done. This was Paul's fault since he had not kept the ceremony a secret from their friends. Ian tore his eyes from Amie's, his awareness of her too much. He needed to get a grip on his emotions. He looked at Miles instead. This was his fault too. This curly-haired man of the cloth. Their surprise vicar.

Ian glared at him.

Miles grinned back. Then, without further ado, Miles threw his arm around Ian and slapped his other hand on his chest. "I never thought I'd see the day, let alone officiate. It was an honor."

Ian shrugged his arm away. "I ought to kill you."

"But you won't."

"No, but I suppose I should thank you for coming instead."

Miles laughed. "You're welcome."

"Amie," Ian said, trying to look at her but nowhere near her mouth. "This is Miles Jackson, an old friend, who is usually more reverent than he just now demonstrated."

Miles dipped his head. "It's an honor to meet a woman who can put Ian in his place."

Ian skewered Miles with another glare.

"Me?" Amie shook her head as if completely ignorant to what she had just done.

Before Miles could expound and earn himself a punch to his mouth, Paul interrupted. "Congratulations to the happy couple." Paul's russet hair fell onto his forehead. Louisa, his wife, who was heavy with child, reached up and fixed it for him.

"I ought to kill you too." Ian took a step toward him, but Louisa slid between them, her large stomach creating ample space.

Louisa blinked her smiling eyes at him. "I have been anxious to meet your wife. Be a dear and introduce us."

His wife. That word froze him in place and momentarily made him forget his ire. He was married. His worst nightmare had come true. "Uh, Miss Tyler . . . I mean, Lady Reynolds . . ." He hesitated, more flustered than he'd ever been in his life. He had never imagined a Lady Reynolds in existence after his grandmother. It took him a moment to remember what he was saying. "This is Mr. Paul Sheldon and his wife, Mrs. Louisa Sheldon."

"Better known as Fisher and Nymph," Tom said, squirreling into their circle. His wide grin swung toward Amie. "Would you care to know what we call your husband?"

Ian sighed. "And this is Tom Harwood, an obnoxious tease, and he is married to . . ." He glanced around just as Tom's wife stepped away from Ian's mother's side and hurried to join them.

"Cassandra, if you please," she said. "I know we are meeting for the first time, and it seems highly unusual to address us by our given names, but I assure you, we will all be fast friends very soon." Cassandra dipped a curtsy and reached for one of Amie's hands while Louisa took the other.

"Several of the group came all the way from York to catch the wedding, but Paul and I are in London until the summer if you need anything," Louisa said, her ever-present smile beaming. "You must know, you have exceeded all our expectations. Not just anyone could be the right match for Ian, but you are perfection itself."

Paul must've neglected to tell them the specifics of their arrangement, though Amie did look perfect today, didn't she? Each curl by her face was flawlessly coiled, and her cheeks bore a rosy bloom. Her gown was exquisite. Her lips a crimson red . . .

Ian gulped.

Tom must've sensed the direction of his thoughts, for he said, "I didn't get a kiss like that at my wedding." His mouth turned down in a ridiculous pout.

Cassandra elbowed him. If she hadn't, Ian might have. Ian's neck burned at the mere mention of that kiss.

Cassandra started telling Amie a humorous story about Tom to put him on the spot instead. Paul took the opportunity to lean over and whisper, "I couldn't keep your wedding from the Rebels. They would have revolted."

Ian knew he was right, but it still rattled him. "You broke my trust."

Paul's gaze was far too humble. "I did, and I hope someday you will forgive me."

How could he stay mad at such a genuine effort? He forced some bluster into his voice, though he knew Paul would see through it. "What's done is done, but I won't be keen on sharing secrets with you in the future."

An arm swung around his shoulders again. "That's because in the future, all your secrets will be with your wife." It was Miles again. Miles, who was far happier than Ian had seen him in years. At least marriage agreed with someone, even if it would never agree with Ian.

Ian sighed. He had hoped to prevent all this marriage advice. There was one secret he planned to share with his wife, and that was the specifics of their contract. "Don't you have any other vicar duties to attend to?"

"I've been demoted to *just* the vicar?" Miles laughed in the quiet way he always did and motioned to Jemma across the room with Mrs. Tyler and Mr. and Mrs. Nelson.

Jemma caught the gesture, gave her excuses, and moved to join their group, her latest dress creation the color of a green apple. The circle expanded to include her. "Lady Reynolds," Jemma gushed, "we are so pleased to share your special day with you."

"This is Mrs. Jemma Jackson," Ian clarified. "She is married to this lowly *just* vicar."

Tom cleared his throat. "No offense, but you aren't very good at this nickname business. You mean Vixen is married to Mr. Romantic. I've been saying these names for years. When will they catch on?"

"I am all of the above," Jemma said with a laugh, "and I was once against marriage myself, so I can give hope to everyone everywhere." She tapped Ian's arm. "Even this one."

Amie's brow rose, and Ian squirmed. She seemed a little overwhelmed, but he could tell she was making note of every detail and wasn't in a hurry to be pulled away.

Jemma glanced up at him. "I'm afraid Lisette and Walter Bentley were unable to make it. They had a few fields burn, and a tenant home was destroyed. They didn't dare leave until everyone was cared for, but they sent their love and felicitations."

Alarm struck him. "Was anyone hurt? What needs do they have?"

Miles slapped his back, his voice steady and calming. "Relax, we have it well in hand. You take care of Lady Reynolds, and we will take care of the Bentleys. You were there for all of us; now it's your turn for a break. Enjoy yourself for once."

Ian took in his friends' supportive, loving faces, and the last of his anger dripped away. Louisa and Cassandra still flanked Amie's sides, each of them eager to bring her into the fold of the Rebel Society.

How could he have wanted to keep his own wedding from them? All his many reasons about gossipers gathering seemed paltry now. His friends were the best part of his life. Each one had already written to him offering help, ideas, or support for his criminal law research without any hesitation. And now this. "Thank you. All of you. I'm sorry—"

"We know," Tom said quickly. "You love us. As much as I hate to cut short a sincere apology, your parents are anxious to speak to you. After the years they've been made to wait for this day, I don't blame them."

Ian looked past Cassandra's curly blonde hair to see his father with his arms folded across his chest and a mixture of annoyance and disappointment on his face. Ian's mother was whispering something to his father. He would guess calming words.

Anxious, indeed. More like on the verge of a fit of temper. He steeled himself and stepped away from his friends.

A petite arm encircled his elbow. He glanced down to see Amie. Her timid smile eased the rising tension inside him.

She motioned with her head to his parents.

He nodded and extended his arm more fully to her. His awareness of her beside him was stronger than ever before, especially her soft touch. His wife's touch.

He set his jaw, willing himself to keep his mind clear, and together they walked to the bench his parents were standing in front of.

His mother embraced Amie and kissed her cheek. "Welcome to the family."

When Mother stepped back, his father took her place. He stood there frowning at them.

Amie, who must've been intent on being an unruly wife, did not hesitate to greet his father. She threw her arms around his shoulders. "Thank you for giving me away."

Ian had been completely dumbfounded when Amie had walked into the church on his father's arm. He still did not know who had put him up to such a task. He had not expected him to attend, let alone come in with Amie on his arm, as if he were somehow controlling the wedding too.

Ian couldn't wait to find out who was behind it. Even Paul wouldn't have stooped so low. Thankfully, Amie did not hold on to his father as long as she had to Ian during the ceremony. He hadn't even realized his hands had fisted at his sides until his nails started digging into his palms.

He wasn't jealous of his father's touch. No . . . it was something else—a surge of protectiveness.

His father reached for his throat, clearing it several times. "Yes, well, if your husband is content to not secure his career, I suppose you will do," his father said. And then he surprised Ian even more than Amie by kissing her on the cheek with a muttered, "Congratulations."

How that one word must have cost him when, in all honesty, he was disgusted that his son had married the wrong woman.

His father stepped back and extended his hand to Ian. "Son."

Ian stared at it. What was his motivation behind shaking hands? His father always had a motive for every act he made. Ian wouldn't shake it.

The next thing he knew, Amie lifted his arm at the elbow just enough that his father caught his hand and shook it. The contact was short, abrupt, and completely unwanted. Amie had some explaining to do. She was breaking all the rules.

His mother beamed and wiped moisture from her eye. "I cannot stop tearing up. I've cried more today than I did at my own wedding. I cannot remember being so happy. Thank you, Amie, for completing our family."

Mother was right. Her happiness was all because of Amie and not at all because of him.

Amie ducked her head. "You are too kind."

At least she was not confessing to their arrangement. He wasn't prepared to face the barely concealed ire of his father right now. There were too many emotions battling inside Ian as it was, and he did not care to feel any of them.

"I have invited everyone over to the house for a wedding breakfast," Mother explained. "But I think there are three people who have been very patient behind you."

If his mother had been teary-eyed, Mrs. Tyler was positively weeping. Amie held her mother for a good five minutes before Ian tried to separate them.

Mr. and Mrs. Nelson looked honored to be in his presence and mentioned three times how they were now related to the Earl of Kellen. When Ian finally pried Amie away from her family, he took her outside to his carriage.

He helped her inside, directed the driver, and then climbed inside himself. He collapsed onto the bench next to Amie and sighed. It was over.

He blinked. Why had he sat beside Amie instead of across from her? When the carriage lurched forward, their arms bounced against each other, sending heat waves through him.

"It is kind of your mother to throw a wedding breakfast for us," she said.

He willed her arm to stop touching his, but it didn't work. "We won't be joining them."

"We won't?"

"We are starting our wedding trip right away." Away from prying eyes. Away from well-meaning friends and relatives. And hopefully, away from each other.

Amie looked over at him, surprise etched on her face. "Where are we going?"

"First, to my townhome to collect Tiny and on to my hunting box. Your future home."

"Oh." Her quiet voice drew his full attention. Was she disappointed? What did she expect? This was part of their plan. Throwing a large wedding party and kissing over the altar was *not* the plan.

"You broke rule number one," he blurted.

She squirmed. "I thought it necessary."

He gave a nod, willing his cheeks not to burn again. Dashed all, he was a grown adult and could talk about kissing without melting like a puddle. "I suppose it was." She *had* been convincing. Or he imagined she had been. She had convinced him, at least.

"I hope I did it right," she whispered.

His brow rose. "What do you mean?"

"I've never kissed a man before."

"Oh, well . . ." He was not prepared for a discussion on the topic. "Uh, it was satisfactory." An understatement if ever he had said one. His heart had stopped. In fact, the entire world had been thrown to a halt.

She had a gift. One she must keep to herself for the rest of her life.

"Then," she said carefully, "you aren't angry?" She looked up at him, those soul-filled eyes begging for forgiveness, and her mouth and chin tilted toward him at the most innocent but becoming angle.

He leaned forward almost reflexively, needing to be closer to assure her. He stopped halfway with a start. He yanked his head back and faced forward. He had plans! His new wife wasn't going to distract him again. "Of course I'm angry," he growled. "You broke rule two and three as well. What is the point of a contract if you cannot keep it?"

She held up her hand and pointed to her wedding band. "Does not the contract with God supersede the first?"

He stared at the ring. At her hand. At her.

Blasted logic.

And why did she have to look so beautiful? "I suppose I had better write down the particulars so there is no doubt in the future." He would need the reminder.

She dropped her hand. "If you insist. For better or worse, I suppose you're stuck."

The carriage took a hard turn, no doubt avoiding an oncoming carriage, and Ian was jolted to the side. His arm came up, and he caught himself on the carriage wall before he slammed into Amie.

She was pinned behind his arm, and their faces were close. Even closer than before. Like the tide of the sea toward a raging sunset, her brown eyes captivated him, held his complete attention, and dragged him into their depths.

Stuck? Ian swallowed. They were far from stuck. He feared it was much, much worse than that.

CHAPTER 12

AFTER STAYING THE NIGHT AT an inn in neighboring rooms, Amie learned firsthand that Ian meant to live by his three rules for the duration of their marriage. It was fine by her since her new husband made her increasingly nervous. The second day of their marriage proved to be just as awkward as the first. She carefully avoided looking across the carriage at him. It would do no good to remind herself how intriguing his aloofness made him or how strong his hands appeared as they rested on the seat next to him—she had to look somewhere, and his hands were supposed to be a safe appendage . . . but apparently not.

If she had been intimidated before, it was far worse now that she had kissed him. Her actions had pushed him to reclaim his title as Lord Grumpy. He was more standoffish than ever. Keeping her distance seemed not just necessary but imperative.

Even if her heart had moved during the solemnity of their wedding vows and those exhilarating few moments of their first kiss— and their kiss *had* been exhilarating—breathtakingly so; she discreetly clutched her chest, the sheer memory of it causing her pulse to race—she was determined to respect their initial agreement forevermore. Though she feared her heart would never shift back to its previous protected position. Why did she keep feeling emotions— imagining yearnings—she couldn't stop?

This was not love. To be loved was to be known, and no one had ever truly known her. Any dreams of such a future died the same night as Papa, her dowry and opportunities to marry gone overnight. Or so she'd thought. Without her permission, a sliver of hope had bloomed somewhere deep inside her. Maybe somehow, sometime, Ian could learn to care for her. She shook her head. No, no, that was ridiculous. Ian would never love her.

She had married the wrong person if she wanted affection.

"We're here." Ian's tired, irritated voice more than solidified her thoughts.

Tiny's yapping had further tried his patience, and blessedly, the little thing had finally fallen asleep on his lap. Her one goal for their marriage should be not to annoy him. Between her and Tiny, that would be challenging enough.

Ian hopped out first, waking the dog and setting him down to scamper about. Ian turned back and offered his hand to help her down. She reluctantly took it, hesitant to start her new life. Once her foot took purchase, he released his grip and stepped away from her like she had some contagious disease.

Focusing on her surroundings helped her not to take offense. They were deep in the North Wessex downs, outside of Marlborough, near a small town called Oakdell, far from anyone she knew. Through the filter of dusk, she took in the house. The two-story hunting box sat tucked against the edge of a forest. Ravens squawked from the trees, and Amie wanted to look everywhere at once. Green countryside stretched for miles on one side, broken up by a rambling road lined with a half dozen small homes and an occasional cluster of trees. She would make a point to meet their neighbors soon. On the other side of the house was a wooded grove, untamed, with wildflowers and ground cover reaching to fill the empty spaces. The unbridled beauty surprised her.

"Welcome to Oak End," Ian said.

She swallowed. This was her home. Their home. Would her life be better now? Or had she made a terrible mistake? "It's lovely," she forced herself to say. "The wildflowers are breathtaking."

He scratched the back of his head and stared at the flowers dotting the grass. Had mentioning the flowers been in poor taste? "My mother likes the flowers here too," he said after a moment. "She loves how the purple blossoms on the wild thyme and the small yellow horseshoe vetch look when brought together into a bouquet."

"You know the names of the plants?" She had not expected it.

"Not all of them. Just her favorite ones. The blue round-headed rampions should bloom soon, and there are purple orchids around here, if you search for them." Ian gestured with his chin toward the house. It seemed he was eager to end their conversation and hurry inside—away from her. She followed beside him up the path toward some short stairs to a broad door with a heavy brass handle.

They did not quite make it before it burst open, and the household staff bustled out. They were led by who she guessed was the butler and housekeeper. They formed a line followed by a handful of other servants. Ian led her to stand in front of the butler.

"Lady Reynolds." Her new title clearly took effort for Ian to say. "This is Mr. Hamburg."

Mr. Hamburg possessed an average face, but his friendly smile endeared her to him immediately.

After his bow, he said, "Welcome, my lady."

"And this is Mrs. Hamburg," Ian said. The housekeeper was a stern-looking matron with wiry black hair—an antithesis to her husband in personality, it seemed. "It's a pleasure to meet you," the servant said, her words short but surprisingly not unkind.

Mrs. Hamburg had the other servants state their names and positions, and Amie tried to keep track of them all in her head.

"The lady is tired," Ian said as soon as they were finished. "Please, show her to her room, Mrs. Hamburg." He turned to Amie. "I will see Tiny settled in the kitchens."

"Thank you." Amie wasn't tired at all anymore, not with so many new things to see. Even so, she was shown to her room on the second floor. She noted Ian's possessions through the open door of the bedchamber beside her own. They would be sleeping so near each other.

It had been the same at the inn the night before, but there had been dozens of other people milling about. This felt far more intimate. At least there did not seem to be a connecting door between their rooms as was the case at larger estates. On the other side of her room, there were two other bedchambers in the corridor and a set of stairs that led to the attic space. The housekeeper coughed, and Amie forced herself into her new room, where she was left to herself.

Her trunk had arrived before they had and was already sitting at the foot of her bed. She glanced around her spacious room, noting the simple furnishings—a dressing table and a set of drawers beside a narrow closet. The neutral colors blended into the walls and drew her to the stark colors out her window. She pushed the glass panes open and sighed. So, this was married life. It was new and terrifying.

She set to unpacking, needing a project to occupy her mind. A half hour later, her new lady's maid, Edna, came in to help her dress for a late dinner.

"Good evening, Edna," Amie said, grateful for a familiar face. She had met Edna the night before at the inn, a talkative young woman who had traveled ahead in a separate carriage with their luggage. "I haven't the faintest idea of what to wear tonight. What do you think?"

Edna flashed her sweet, toothy smile at Amie. "Let's 'ave a look, eh?" Her slender body moved lithely about the room as she set aside a dress and pair of slippers for the evening. Amie hadn't had a lady's maid of her own before, and Ian had arranged for one without her even knowing. It was a luxury she was not going to complain about. For a man so against marriage, he'd been meticulous in his planning.

"This dress is perfect. Shall we see what you can do with this mane of mine?" Amie lifted one of her stubborn curls by her face. She had never learned to fix her own hair with any talent.

Not a quarter hour later, Amie admired her tamed hair. Edna had as much expertise as Aunt Nelson's expensive lady's maid. Ian had chosen well. While Edna fussed over her, she chatted about the staff, but Amie was too distracted to remember the names of the servants to place in her mind who Edna spoke about.

When her toilet was complete, Amie crept from her room and down the stairs, anxious about running into Ian. She took in the nuances of her home. Dark walnut trimmed the walls and the staircase. To the right was the entrance hall, and to the left a small library. She stayed straight and found herself in an open salon. The room on the same side as the library was the drawing room, and she supposed the opposite end of the salon would be the dining room. The house was not overly large and would be easy to learn.

"Are you ready for dinner?"

Her skirts pulled around her ankles as she whirled to face Ian, her hand going up to still the sudden, wild beating in her chest. "I . . . I am."

"Good." He clasped his hands behind his back and rocked on his heels. He was acting hesitant and not as confident as normal. He pointed to where she had guessed the dining room to be. "This way."

He didn't take her arm, but she supposed there was no need to be formal any longer. And beyond that, no one to pretend for. The dining table, covered in white linen, sat eight and was much shorter than the one at his parents' home. Would they ever have friends to join them? Perhaps some of Ian's friends from Town would visit, or she would make new friends of her own.

Ian pulled out the chair at the end of the table for her before taking his own seat at the other end. Suddenly, the table appeared much larger with all the open space between them.

They ate quietly, Amie hardly tasting her food.

When they finished, Ian set his napkin on the table. "I've been thinking about our arrangement."

Her heart lurched. Did he want to change it? Did *she* want him to change it? She forced out the first words she could think of. "You have?"

He fingered the stem of his glass. "I will stay a fortnight and see that you are situated before I return to London."

A fortnight. That was all they had together? And then she would be alone. But she would have a roof over her head, just as she wished.

Why was she not more thrilled with her prospects? "When will I see you again?"

"I will not plague you with my presence too often. I know you wished for a house, not a husband. However, we should probably be seen together over the holidays."

"Of course." She poked at her food with her fork. The holidays were months away. By then, the world would know their marriage was a sham, and it would hardly matter if they were together or not. But she would have the house, and that was no small thing.

"I am happy to send for your mother," Ian said, "if you would like her to reside here with you. We didn't go over the details, but Oak End will be yours to run as you see fit. Please feel free to have whatever company you desire."

"Mama would be glad to come." What would she think when she arrived and found Ian had no intention of visiting? Would she be proud Amie had done well for herself, or would she be disappointed that her only daughter had not found love and never would? Regardless of what Mama or anyone else thought, Amie must stick to the plan. She had a home now. What more could she ask for?

After dinner, Ian handed her a folded piece of parchment. "This is a copy of our verbal contract. It lists the same three rules we discussed that day by the orchard. You may keep this copy. I have my own."

It felt awfully official written on paper. She fingered it. "Would you like me to sign it?"

"This is a mere formality, so neither of us can claim to forget anything. But perhaps you had better sign it for good measure."

It wasn't a very good contract if both of them didn't sign it. She wondered if he had added any consequences. If he'd been smart, he would have, and she suspected him to be a very thorough man.

"Thank you."

He nodded and added a curt, "Good night."

She waited until she was in her bedchamber to read the contract. But when she shut the door behind her, her eyes caught hold of a bouquet of flowers by her bedside. Not just any flowers. Wildflowers.

Purple, blue, yellow, and green blossoms tied together with a piece of twine pooled out of the short, white vase.

Had Ian arranged for someone to bring flowers for her? She held up the contract, confused. It had to have been one of the staff members because flowers weren't a gesture from a man who didn't want anything to do with her.

She quickly opened the contract and read through the contents. It was short, with the same strange rules and nothing more. He was a particular man, that much was clear, but he had not added anything more to their conditions.

Shaking her head, she found her writing supplies and signed it. This time, she would not venture to forget any of the rules, even if a vicar stood over her and an entire room of people expected an allowance. She tucked the folded parchment into her diary, which she failed to write in more than twice a year, and shoved the book under her mattress, far enough that no maid would accidentally find it when changing the bedding.

There. It was done. From this point forward, she would obey his rules of matrimony.

CHAPTER 13

IT TOOK AN EXCEEDING AMOUNT of effort to avoid another person living in the same house. Being a married man was hard work. Ian kept himself busy between exercising his horse and closeting himself in his office. During the latter, he sent letters to rally support for altering criminal law, sent ever more letters to learn what was already being done, and generally did whatever was required to dodge his wife.

Not for his sake, of course. He wasn't at all nervous about running into the woman who confused boundaries and broke terribly specific rules. Not completely nervous, at any rate, but he would continue to lie to himself until he believed it. He told himself he avoided her because he didn't care to be in her way. This house was to be hers now. A promise was a promise. Besides, the men in his family had never been ideal social companions. Their failings were not isolated to one or two faults, which was unfortunate for anyone who had to put up with them.

And perhaps there was a small secondary reason. He didn't care to admit it even to himself, but the truth kept interrupting his thoughts despite all his efforts to the contrary. Ian feared feeling something again when Amie came near him. He had to believe that if he didn't give in to the sensation of wanting a woman, he wouldn't succumb to the possibility of the accompanying temptation to live an immoral life, as his male relatives had done. He had only to think of the heartache his mother experienced year after year as his motivation to hold his ground. Distance from Amie was the simple, viable solution.

This left him and Tiny to hold down his office, not unlike a military fort protecting them from the enemy. His enemy being Amie, of course. An attractive enemy who had made surprise attacks at his wedding and permanently dismantled his presence of mind.

"I know." Ian sighed. "We aren't enemies; we're partners. But it's not so bad, just the two of us, is it?"

Tiny looked up at him from his posterior position with sad, bored eyes.

"We'll survive," he said. "A man can do anything for a fortnight."

The following week passed with agonizing slowness and death might have been preferable. He was acutely aware of Amie's presence at all times. She was like a phantom, leaving her scent behind in every room, humming tunes that remained in his head long after she finished, and laughing in just the right way so it carried through the corridors. He'd never known any of the staff to have a sense of humor, but Amie had discovered what he had not.

Out of good manners, he and Amie ate together every evening and talked a little about their days. He kept a business tone and sat on the opposite end of the table. Amie didn't seem to mind. She had adopted her own routine. She took a morning walk each day in a new direction. In the afternoon, she read from the collection in the library, alternating genres. He hadn't meant to watch her movements, but she was a curious thing.

By the beginning of the second week, he observed that she was coming home later and later from her morning walks.

"What is keeping her?" he asked Tiny, pulling back the drapes to peer out the window again. Tiny yapped a response, then Ian said to him, "I know you're concerned. She's hard to predict." He took out his pocket watch and checked it for the hundredth time. Was she meeting with someone? She couldn't have made friends so quickly. Was it a man? He rubbed his eyes. "This is ridiculous," he muttered under his breath. What nonsense was he imagining now? Amie wasn't the type of woman to gallivant around the countryside wooing the neighbors. Though with her hair tamed and gowns fit properly to her shape, she wouldn't have to do anything to attract attention.

The men would come to her.

He folded his arms across his chest and turned to his only companion of late. "I'm going to get to the bottom of this, Tiny. I'll ask her at dinner where she's been. It's the perfectly responsible thing to do."

With a solution prepared, he could finally work again. Eventually, Amie returned, and the hours waned until dinner. As soon as they were both seated across from each other, he stared intently at her between the silver candelabras. She was wearing a pretty white muslin and her hair was coiled on her head with a single delicate curl just above each ear. Her creamy skin appeared a little rosier tonight, no doubt from the warmer spring weather. Her neck . . . he blinked. He shouldn't be looking at her neck.

He cleared his throat. No use procrastinating business. "Amie," he hedged, "are you enjoying your walks?"

Amie removed her gloves and set them in her lap. "I am."

"They aren't too long or tiresome?"

"I've always enjoyed regular exercise and fresh air."

He leaned into the arm of his chair. "And where is it you go?"

She gave a dainty shrug. "All over."

He clenched his jaw. He didn't want to sound like he was hounding her, but her vague answers were extremely trying. He kept his tone as conversational as possible and asked, "Nowhere specific?"

"Oh, just here and there."

She was being impossible. "And no one walks with you?"

The footman held a plate of steaming mackerel out for her, and she helped herself to a small portion. "I was not aware that I needed a chaperone. A married woman is generally free to come and go as she pleases."

"Chaperone? No, I suppose you are right." He couldn't think of another question that did not also include an unfounded accusation. It was settled. If he wanted to know what she was about, there was one simple solution: He had to follow her.

And no, he was not losing his mind from locking himself in his office for over a week and primarily speaking to a dog. Once he had assured himself that she was well and safe on her walks, he could leave her to herself. It was the least he could do . . . as her husband. Weren't husbands supposed to be protective?

CHAPTER 14

THE NEXT MORNING, IAN WATCHED through his study window as Amie left the house. He kept her blue spencer and red bonnet in sight until an easy distance separated them.

"It's time," he said to Tiny.

Tiny jumped to his feet, as if anticipating the walk together.

"Sorry, not this time chap. I can't have a single bark giving me away."

Tiny whined.

"I'm merely ensuring her safety. Try not to misunderstand." He bent down and scratched behind Tiny's ears before heading out after Amie.

He kept off the road, tromping through the dew-glossed grass and tucking himself behind trees. She walked without suspicion, holding a small woven basket on her arm. No more than a half mile from the house, she stopped at the gamekeeper's cottage. Ian had met the older couple who lived there several times over the years but could not profess to knowing them well. Was Amie requesting a certain game for the table? Couldn't she ask the cook to do that?

He held back, watching from a distance as the gamekeeper's wife waved Amie inside. Amie shook her head but said something that made the woman wrinkle into a full smile. When the door closed, he fully expected Amie to turn around and return home, but she was off again, holding her basket to her as she continued down the lane. Unable to resist, he followed her again.

To his surprise, she stopped at the very next cottage. Ian crept closer, ducking his long body behind a stone wall that came up to his waist. He lifted his head enough to see her hand something to someone inside the house.

Amie stepped back and waved. "Enjoy the broth, Mrs. Turner!"

Broth? Ian frowned. Was she playing nursemaid?

A moment later, Amie continued on, swinging her basket happily at her side. There weren't many houses along the road, but Amie stopped at every last one of them. Depending on where he could secrete himself, Ian couldn't always observe her interactions. It seemed she was . . . helping her neighbors. But how did she know them so well in such a short matter of time? Regardless of how, she had made fast friends with everyone. She was a marvel. There had been no need to worry about her at all. If she could take care of everyone, she could certainly take care of herself.

If he had possessed an ounce of guilt at walking away from Oak End, it slipped away with the morning sun. Indeed, her behavior now reminded him of their visits with her neighbors in Chestervale, where everyone had raved about her kindness. She'd even rescued Tiny, and Ian supposed he could include the mint leaves she'd so helpfully given him. A sudden grin played on his mouth. There was no denying that Amie had a bit of a Rebel spirit.

He tilted his head, trying to get a better look at her position. She stood on the front step of a stone house with a thatched roof, nodding and speaking little. Why was she lingering at this particular house? What were they conversing about? He couldn't make out a thing. He and Amie had certainly never spoken this long together. He shifted, his legs starting to cramp.

While he didn't mind freely observing her, he felt a trace of frustration. Shouldn't she have told him where she was spending her time? All these people—these strangers—were spending time with *his* wife, while he had to hide behind a shrub to get a good look at her before dinner.

He scoffed at his own unjust reaction. It was exactly how it should be. The neighborly interactions seemed innocent enough, and his thoughts were borderline jealous. The whole arrangement was confusing him, and he was not an easily confused man.

Amie stepped away from the cottage and finally began to return the way she'd come. He sucked his breath in to narrow the breadth of his chest, realizing this particular tree would not hide all of him should she look over.

When she passed, he stepped around to the back of the tree, but he should have looked at his feet and not at her. His boot caught on a raised root, and he went crashing down to the grassy undergrowth.

Someone gasped. He wasn't sure if it was him or Amie.

"Ian? Good heavens. Are you well?"

Blast. It was Amie. He hurried to his feet, brushing his trousers off. "Of course." His knee was smarting, but he wasn't about to admit it.

"What are you doing there?"

He pointed to himself. "Me? I'm . . . hunting." He forced an amiable smile.

She frowned, clutching her basket with both hands by her waist. "Hunting? For what?"

"Squirrels," he blurted. Because grown men always hunted squirrels. He barely withheld his grimace.

Her charming brown eyes blinked rapidly. "With no gun or weapon?"

He reached to scratch his neck and paused with his arm in the air. "I prefer to use my bare hands." He waved his hands like it was the obvious answer.

"I see." She shook her head. "Actually, I'm having trouble visualizing how this is done. My curiosity is piqued. Might I watch?"

He looked up into the tree and bent to reach for a rock. No, this was going too far. "Forgive me," he said, straightening. "It's not a sight for a lady."

"I suppose not." She relaxed her grip on her basket, letting it fall to her side. "I suppose we will have squirrel for dinner. I will congratulate you then. If you will excuse me, I will continue on my walk."

He nodded and waved her forward, his smile dropping when she was too far to see. Squirrel? Really? Was he ten years old again? Even then, that was the last thing he wanted to eat for dinner. But neither was he going to disappoint her. He had too much pride for that. He looked around, not seeing a rodent in sight. With a sigh, he went in search of the gamekeeper.

Once he finally returned to the house, it was already dark, and storm clouds gathered overhead. Eager to change and forget about his tiresome afternoon, he hurried inside. Mr. Hamburg met him at the door with a letter. Ian accepted it, broke the seal, and scanned the contents.

By Jove! This was exactly what he'd been hoping for. The new home secretary, Robert Peel, was intrigued about Ian's ideas for reform and wanted to meet. The House of Commons currently possessed more power than the House of Lords. He could almost taste the change on his lips.

How soon could he arrange to leave? The fortnight had not passed, but surely Amie would not begrudge having the house to herself sooner than planned. He committed to telling her at the first opportunity and leaving after breakfast.

He dressed for dinner and, once seated, grimaced at his plate. The small squirrel the gamekeeper had miraculously managed to catch lay cooked on his plate and sprinkled with herbs. Glancing at Amie, he caught her smile.

"I cannot wait to try it," she said.

Good. The squirrel had been worth the long afternoon if it meant pleasing her, especially since he meant to leave in the morning. He hoped to part on amicable terms.

If he had learned one thing about Amie in their week together, it was that she deserved to be happy, and she would be much happier when she could finally rid herself of him. Independence would finally be hers.

Her dream come true.

Whereas, he was oddly reluctant for dinner to end, despite the eagerness his earlier letter had lent him. Even if he did not plan on touching the main course, let alone tasting it, he had grown used to seeing Amie at this hour every night.

Perhaps that was why he needed to hasten his departure. No more habits like this needed to be formed before he returned.

CHAPTER 15

AMIE DID NOT CONSIDER HERSELF to have a picky palate, but no matter how she tried, she could not bring herself to eat more than a single bite of squirrel. It was . . . disgusting. She poked at the white meat on her plate, and when Ian bent to take a bite of his own dinner, she lifted a bare fork to her lips and pretended to chew. "Delicious, Ian."

He looked up at her. "I'm glad you enjoy it."

She couldn't even force a smile. The nutty taste of her first bite still tempted her to gag.

Instead, she nodded.

Vigorously.

They had had such strained interactions all week, and today was the first sign that Ian was no longer angry with her. He had followed her all morning, after all. She did not know whether his hunting had had any part of it, but she did know that she had caught sight of him several times while meeting with the neighbors. His large body wasn't terribly capable of masking his heavy footfalls either. Then Edna had told her that the gamekeeper had delivered squirrel for dinner but had stayed a half hour to complain about how his lordship had been so insistent that the gamekeeper had lost half a day's work chasing down the little varmint.

Amie wanted to smile thinking about it. Had Ian gone to such efforts because she had said she expected him to catch one? How strange and amusing. She wanted to encourage this camaraderie, whatever his motivations. It had seemed foolish to ever hope for love after their wedding. But friendship? Surely they could find some semblance of it. And there were the flowers too. Edna had said Ian had insisted Amie have fresh wildflowers brought to her room regularly and that he had prepared the first bouquet himself. His thoughtfulness had touched her. Could they not find some way to get to know each other better?

"Amie," Ian said.

She stopped her fake chewing. "Yes?"

"I'm leaving for London tomorrow."

Her fork dropped, clanging against her plate. Leave? Now? Had he not promised another week with her? She fought down her surprise and tempered her voice. "So soon?"

He frowned. "I promised you independence, and I see no reason to prolong my stay. There will be a carriage here at your disposal for any trips you should take to the shops in town or to visit friends. You have already done an admirable job at acquainting yourself with the house and the neighborhood. I hope you will be comfortable here."

Is that why he had followed her? Not because of any curiosity on his part or desire to know her better but because he'd wanted to see if she was capable of being left behind?

"Yes," she said quickly. "I want my independence." Her dream now felt like a lie on her lips. She felt compelled to say something more, even if she could not admit the truth to her changeable heart. "Please, don't rush out the door on my account. This is your home too. I can distract myself whether you are here or not. I hardly notice your presence." Another lie. It tasted worse than the squirrel. Of course she noticed Ian in the house. She sensed his movements almost before she heard him. It had been the same today on her walk.

She might be married to him, but admitting her strange feelings was unfathomable. Not after how he'd reacted to her kiss. She knew the difference between blind faith and sheer stupidity, and hoping for Ian to see her as anything more than a wife of convenience was clearly the latter.

Let him leave her. Then she might finally rid her thoughts of him.

Ian played with the stem of his glass, as he often did. "Is there anything I can do for you before I leave? I want to see that you're comfortable while I am away."

What did she need? She had more than she had ever had in her life. Finally, she thought of something. "Would you be willing to make travel arrangements for my mother? I do not know where to start."

"I would be happy to do so. How soon would you like her to come?"

"Perhaps in a month? I thought to fix up the bedroom next to mine, if you agree to it. The paint is chipping, and there is a tear in the drapes."

He pressed his lips together, humming his agreement. "I have left you a sizable allowance and credit at all the stores in town. You may make whatever changes you desire. The mercantile can help you order anything you cannot find readily stocked."

She had seen the piles of letters sent out for the mail. When had he had the time to do this for her? "Thank you. You are most generous."

"If you need more, you need only to write to me."

They ate quietly for another few minutes. She did not even pretend to touch the squirrel again. She had lost all motivation to please him, even if he had left her a never-ending allowance. He was leaving anyway. It seemed even a friendship would be too much to ask for.

After dinner she said a polite good night and wandered back to her bedchamber, her steps dragging. She did not know if she would see Ian in the morning. He often kept his distance until dinnertime. She shut herself into her room and shivered. Was it her mood, or was it colder than normal? Setting her evening gloves on her bedside table, she rubbed her bare hands along the gooseflesh on her arms before reaching for the bell pull to call for her maid. A howl sounded from the direction of her window, and she startled.

Crossing the room, she realized the glass had been left open. She peered out into the night, the trees swaying angrily.

"No, no, no." It couldn't be a storm. She had not seen any sign of the change in weather that morning on her walk. After she pulled the glass shut tightly, she backed away from it and shivered again. Surely it would blow over. There was nothing to worry about.

Her chest tightened.

It was just a little wind.

Just wind.

CHAPTER 16

IAN FELL INTO A COMFORTABLE sleep, hopeful for a chance to further his latest project and to have a reason to think of something other than dratted squirrels or a pair of luminous brown eyes. Everything was finally falling into place.

Sleep, however, was short-lived. A crash somewhere in the house startled him awake. And a shriek followed directly after. He bolted upright in bed, his heart pounding. A rumble of thunder roiled through the sky outside his window, and a flash of light filled his room. Had the storm woken him? Or had it been Amie? It took a moment for his mind to process what he'd heard.

The shriek had been distinctive.

Digging around for his trousers in the dark, he located them on a chair and shoved his legs inside. He tucked in his nightshirt and ran barefoot through his door toward Amie's.

In his eagerness to check on her, he didn't bother to knock but threw the door open. His eyes began to adjust to the dark, but it wasn't until a second flash of lightning that he saw that Amie's bed was empty.

"Amie?" His whisper was lost in a resounding crack followed by a torrent of rain against the house and window. He moved inside the room. He thought he'd heard a crash earlier. His foot hit something sharp. Lowering his gaze, he saw pieces of either a vase or a pitcher.

"Amie?" he called again, rounding her bed. The room was empty. She wasn't here. Maybe the storm had awakened her, too, and she'd knocked over the vase on her way to the kitchen for a bite to eat. Or perhaps she'd gone to the library for a book. He was tired, but he couldn't go back to bed without cleaning up the glass. He didn't want Amie to hurt herself. At the fireplace, he discovered the flint. It took a moment to light a candle, which he then held to assess the damage.

A boom like a cannon sounded outside. What a storm. He had observed a few dark clouds with the gamekeeper but nothing this severe. A whimper sounded from somewhere. Whirling around, he saw nothing. His tired mind was playing tricks on him. Shaking his head, he bent to pick up the largest piece of glass when he heard the whimper again.

His gaze flew to the closet door. It had come from that direction. There was no way she was in there, but he could not put the thought aside. "Dash it all," he muttered under his breath. He set the piece of glass on her dressing table and took the candle to the closet. With a yank, he opened it, fully expecting to see nothing.

He was wrong. Amie sat on the floor with something tied around her eyes. She had her hands over her ears and was rocking back and forth. Another whimper tumbled from her tightly squeezed lips.

Alarm seized him. "Amie," he said again, not bothering to whisper this time.

She stilled, her head turning to him.

He crouched into a sitting position, set the candle aside, and quickly had his hands on her blindfold. He pulled it off her head with a gentle tug. "What in heaven's name?"

Tear-streaked eyes looked up at him. "W-what are you doing here?"

"I heard a crashing sound. What are you doing in the closet? Was there an intruder?"

"I was just—" Another resounding crack sent her hands over her ears again.

Ian's eyes widened. She was scared of the storm. He scratched the back of his head. What was he supposed to do? He still held her blindfold, or handkerchief, or whatever it was.

After a moment, she lowered her hands again. "I put that on so I wouldn't have to see the lightning. And I came in here so I wouldn't have to hear the thunder." She swiped at the moisture on her cheeks. "You must think me ridiculous—a grown woman in a closet." She turned away from him, clearly embarrassed. "Please, go back to sleep."

And leave her here like this? "Are you certain you will be all right?"

"Yes," she said much too quickly. It reminded him of her hasty answer at dinner when she'd said she desired her independence. He had not dwelt on it then, but now he wondered what else she had meant. Her hesitancy here felt like determination but not honesty. Had it meant the same earlier?

He stood and offered her his hand. With some reluctance, she took it, and her nightdress unfolded like a waterfall. Her long, curly hair hung to her waist. Something in his gut pulled at him. He didn't feel like he should be seeing her this way, but neither could he bring himself to walk away when she was so frightened. "It feels wrong to leave you upset, Amie. Should I call your maid?"

"No. I will go back to sleep." She moved to step past him when a bolt of lightning flashed through her window. Jumping back, Amie snagged his shirt and dragged him inside the closet with her. Her hands trembled, shaking the fabric against his chest. He felt her gaze climb up his neck to reach his eyes. "That, uh, surprised me," she breathed.

And she kept surprising him.

He gulped, not sure whether she planned to let go of him. This was no mere fright. She was terrified. "What helps comfort you when there's a storm?"

"Oh, I'm not afraid of storms. I just don't care for the lightning or the thunder. It keeps me awake."

"Are you certain I cannot call for Edna?"

She gave a furtive shake of her head. "I don't want to trouble her."

Not even the dim light of his flickering candle could obscure her true feelings painted so plainly on her face. He was beginning to learn her mannerisms and expressions, and she was a terrible liar. His problem was guessing what she wanted to say instead but couldn't let herself. "Then, trouble me instead," he said.

"You?"

He nodded. "Tell me, what helps you sleep?"

She slowly released her grip on him. "Mama usually strokes my hair and sings to me." She shook her head again, lowering her eyes. "Oh, please leave me. This is humiliating."

He had been about to leave when she had dragged him into the closet, but he couldn't do so now. His shoulders sank with the reality of what he was about to offer. "I can . . . I can pat your head." He groaned inside. *Pat your head?* Had he really said it like that? Life had never been this awkward before he'd entangled himself with Amie. Now he was volunteering to break one of his own rules.

She scoffed, though it sounded choked from emotion. "Do viscounts pat heads? It seems more appropriate for a nursemaid."

He smiled. "Do not underestimate this viscount's abilities." The words were teasing, almost flirtatious. He was scaring himself.

"No, it's too much to ask. I couldn't."

"Amie." He said her name like a whispered command. "Let me help."

She held his gaze for several beats before giving an almost imperceptible nod. "Since you seem determined, I suppose we could try it." She took a deep breath and moved around him. She went straight to her bed and practically jumped beneath the covers at the sound of more thunder.

He scrubbed his hand over his jaw. This was going to be a long night.

He bought himself a few minutes by cleaning up the glass before inevitably returning to her side. There was nothing else for it; he had to stroke her hair. This storm wasn't going away anytime soon.

Amie laid on her side, turned away from him, her face half hidden in the covers. Kneeling beside the bed, he reached for her tangled hair. His hand wavered just before it made contact. The texture surprised him. Soft, silky strands coiled beneath his fingers. He lost his hand in the long tresses, completely absorbed by them.

It took another crack of the night sky and a jerk from Amie's body for him to remember why he was touching her hair. She was likely keeping her tears at bay sheerly because of his presence. His hand on her hair wasn't putting her to sleep either.

Her mother had *sung* too.

He squeezed his eyes shut, battling his pride. But Amie was his responsibility. He didn't want her to be afraid of anything, not if she was to survive here without him. A strong urge to protect and comfort her humbled him enough that he found himself humming the lullaby "Lavender Blue" from his childhood.

Lyrics came next, his singing voice a little rusty. Very well, a *lot* rusty. It took a verse or two before he gained confidence. His hand all the while continued to stroke her bewitching curls. The ones by her temple were tighter, and his fingers lingered there, playing with the hair. He repeated the verses he knew over and over again. Amie slowly stopped jumping at every noise or flash of light and relaxed beneath his hand.

He wasn't sure if she had fallen asleep, so when his voice went hoarse, he went back to humming. His own eyes were heavy, his knees ached, but he couldn't stop. She needed him.

And it was nice to be needed.

CHAPTER 17

AMIE FELT A HAND ON her head. Ian? She blinked, her swollen eyelids pulling partially apart with some effort. *Ian!* Her breath caught, and her eyes flew open the rest of the way. It was Ian's hand on her head, and his other hand was curled under his own head. He had fallen asleep hunched over her bed, while she had curled up beside him.

He had stayed here all night. Guilt swirled in her empty stomach. Why hadn't the storm come after he had left for London? Mama was the single living soul who knew about her deepest fears. She knew how storms awakened the horrible memories inside Amie, haunting her with every crack and flash of light. It was mortifying to suffer into her adulthood—to never grow out of her nightmares . . . to always be plagued by her darkest day.

She squeezed her eyes shut. Wasn't she already beneath Ian in every way? Need he witness her every humiliation?

Not certain what to do, she remained impossibly still, afraid to wake him. Looking elsewhere was futile, her attention riveted on his sleeping form. His breath came in a heavy, slow rhythm. Minutes ticked by, and somehow, some of the nervous tension left her.

This man . . . This serious man who wouldn't let anyone tell him what to do had been kind enough to care for her last night. He had shown glimpses of this soft side before but had hid it well recently. The slumbering Ian was different. His features were smooth and his mouth relaxed. Something tugged deep within her chest. The emotion resembled the warmth and affection she'd felt for him when she'd kissed him.

It would be foolish to overthink his thoughtfulness. He clearly felt a responsibility toward her, but she would not hope for him to care for her as a man did for a woman.

He had saved her from Robert and from Mama's lies and from a future doomed to hardship. She could never ask for more.

Despite this firmness of mind, her hand lifted of its own accord. Just one touch. One last feel of him before he left for London. And then she could be strong. Her fingers found the silk tendrils of his hair, and ever so gently, she stroked a lock off his forehead.

What would it be like to be loved by such a man? To feel safe in every storm? To wake up to him beside her every morning? In one breath, she praised God for her blessings, and in the next, she wondered if this were a form of punishment. She finally had the security she'd longed for, but never had she felt lonelier.

She fingered Ian's hair once more, the action comforting her. She wasn't alone right now, and that, in and of itself, was a tender mercy. If only she could memorize the feel of his hair beneath her hand and his presence beside her. Then perhaps the coming months and years wouldn't plague her.

Ian stirred, and Amie pulled back. He lifted his head, moving his arm from above her head, and blinked at her. His reaction mirrored hers, and his eyes widened to twice their normal size. "Amie."

She swallowed. "Good morning."

"Were you able to sleep?" His hand went to his hair, but his attempts to smooth it down mussed it further. She should be more embarrassed about her own state, but her one comfort was that she had to appear far better than she had last night.

She nodded against her pillow. "Thank you for staying with me."

"Of course. I want you to feel safe here." All at once, he straightened, and his easy composure disappeared. "You are forbidden to tell anyone that I, er, sang."

For all her lessons on manners, she could not hold back her laugh. "I'm sorry. You sing very well."

"You don't have to pretend. I am perfectly comfortable leaving that talent for others to possess."

"No, I like your voice. Honest." Her mind had latched on to his deep timbre, letting it flow through her until it had soothed her every fear.

His brow rose. "Then, you must be the first." He pushed himself from the side of the bed to a standing position and cried out as he stumbled forward, his hands landing right in front of her on the mattress. "My legs are cramped." He winced and stood again, stretching his back slowly as he did.

She sat up, holding the blanket to her chest. "What can I do?"

He held out his hand. "Nothing. I need a minute is all." He straightened and hobbled toward the door.

"Ian."

He turned at her voice. "Yes?"

"Safe travels."

He hesitated, staring at her with a solemn expression she could not read well. Was it reluctance? Or did she only wish it were?

Finally, he gave her a nod before slipping out her door.

She didn't sigh with regret or call after him with any hope. This was how it was meant to be. He was meant to leave, and she was meant to stay behind.

CHAPTER 18

THERE WAS NOTHING LIKE GOING up against a secretary of state, and Ian had been doing exactly that. Mr. Robert Peel was an intelligent man, but he was also a politician, and there were procedures to changing law and timelines to follow. Not to mention, Peel had previously committed to other causes. Ian's persuasions were hitting a brick wall, but he would not give up. "I've gone over to the Old Bailey courthouse and seen the records. Our executions have increased dramatically over the last century."

Mr. Peel sighed. "So has crime, unfortunately."

Ian hunched over Mr. Peel's desk, hoping the increased proximity would help the man see the urgency Ian felt. "Yes, yes, especially after the end of the war. But our system isn't creating more order, is it?"

Mr. Peel leaned forward, too, apparently not one to be easily intimidated. "We have limited resources to police and keep order in our country. Our prisons are overflowing and disorderly. I want change as much as anyone, but it must be done step-by-step. You speak as though you want to overturn it all at once."

"The fastest way to empty a bottle is to break it," Ian said.

Mr. Peel shook his head. "I won't break this country."

"I'm not asking you to. I'm asking you to break a system and save lives."

A few minutes later, Ian left his meeting discouraged. Mr. Peel was sympathetic to the cause, but he was pushing too many of his own platforms to take on this one too. And he, like many others, valued law and order and did not want to worsen the state of the nation by disrupting it.

Returning to his townhome, Ian longed to sit in his favorite leather chair for the entirety of the day and forget about all his problems. But he hadn't made it two feet into his home when his butler, Mr. Jones—a steady fellow with more sense than hair—stopped him.

"We did not expect you back so soon from Oak End, your lordship."

"I had business I had to address in Town." Ian handed Mr. Jones his hat. "How are Edna's younger sisters managing in the kitchen?"

"Cook is quite taken with them, your lordship."

"Very good."

Mr. Jones dusted off the top of Ian's hat. "Will your wife be joining you here?"

Wife. That word never ceased to rattle him. "No, she won't."

He took a step past Mr. Jones, but the man followed him. "Should I send a letter to your parents to inform them of your return?"

Ian's whole body shivered at the idea of facing his father again so soon. "No, thank you. That will not be necessary." Another step toward the drawing room. He was almost there.

"I merely thought to stop their journey if they have not already left, your lordship."

Ian paused and looked over his shoulder. "Has my mother returned to Brookeside?"

"No, your lordship," Mr. Jones said. "Lord Kellen and your mother planned to travel to visit you and your new wife at your hunting box."

Ian whirled fully to face Mr. Jones, his pulse galloping like a herd of wild horses. Frightened wild horses. "When did you hear this?"

"Only this morning, as some of the staff have been given a bit of a holiday, as they won't be needed until your family returns."

"Blast." Ian marched back to Mr. Jones and took his hat from the man's hands. "It looks as if I am returning to Oak End post haste." As much as he couldn't let his parents discover the truth behind their sham of a marriage, he also didn't dare leave Amie unprotected with his father. He could hear his father's condescending voice without any effort of his own, and he didn't want his father's negativity hurting Amie's feelings or leaving her insecure. If Ian left now on horseback, he could beat their carriage.

His marriage had made it this far, and he would protect what was his.

CHAPTER 19

AMIE HAD SPENT SO LONG living with other people that she'd thought she would like living alone. The first day was tolerable, but by the second morning, the emptiness of the house began to press in upon her. Even Tiny was feeling Ian's absence. She'd had to banish the dog to the kitchen to keep him from whining at the door for hours on end.

He needed to learn that there was no use wallowing in what could not be changed. She'd learned that precise lesson plenty of times in her own life—and it seemed she was about to learn it again. Staying busy was the best cure she could think of, so she threw herself into preparing Mama's room, determined to turn the house into her own.

She called a footman and maid up to help her, assigning the footman to move the furniture away from the walls while she covered each of the pieces with Holland covers. She instructed the maid to take down the sun-stained curtains with the tear.

"And what would you have me do with them when we're finished, my lady?" Gwen was a stout maid with ruddy cheeks. She didn't say much, but she had proved herself to be a hard worker.

"Excellent question, Gwen. The fabric is poor enough that it's only fit for the fire. The bedding is salvageable. I think I know a family who could use it."

"Yes, my lady," the maid replied. She pulled over a chair to the window to start taking down the drapes.

Amie finished putting a cover over the dressing table when a scream sounded from behind her followed by a loud thud. Whirling around, Amie found Gwen on the floor with her leg twisted at an unnatural angle. Amie rushed to Gwen's side as another servant who had come running at the scream left again to call for the doctor. As the servant rushed for help, Amie and the footman worked together to set Gwen up in the last spare bedroom on the upstairs floor.

"It's a bad break," the doctor informed them once he'd arrived and had a chance to exam her. He closed his satchel. "I wouldn't recommend any servants carrying her down the stairs for at least a week as the bones sets. And no weight on the leg for another five after that."

Gwen whimpered behind them. The poor thing was miserable.

It was late afternoon when Amie finally had a moment to sit down and catch her breath. The small library had quickly become a solace to her, and her feet moved toward the serenity she would find there. She'd not made it past the staircase when the front door flew open.

Her next breath did not come. Or the next. "Ian?" The name came out in a suffocated squeak.

His face was lined with fatigue, but his eyes were bright and alert. He shut the door behind him and strode toward her. Her heart raced the nearer he came. Stopping abruptly in front of her, he said in the velvety timbre she had missed, "Amie, we must speak."

She nodded, unable to find her voice. He set his hand on her back and directed her toward the library. Ironic that they had both thought of the same place. But what did he possibly want to say? Had . . . had he missed her? Is that why he had returned so quickly? There was such a determined look about him that it sent a thrill through her middle.

Could he . . . could he care about her?

After shutting them inside the library, Ian put a hand on each of her arms, completely breaking the rules. If her heart had raced before, it was erratic now. "What is it, Ian?"

"I had to come back. To see you."

She bit her lip. Was this love? She'd wondered her whole life about it, and now she was experiencing it. "You did?"

He gave a long nod. "Before my parents arrived."

She smiled, unable to help herself. And then she blinked. His parents? Her mouth drooped as quickly as it had risen. No, he was not in love with her. "Y-your parents are coming here?"

"Yes," he said, as if that one word could convey the seriousness of the situation. "I don't know how far they are behind me. They had a decent head start. I only beat them because I was not in a carriage but on horseback. There is much to speak of before they come. My father hinted that he did not think of us as a love match. If he does not believe we are married in every sense of the word, I believe he will try to have the wedding annulled."

A panicky feeling landed in her chest. "I don't understand. Is he coming here for that very reason?"

"I don't see another reason for him to come. He is not a man to pay a social call without good reason. If it doesn't benefit him or Parliament, he won't do it."

Apprehension started to spread from her chest to her stomach. She had thought Lord Kellen tolerated her, but she should have known better. People did not soften overnight. Certainly not for small things such as walking a person down the aisle at a wedding. What he'd said to her that day came to her mind—his comment about how Ian must care more for her than furthering his career. Regardless of Ian's lack of feelings for her, his father saw Ian's decision to marry her as wrong. He had been unable to prevent the wedding, but perhaps he would try to prevent their marriage from lasting. And now she was to play hostess to him.

"I should tell the cook that we are to expect more for dinner tonight." She chewed on her lip, wondering if there was anything else she could organize. She thought of Mama, wondering what she would do. They might not have had a home of their own, but Mama had subjected Amie to lessons on the ways to run a household. Without a dowry, it had seemed impractical at the time—silly even— but now Amie was extremely grateful.

Ian released her. "I did not think of dinner. An excellent idea. And we can have a maid air out the bedrooms upstairs and make certain clean linens are placed inside."

Amie felt a little faint. "Upstairs?"

He nodded. "We should prepare both bedrooms. My parents often sleep separately."

"Oh, fiddlesticks," she breathed.

Ian's frown deepened. "Fiddlesticks? It is not uncommon for a husband and wife to prefer separate bedrooms."

"No, that is not it. It's another matter entirely. A big matter, actually. There aren't any bedrooms available for them."

"What do you mean?"

He wasn't going to like this. "I mean that Gwen broke her leg and is confined to the bedchamber on the end."

"Gwen? Who is Gwen?"

"One of our maids."

"And she is in one of the bedrooms? Upstairs?"

Amie winced. "Yes."

Ian sighed. "I suppose they must share the other spare room, then."

Amie shook her head. "I thought to prepare it for my mother. I had the bedding donated and the drapes burned."

Ian's mouth fell open. "Good grief."

Amie was reluctant to continue, but she had to explain. "We spent all morning pushing the furniture to the middle of the room and covering it so we might paint."

Ian pinched his nose with his hand. "Stop, please stop."

She held her tongue, though her mind raced for a solution. Surely they could find more bedding, though it would take time to put the furniture back. They couldn't order new drapes fast enough, but maybe they could tack blankets to the wall? What was she thinking? When had tacked blankets been acceptable for an earl and a countess?

"They'll have to have my room," Ian finally said, dropping his hand with a long, weary sigh.

Amie frowned. It didn't seem fair that he should give up his room when she had created the bedchamber dilemma to begin with. "But where will you sleep?"

His brow rose, and he gave her a pointed stare.

She scrunched her nose. "In the library?"

He shook his head.

She thought again. "The sitting room?"

He shook his head again.

There was no room in his small office. Not for a man as tall as him. Then it dawned on her. "Wait." Her eyes widened. "With . . . me?"

Ian gave her a concise nod, his face grim.

Her mouth formed the shape of an *O*.

Ian stepped back from her and took a seat on the sofa, facing the fireplace. "I never imagined I would put you in this situation, but you did agree to help my father believe our marriage is legitimate. I would not ask if I knew a better alternative."

She forced her gaping mouth to close. She couldn't just stare dumbly at him all night. He deserved an answer. "I suppose it is a fair solution. It's not like we haven't spent the night together in the same room before." Heat filled her cheeks as she added, "You can depend upon my help."

"Thank you," Ian said. "I shall speak to the housekeeper about the arrangements, if you can inform the cook."

She nodded, clasping her hands together like the brave little viscountess she wasn't. Ian pushed away from the sofa and made to leave, but she wasn't ready for him to abandon her. Not yet. Before he could grasp the door handle she blurted, "Were you able to finish your business in London?"

He looked at her over his shoulder, his frown deepening. "No, but I am more anxious than ever to see it through." He did not expound, but she could see that whatever it was that he was working on weighed heavily on him. She filled in his unsaid words: When his parents left, he would leave again too.

Once he vacated the room, her shoulders slumped. She rubbed her forehead with one hand and hugged her waist with the other. Why had she immediately assumed he had returned to confess his love to her? She was an idiot. She would play the part of a dutiful wife, but she would not grow any more attached. There was no reason to miss someone who did not miss her in return.

CHAPTER 20

IF HIS WEDDING HAD BEEN awkward, dinner with Amie and his parents was far worse.

"We must apologize again for coming unannounced," Mama said to Amie across the table. Amie had dressed the part with a pretty pale-yellow gown and her hair pinned neatly to her head. Too neatly. He suddenly wished it were down, which would be, of course, completely inappropriate. His tired mind was abusing him again.

"You are always welcome," Amie said. She met Ian's gaze, almost as if she sought approval of her statement.

He smiled at her and gave a small nod. She had done exceedingly well for her first time hosting. He knew she had little experience with gatherings to the level his family was used to, but no one would know it by how she performed her role. She carried herself with an air of grace and said all the right things.

Was it wrong of him that he was half afraid of another unexpected occurrence? Something like finding a maid convalescing in the family rooms. He still couldn't believe how the house had been turned upside-down in the mere two days of his absence.

After dinner, his mother took Amie's arm, and the two of them left to the sitting room together. He heard Amie whisper an apology about missing the wedding breakfast. He cringed inwardly. He should have been the one to apologize for it, but he was grateful she had done it for them. He tried to relax back in his seat, but his muscles were stretched taut. It was just him and his father now, and Ian wasn't prepared for it.

"Lady Reynolds has exceeded my expectations," Father said flippantly.

Ian resisted slamming down his glass at his father's impertinent statement but instead rested the glass as gently as he could on the table. "I do not think you need any expectations for my wife since your opinion holds no weight on the subject. We are already married."

Father pressed his lips together. "All I'm saying is you could have done worse in your rush to disobey me."

Ian's grip tightened around his glass. If he gripped it any harder, he knew he would crush it. This was no backhanded compliment. It was a reminder that his father was wise to the situation and an even greater reminder that Ian was a continual disappointment. Unless he wanted glass shards stuck in his hand, continuing this conversation seemed pointless. Ian pushed back his chair. "You must excuse me. I am eager to be by Amie's side." He strolled purposefully from the table. His father's voice stopped him before he made it very far.

"Did you miss her so terribly when you took off to London in the middle of your wedding trip?"

Ian ground his teeth together, fighting against all the frustrated words he wanted to throw at his father. He turned, just enough so his father could see his calm expression—albeit incredibly forced. "I had important business in London. Is that why you rushed here? To ascertain if I regretted my choice? You can see for yourself, Amie and I are happily wed."

He did not wait for his father to respond. With a controlled hand, he pulled the door open and strode into the sitting room. His breath, however, came in short bursts. Amie looked over her shoulder at him from her seat on the sofa and smiled.

That one smile, laced with her innocent charm, steadied him. His anger melted considerably. He had calmed her in her storm, and she would not abandon him in his time of need either. They were allies, and while it was and would always be a loveless marriage, she was offering her friendship.

And he would take it.

⁓

Ian forced a visage of calm when he felt anything but. His father, annoyed by the sleeping situation, grumbled under his breath about sharing the family rooms with the help. Mama, however, was her usual collected self and did not betray her feelings on the subject. They stood outside his bedchamber, as if waiting for him and Amie to turn in first.

"Good night, then," he said to his parents.

"Good night," Mama said.

Father held his ground, his expression smug.

Ian held out his arm for Amie and led her into her room—their room. The last thing he saw before he shut the door was his father's raised brow. Ian wouldn't give him a single reason to think this marriage a sham.

A trembling hand on his arm altered his attention away from his father. He glanced down at Amie. She looked rather pale. Her nerves were betraying her.

Ian cleared his throat and whispered, "I am sorry."

Amie released him and took a step away. "It isn't your fault."

"I won't forget the first rule of our contract tonight," he said.

She nodded, but by her noticeable gulp, she wasn't ready to swallow this situation he had served her.

He looked around, wondering how to proceed. Neither of them was dressed for the night. "I will step out for a moment and let your maid attend to you."

She nodded too many times. "That would be kind."

He almost laughed but more from awkwardness than humor. He nodded and let himself out. When he turned, he saw his father standing there with his arms folded, looking not at all surprised to see him.

"I . . ." Ian started, searching for some excuse. He spoke the first thing that came to his mind, something that was in truth about himself. "Amie sometimes has trouble sleeping. I'm fetching some warm milk from the kitchen."

"Can't a servant do that?"

Ian straightened. "A husband ought to serve his wife when he can." He moved to the staircase before his father could laugh in his face. Even if Ian didn't love Amie, he would stand by his statement, regardless if he was in the minority in his opinion.

After stalling in the kitchen, taking a moment to play with Tiny, where they had decided he'd best remain with company in the house, Ian returned upstairs with the warm milk. He'd been gone at least a quarter hour, but his father was still standing in the corridor. Father leaned against the wall, examining his fingernails, obviously waiting for him. Ian gave him a curt nod and marched toward Amie's bedchamber door. He wanted, with everything he possessed, to knock, but to save face, he did not. When he entered, he kept his face down, and once the door was closed, he hastily turned toward it.

"Are you decent?" he whispered.

"Yes," Amie said.

He turned and found she was already in bed, with covers pulled up to her neck. The second thing he noticed was a line of pillows beside her, right down the middle of the bed.

Once again, his frustration melted at the sight of her. He fought his smile as he blew out the candles by the fireplace and, though she might not appreciate it, approached her on her side of the bed. He handed her the warm milk.

She sat up and accepted it. "Thank you. This is very thoughtful."

"You're welcome." He pointed to the pillows. "The boundary line is most creative."

"I didn't want to accidentally touch you. I know how sensitive you are about rule number one."

His brows rose. "Me? Sensitive?"

She nodded.

He wasn't sensitive about anything. He opened his mouth to argue, but there was no point. She was right that he didn't want her to touch him, but not because he was afraid she would give him a disease. In truth, he wanted her comfort more than his own. "My sensitivities are not as important as yours. Is there anything else I can do to make this night easier for you?"

She studied the bed that looked a great deal smaller with her in it, especially with the pillows. He would be sleeping on the edge all night.

"Perhaps you could sleep upside-down?" she asked.

"What?" The word came out louder than he'd intended. He looked at the wall separating them from his parents and, in a lower voice, repeated, "What?"

"You know, put your head on the opposite end of the bed and your feet near the top?"

Of all the ridiculous ideas. He bit down his natural response once more. "I can certainly do as you ask." It trumped sleeping on the floor.

Amie finished her milk and set it aside. "I'll turn away while you undress." She blew out her candle beside her and put the blanket over her head.

She made it sound like he was stripping down to nothing. He held in his chuckle and moved to his side of the bed. He cast off his boots, jacket, cravat, and waistcoat. Then he unbuttoned the top of his shirt so he could breathe better. Neither it nor his trousers were going anywhere. He didn't want to shock Amie more than the circumstances already were.

He blew out the candle on his side of the bed, the last one lit, before flipping his pillow to the bottom of the bed and slipping under the covers himself. "You can take the blanket off your head now. I'm decent."

Amie pulled the blanket off, but even in the dark, he could tell she did not move to glance at him. "Good night."

"Good night."

He lay there for several minutes, sleep evading him. Devil take it, his pillow smelled like Amie—an intoxicating vanilla that would haunt his dreams.

Amie stirred on her side. "Ian?" she whispered.

"Hmm?"

"You don't have to tell me, but I am curious why you and your father do not get along."

"It's a long history. I am not certain where to start."

"I see. Is there anything about your father that you admire? Or does everything about him bother you?"

What a question. "Must I answer?"

"No, you don't have to."

He thought about it for a moment. So much of his father bothered him that he hadn't spared a moment to look for any good qualities. He supposed the man had a few, as most people did. Ian thought she might be asleep by the time he answered. "I suppose he is decisive and not easily fooled." *Unfortunately for them.*

Amie stirred a little. "It seems he gave his best traits to you."

He gave a half smile against his pillow. "I'm glad you see something in me worth admiring after what I've put you through tonight."

"I see more good in you than that," she said. "Though sometimes I don't think you want others to know how good you are."

He shook his head against his pillow. Amie could be extremely honest when she decided to open up to a person. "You sound like my friends in Brookeside. Sometimes, I think they're the only ones who know the real me." He didn't know why he'd said it, but there was no taking it back now.

Her quiet voice answered back, "I am happy you have people like that in your life."

Her words touched him. More than she would probably ever know. "What about you? Who knows the real Amie?"

"I . . . I don't know." He hadn't expected for her to stumble over her answer. "Tell me about Brookeside," she said quickly. "You mentioned you have a house there that you might return to at some point.

Do you love it because your friends are there, or is there something special about the location that draws you in?"

It didn't escape him how she'd turned the subject back on him. He didn't mind. He could talk about Brookeside all day. "Bellmont Manor is a picture, but the land is what is truly beautiful. We have two ponds, where we swim, fish, and picnic. My friends and I prefer the farther one because it's larger and removed from onlookers."

"What else?" she asked, a yawn nearly cutting off her words.

It was like she was asking him to talk her to sleep. He did so little for her that he would oblige her in this. "There's the Dome."

"The Dome?"

"My hideout—a Palladian-style temple." He couldn't believe he was telling her this, but it was as close to a bedtime story as he could think of. "The place where my friends and I scheme about escaping our mothers and saving the world."

"It sounds perfect."

"It is to me. The Rebels and our missions are my life."

"Rebels?"

He nodded against his pillow. "That's what we call ourselves— Rebels against Society's injustices." He had never told anyone about the secret work he and his friends did, but it felt right telling Amie.

After a moment, she asked another question, breaking the stillness in the room with her quiet voice. "The friends from your wedding. Are they Rebels?"

"Yes, along with Lisette and Walter Bentley. You might have heard, but they remained behind in Brookeside for personal matters. Five of us grew up together, but now their spouses have joined the cause too."

"And you help people?" There was awe in her voice, and her respect made him feel like twice the man he was.

"We try to."

"Your life in Brookeside sounds like an adventure."

"At times, it has been." In an attempt to help her relax, he shared a few stories of his getting into scrapes as a child. He added other information about his home and his friends, mostly insignificant details. When he heard her soft breathing, he knew she was finally asleep. He forced his eyes to close and his mind to empty, but Amie's question about his father circled in his mind again, pushing away all the sweet memories of Brookeside. He rotated from his side to his back, but the question persisted.

What did he like about his father?

The man wasn't all bad. Outside of his personal life, he supposed his father had been a bit of a Rebel himself. He'd done a lot of good with his career in Parliament. Ian had noticed, but he hadn't wanted to believe it. What good was a man's work if he neglected his family?

Ian willed that question to linger in his mind instead, and for some reason, it made him think of Amie. He drifted off to sleep before he could figure out why.

CHAPTER 21

AMIE TOSSED AND TURNED ALL night from an upset stomach. She woke in the morning feeling groggy. Pillows were sprawled across the other side of the bed. Ian's side. She hadn't heard him get up. Easing out from under the covers, she went to the bell pull and gave it a tug. Edna had better hurry. If she dressed quickly, Amie could begin playing the dutiful role of hostess and smooth over some of the awkwardness of the night before.

When she turned around, she noticed something sticking out from under her bed. She moved toward it, curious about what it was. Stopping suddenly, she realized the subject of her gaze. It was a foot! She hurriedly crept over the bed. Ian hadn't woken. He was asleep on the floor! He had one leg tucked under the bed, and the smallest corner of the quilt draped over his chest and one arm. How cold and hard his night must have been.

Oh dear. Edna would be here any moment. Her chatter would wake up Ian in an instant. Sucking in her breath, she realized something worse. Edna felt it her duty to report the comings and goings of the house to Amie. She was a bit of a gossip. If Edna witnessed Ian sleeping on the floor, Amie wasn't certain she trusted the maid enough to keep such a matter a secret.

After donning her robe, Amie moved to Ian's side and crouched beside him. She took his arm in her hand and gave it a nudge. "Ian. *Ian!*"

Ian's eyes flew open, and he sat up quickly. His hands came up around her arms. "What is it? What's wrong?" His eyes darted around her face, neck, and nightgown.

His instant concern made her forget what she was doing for a moment. "It's Edna. My maid. I didn't see you here on the floor, so I called for her."

Dropping his hands, he seemed to understand her halting sentences and climbed to his feet. Amie tried to look away, but she wasn't fast enough. She should have been relieved that he was still fully clothed, but even though this was the second time she had seen Ian in just his shirtsleeves, this time, she had a much better view of him.

Although his half-dressed attire emphasized his well-built shoulders and chest, it wasn't exactly indecent. No, that was not what she would call it at all. It was a state of vulnerability—of normalcy. In his shirtsleeves, he wasn't the viscount or the imposing man who wouldn't let anyone dare try to control his life. With his shirttails sticking out and his hair ruffled, he was human. And so utterly real it nearly stole her breath.

"What is it now?" Ian asked, taking up his discarded waistcoat.

She'd been staring. But how could she not? In one moment, one of the many walls between them had simply vanished. She didn't know the removal of fine clothing could do that. It was just the two of them, her in her nightgown with her tangled curls in a haphazard braid and him—the man who had slept beside her—standing thusly.

"Nothing." She blinked and looked away. Their strange, guarded relationship hadn't prevented them from finding themselves in another intimate situation. It was as if fate were trying to tell them something. But perhaps fate would be better off focusing on a more willing couple in less trying circumstances.

Clearing her throat, she suggested an idea while he put on his waistcoat. "There is a dressing screen in the room next door covered in Holland covers. Could we not bring it in here? That ought to solve some of our problems for the next several days."

"Brilliant." He arched his back and groaned.

"Was the floor more comfortable than the bed?"

He pinned her with a glare. "The floor does not kick me in its sleep."

She blinked. "Oh my. I did have a restless night. I apologize."

Ian shook his head. "You didn't move more than an inch the night of the storm, but last night, pillows were flying as though someone had dragged a catapult in here."

She wanted to disappear into the cracks in the floors. "How . . . mortifying."

"Nonsense. You cannot control what you do in your sleep. At least, I don't think you can. Perhaps you subconsciously wanted to abuse me." He moved to her dressing table and looked at himself in the mirror. "No bruises on my face, thankfully."

"I kicked you in the face?" Her hand went to her mouth.

He turned to her, his defined jaw clenching. "You weren't asleep, were you? You broke rule number one again, and I daresay you're getting more creative in how you do it. Was this my punishment for imposing on you?"

She quickly shook her head.

"Now I understand why you asked me to sleep upside-down. I did apologize for this situation I put you in. Why couldn't you have merely told me that you hated it?" He set his hands on his hips and stalked toward her, stopping just in front of her. His eyes peered steadily into hers, searching for answers he surely would not find.

Last night, she had felt as though they were two members of the same team—partners, so to speak. He had even answered her question about his father, even though it couldn't have been easy. How could she have kicked him in the face and ruined all their progress? Now he thought she wanted to abuse him?

Annoyed at herself, she blurted in a frustrated tone, "If I'd wanted to kick you, I wouldn't have done it covertly."

One thick brow rose. "What does that mean?"

"It means if I had wanted to kick you, I would have done it just as we are and not while you were unconscious." Maybe. With the way he looked at her, rendering her nearly breathless, she wasn't sure her weak knees could produce a kick at all.

Ian put his hand up against the wall behind her head. When had she stepped back against it? "I see. Are you feeling particularly like you want to kick me just now? Because I would rather have it done here in private than anywhere else. Could you please give your generally nice husband such a courtesy?"

"I . . . I . . ."

"I'm tired, Amie. If you're going to get out any aggression, do it now. I'll let you."

Her eyes flicked to the grim line of his mouth. It was easier to look there than meet his gaze while it peered into her very soul. A sudden memory came to mind—one where she had experienced touching that mouth before. Fiddlesticks! She shouldn't have looked at his lips either. Heat flooded not just her face but her entire being, too, and she glanced back up at his eyes. "I . . . don't want to kiss you."

His eyes smoldered. "Who said anything about kissing?"

She frowned. What had she said? *Kiss* you? She frantically shook her head. "I mean, kick you. Not kiss you."

"Really?" His words came out low. "Because you seem to have an affinity for both." His gaze dropped to her mouth.

"Who, me?" She gave a nervous laugh. She started to explain herself but her words died. Was it her, or was gravity pulling them closer together by the moment? Either there was no air in the room, or she had forgotten how to breathe.

A knock on the door sounded, and Ian's eyes met hers once more. He didn't pull away like she thought he would but stayed in that same position, with his hand on the wall beside her head, studying her. The heat in his gaze seemed to burn her cheeks.

She blinked, and the spell broke.

He pulled back and cleared his throat.

What did it mean? Did he resent marrying her? Or had his thoughts gone the same direction as hers?

But surely he would never kiss her again . . .

It wasn't as though he were as affected as she was. He had so much control over himself—over his emotions. But did he ever think of kissing her? Was he thinking of it now? Ian raked his hand through his hair and finished buttoning the top of his shirt. "I'll see to the screen," he said before he stalked away.

CHAPTER 22

AMIE DIDN'T CONSIDER HERSELF TO be hiding in the library. The servants knew where she was. No, she was staying out of the line of fire. Lady Kellen had gone to visit a friend she knew who lived a short carriage ride away, leaving the two men to spar with words freely whenever they were in company together. Amie had tended to Gwen, brought a treat to Tiny, and overseen any other hostess duties, but in the end, she had needed a retreat.

Even sewing was preferable to either of the men's company at the moment. Especially Ian's. After this morning, she didn't know what to think of him . . . of them. Somehow, something had shifted again, much like it had after their wedding. There had been a heated tension pulling between them all day. They were either looking at each other or trying not to. She needed time to sort it out.

Amie unpacked her sewing basket in search of the handkerchief she was embroidering with her new initials, in case she ever attended any parties or public outings. She shifted her basket and dropped her needle on the ground. Sighing, she set the basket aside and climbed onto her hands and knees to search for her needle. While brushing her hand along the blue Axminster carpet, the door to the library opened. Her tea, finally. The sofa blocked her view of the entering maid, and Amie didn't dare move her hand from her search to stand or wave her in. With a few more swipes, she finally secured the needle and returned it to its place in the basket on the floor. Suddenly, a voice behind her spoke.

"I haven't forgotten what's happened," Ian said. "How could I?"

Ian? Amie's whole body cringed. He had found her. And on her hands and knees, as though she were some idiotic baboon! Maybe asking him to sleep upside-down had been too much. Didn't he realize that she'd done it only to keep his silly rules? She felt like a disobedient puppy ready to be chastised by its master. She kept her head ducked, embarrassed to face him.

His gruff tone changed to a softer one. "My words might take you by surprise since we are little acquainted, but a change must be made."

A change? Her head tilted an inch to the side.

"You and I are not so dissimilar. In fact, a union between us—an intimate union could make all the difference. I believe—I hope—we feel the same on this subject. Do we not?"

Sweet hope rushed through her. She thought about their almost-kiss that morning. She hadn't admitted that it had been just that until this moment, but she realized that it meant he had felt something too. Still, she couldn't move out of her crouched position behind the sofa. Couldn't answer him. Couldn't even look at him. As awkward as she was, he was asking her to confess before he did, and she didn't have the courage. Her heart raced all the same. Could he really want to stop pretending and make a go at their marriage?

"I know so many others hold higher qualifications than I do," Ian continued, "but the passionate state of my heart is what matters."

She felt her lips curling into a smile. How modest of him. She did not imagine he had ever been so forthright with his feelings before.

"Please, give me a chance to prove myself," he begged. Yes, begged. It was nearly Amie's undoing. "I've never asked anything of anyone, but this small favor would mean a great deal to me."

Her smile came fully this time. She forgot all about wanting to hide and stood up. "Your eloquent words have persuaded me. My answer is yes."

Ian yelped. His back hit a bookshelf, and a few books tumbled out onto his head. He winced and rubbed a hand through his hair. "Amie, you startled me."

"I did?" Did he not like her answer? Had he not expected it? But surely he had seen the desire in her eyes that she hadn't been quite able to hide.

He reached for the books to replace them. "I did not see you there. You were like a ghost, jumping up the way you did."

"You . . . you didn't see me?"

He shook his head. "What was that you were saying about an answer?"

Her confidence wavered. Had he been practicing his speech to her? "I gave you the answer to your question: yes."

"My question?" He stared at her, wide-eyed. "Oh, you mean the letter I was dictating to Sir James?"

She frowned deeply, to her very slippers. "Who is Sir James?"

Ian scratched under the cravat at the back of his neck. "Sir James Mackintosh of the House of Commons. Did you think it sounded all right? After my fruitless interview with Robert Peel, I need this to work. It's really imperative that we work on amending the criminal law together."

A member of Parliament? Criminal law? She squeezed her eyes shut. How many times must she humiliate herself in front of this man? And on the same day! She had to rethink the particulars of the conversation to see how she possibly thought he was speaking to her, and about them, before she could answer him. Was her heart so deluded that she actually believed he would ever want her? "Oh, fiddlesticks," she muttered under her breath. "Do you always dictate your letters like this? Or do you usually employ a scribe?"

"No, I prefer to do my correspondence myself. I hoped to get the particulars right before I took up my pen. But the letter seemed to excite you. You must have thought it convincing?"

Too convincing. She had been ready to overlook his failings and try for a real marriage. It was like her father had always told her—she was too soft-hearted. What she needed right now was a trip to see her father's headstone so she could talk this confusing situation out. She cleared her throat, a very unladylike thing to do, and forced herself to answer him. "I am only convinced by your dictation that you need my help."

"Oh?" He gave a short laugh. "Do you have experience with writing to members of Parliament?"

She shook her head. She was talking about something else entirely. This was twice now that she had imagined he was saying one thing when he had really meant another. She feigned a look of confidence. "I shall be your scribe and will write what you say until you get it right. You wouldn't want to confuse Sir James."

He scowled. "What part was confusing?"

"All of it." *Every last word.* "Trust me when I say, you need my help."

He eyed her as if he could see all the trouble she had ever caused him embodied before him. It wasn't her fault that he always witnessed the worst of her. Some people thought she had the kindness of angels. They were possibly old or sick, but that wasn't the point. Either way, she doubted that kindness was what Ian saw when he looked at her.

He rubbed the crease in his chin. "I suppose you may help."

Her brows rose. He had actually agreed? She had better do something about it before he changed his mind. "Brilliant, I will collect some writing materials." She rushed past him and out the door to collect parchment and her writing box.

A half hour later, she had written two different versions of the letter, and neither of them could be mistaken for a love letter to herself. She couldn't decide if that was fortunate or unfortunate. But as she had never received a letter even remotely on that subject, she reminded herself to pay attention. There was a lot to understand about Ian's interests, and she was determined that this activity would help her puzzle him out. She had never guessed that he would pick such large battles to fight.

Without disclosing too many details, he'd told her about meeting a servant girl caught in the act of thieving and how the thought of her dying had shaken him. Amie had lived in England her entire life and disliked plenty of political and social positions but had never thought about doing anything about it. There was something about Ian's story that made her see him in a whole new light. He wasn't out to start a ripple but a tidal wave of progress, and she believed him equal to the task. She wanted to know how he would do it and to watch every moment as history was made.

"This Sir James Mackintosh"—she began—"do you really think he is capable of lowering the number of reasons for hangings?"

"Not just him. He's on a committee that has been reviewing the criminal law for nearly four years, and before that, others were doing so. I *must* join their cause. At the risk of sounding like a braggart, my friends and influence could possibly expedite the results. Robert Peel might be the prime minister one day, but he's biding his time—a true politician. Change will come, but not fast enough. Mackintosh has the tenacity for the subject. He's going to be the push Peel needs. Every minute counts, and lives depend upon it."

Amie couldn't fathom such passion—such commitment. She understood better now what he'd meant on their drive in Chestervale when he had claimed to rebel against the societal rules he did not care for and again last night when he had said he tried to help people. He did not mean it in a flippant, reckless way but in an honorable, just manner. He really did want to make England better. It was a quality wholly without guile and truly admirable.

One question led to another, and Ian patiently answered each one. The time passed quickly, but it was not long enough. Everything he said fascinated her. Many would frown on discussing politics with a woman—they were too delicate a creature—but not Ian. He was un-fettered in the knowledge he bestowed.

"You've been so kind to answer my questions," Amie said when no more nagging thoughts came to mind. "If it was not obvious how ignorant I am on matters of state before, it is now."

"The only crime of ignorance is if you willingly choose to remain in that state despite the opportunity to do otherwise. It's an admirable quality to seek after knowledge, Amie."

Her cheeks warmed at the compliment. "I do not know many men who would share your opinion."

"Then, be grateful that I am your husband and not any other man." He winked at her, sending a flutter to her middle. *Ian* had winked at her. Lord Grumpy himself! How was she supposed to respond? After confusing his letter as a declaration of affection, she willed herself not to read into this gesture.

Conversation. They needed more conversation. "You speak as if you often immerse yourself in giving charity and righting Societal wrongs," she began. "When did you decide to spend your time this way? After all, you are not in Parliament yet and do not have to spend your hours aiding various causes."

Ian sank down onto the sofa beside her, making her writing lap desk wobble on the other side of her. His arm came up on the back of the sofa but did not extend to her. Giving her a sideways glance, he said, "I was waiting for your questions to turn personal. You have a tendency to pry." His voice was half serious and half amused.

She looked down sheepishly. "Forgive me."

"No, I will answer honestly, as I did last night. There are some matters I prefer to keep private, but this does not need to be a secret between us. You might as well understand why I am the way that I am. And I admit, telling you so prolongs facing more conversation with my father."

Lord Kellen had stuck his head in once, shaken it, and disappeared again. He was a suspicious man. She did not blame Ian for avoiding him.

Ian sat for a moment, lost in his thoughts, or perhaps gathering them. When he began, his words were slow, almost as if he were testing out whether he wanted to share them or not. "Do you remember Mr. Jackson, my friend and the vicar who officiated at the wedding?"

"Yes, I remember him. One of your Rebel friends?"

"He was one of the original five I spoke of last night. Miles Jackson was just a child when he lost his father. He was going to have to move away from Brookeside. Everyone who knew the family was devastated. I was no less upset than anyone. My friends, you see, represented my stability. But a widow without any living must often look to the charity of her relatives, as you well know. It's the way of Society. My friends and I loathed the unfairness of the situation. So we banded together and found Miles's mother a new husband so she would not have to move."

Amie bit her lip to keep from laughing. "You played matchmaker?"

His expression was like a guilty child caught sneaking sweets. "I suppose you could put it that way."

"Then what happened?"

"It gave us confidence that we could help others in difficult situations. We had been given a second chance to grow up together, and we wanted to give back. And we did. We've aided more people than I can count. Some situations were dire, others small, but every trial is significant to the one who carries it. The feeling is addictive and never quite satisfying. The more you help, the more you see who is suffering and needs you. I want to help them all if I can. Some directly, others indirectly. Whatever God allows me to do. It's why I raced to London to meet with Mr. Peel. I can't bear the thought of seeing another starving person desperate for food swinging from the gallows. I must do what I can."

She stared at him. Lord Grumpy had been hiding a heart the size of England. "Ian, I had no idea."

"What?"

"That you were a hero."

Astonishment crossed his features. "Me? It's nothing." He seemed embarrassed by her admission and quickly stood. "My paltry efforts should never be applauded. I live a privileged life and have a duty to perform." He dipped his head in a formal parting. "Thank you for all your help today. I should see if my mother has returned."

He turned and left her alone with her thoughts. Thoughts that swirled in her mind like the inkwell she picked up to put away. How could a man with such a capacity for love push away the attempts from others to love him in return? She saw it first with his family and then with his friends. Why couldn't he find room in his philanthropic heart to build a relationship with his father? And why did he shy away from the very thought of his own marriage?

She put away the last of her writing tools and lifted her handkerchief once more, rubbing her fingers over the embroidered initials. They didn't feel as if they belonged to her. It didn't seem likely that they ever would either. But she did feel prouder to carry the title that belonged to Ian.

Even if he could not give her love, he gave as much as he could. And for now, that was enough.

CHAPTER 23

IAN HANDED AMIE A GLASS of warm milk—the same excuse he'd used the night before to give her a moment of privacy before bed.

"Thank you." She did not even look at the glass before dutifully drinking it from her propped-up position in bed. Another thing that was the same as last night was her guarded position, huddled under her covers. It was not as if he hadn't seen her in her nightdress, but he appreciated the quilt just the same. It was a firm reminder that they were in a business relationship, and they must maintain proper boundaries.

"Do you mind if I read for a few minutes?" he asked. He didn't dare face his father again in the corridor to return to the library, so he had brought some papers with him instead.

"No, I don't mind. I actually prefer to read for a few minutes before I go to sleep too."

He didn't know that about her. She did seem to be a great reader though. "What will you read?" He didn't see any books in the room. There were few personal affects anywhere, besides the minimal items on her dressing table. The room suddenly struck him as bare and lonely.

She pointed behind him. "I have a few favorites on a shelf in the closet that I always keep with me. What about you? More work?"

His gaze trailed back to hers. "Some copied essays by a man named Samuel Romilly that were sent to me by Paul, uh, Mr. Sheldon, my barrister friend who you also met at the wedding. He thinks they might help my project."

"The man with the russet-colored hair? How kind of him. He must be a good friend if he is taking time out of his own work to assist you."

Ian shrugged. "I am fond of all my friends, but Paul is probably my closest, even if he did rat out our wedding to the other Rebels."

She smiled. "A very good friend, then."

Amusement pulled at the corners of his mouth. "You would see it that way. You know, you are more sentimental than I first took you for."

"Am I?"

"You talk practically, but I see your attachment to people and ideas."

She smothered another smile. "Yes, I think you're right. Anyway, tell me about this Mr. Romilly. How will his essays help you?"

"Do you really want to know after I jawed your ear off all afternoon? It won't bore you?"

"Not in the slightest. As you said, I ought to improve my mind if I have the opportunity. If you're willing to share, then, isn't this an opportunity?"

He chuckled. She had paid attention, and he ought to reward her for it. "I suppose, although this feels like a very dry bedtime story." He took a seat on the edge of her bed and felt her legs right against him under the covers. He jumped back up. "Pardon me."

It was her turn to laugh. "I told you that you were sensitive."

"I wouldn't call this sensitive. It simply doesn't feel right." The lines between them were already blurring, which was exactly what he'd been afraid of from the beginning. He was too comfortable with her. It was those eyes. They sent out a siren song that lured him closer and made him forget himself. "I'll pull up a chair."

Taking the small wooden chair with the embroidered cushion from behind the dressing table, he set it a few feet from her but close enough to her candle to still read. He lifted one of the papers, finding where he'd left off. "Romilly had the right of it. He had some brilliant criminal law reforms he presented in 1813, but they were rejected. In 1814, he got rid of the ghastly combination of hanging, drawing, and quartering. This man might be my hero." He skimmed a little further, sharing a few lines here and there, not wanting to bore Amie, despite her saying otherwise.

After completing a few sections, he set the papers in his lap. "Well, what did you think?"

She had her long, curly hair in a braid, and she played with the ends of it. "Do you really desire my opinion?"

She had no idea. He was *anxious* to know what she thought, but he didn't want to appear too eager. "I wouldn't have asked otherwise."

"Very well. I think it must be like owning a horse. If someone said an ox were a better choice, more stable, and safer, you might not even care to look twice at it. You're content with your horse. It gets you where you want faster. Tradition is hard to break free from. We have set ideas and like what we are used to."

Ian stretched out his long legs, crossing them at the ankles. "You make a good point, but I am too stubborn to believe England can't see the benefit of this change. I cannot consider failing as an option."

The candlelight flickered, making Amie's eyes sparkle just as she smiled at him. "I want to help you."

He chuckled again, pleasure seeping into his chest. "Will you?"

She nodded. "Romilly accomplished change. While opinions are firm on the subject, there is hope that your efforts might lead to similar progress. That's worth the chance. If you'll let me, I would love to continue to be your scribe. You'll have a great deal of letters to write if you intend to persuade all of Parliament, so I can copy pages, too, if need be."

How could he say no with her so enthused about her idea? "Very well. You can help."

"Good." She leaned forward and wrapped her arms around her knees covered by the quilt. "Now, tell me more about Romilly."

His mouth twitched. "Aren't you ready to sleep?"

She shook her head.

He cleared his throat to keep from noticing how sweet she looked and tapped his letter. "When Romilly died, Sir James Mackintosh, whom we wrote to earlier today, took up the torch. I have a great deal of respect for both these men. They might not have seen the success of their actions, but they have certainly paved the way for us. Sir James is a Whig and Mr. Peel a Tory, but if we can unite them, the two could persuade the different sides of Parliament. It will be our only hope."

She stifled a yawn and lowered herself back on her pillows, curling up on her side. "Does it have a chance if it passes to Lords or on for the royal consent?"

He tried not to notice her new position on the bed. "You're catching on already. I believe our greatest stumbling block will be the House of Commons. I have far more connections in Lords."

Amie yawned again, quickly covering it with her hand. She looked like a rabbit in a burrow of blankets, ready to drift off to sleep.

"Enough for tonight. I've kept you awake long enough."

Amie raised her head. "Please, tell me you won't sleep on the floor again. I promise not to put any pillows anywhere. They're clearly dangerous."

He set his papers on her nightstand. "Sorry, I'm not brave enough to sleep with my head on the bottom of the bed."

Amie frowned, studying the bed as if it had been the reason for her tossing and turning the night before. "What if you slept across the bottom?"

His face hurt just visualizing it. "Need I remind you, you kick in your sleep?"

She had the gall to look affronted. "I have shared a bed with Mama for years, and she never complained about me kicking. I did not feel well last night, and I slept poorly. You have nothing to be afraid of tonight."

Maybe she was right. He reminded himself once again that during the storm, she had hardly moved an inch, and the floor had been terribly hard last night. "Shall I put my head on the farthest side from your feet?"

She grinned. "An excellent idea."

He was glad he had pleased her, but she was not the one risking getting beaten up in the night. Blowing out the candle, he stripped to his shirtsleeves and trousers and lay across the foot of the bed, atop her cover, with a second smaller blanket across his own body. The bed, however, was not square, and his feet and lower legs hung off by at least a foot.

Heaven help him. It was going to be another long night.

CHAPTER 24

AMIE SAT BESIDE LADY KELLEN the next morning at tea in their small drawing room. Lord Kellen sat on the opposite sofa, a newspaper in his hands. Ian transformed back to being Lord Grumpy whenever his father was around and was just now leaning sullenly against the mantel. There was no fire, as the morning was warm, but he seemed content to keep a distance from all of them.

The dark circles under his eyes testified to another long night. She did not think warm milk agreed with her. She, too, was exhausted. It wasn't as if she had planned to kick him all night and send him back to the floor. The very idea forced a small moan from her lips.

"Are you well, Amie?" Lady Kellen asked. She had taken to calling her that at the wedding, and Amie rather liked it. Even if liking it meant nearly breaking rule number two.

She could feel both Lord Kellen's and Ian's eyes suddenly on her. "Yes, perfectly well." She put her tea cup to her lips and took an obligatory sip.

"Forgive me," Ian said, snapping his fingers from across the room. "I had forgotten. I promised Amie I would take her riding." He pushed away from the mantel and came toward her, his hand outstretched. "I apologize for my forgetfulness, darling. Shall we?"

Darling? That was a far cry from the ordinary terms of acknowledgment she received. But he did not have to ask twice. She set her teacup down and eagerly reached for his hand. His large one circled around hers, his grip strong, just as she had imagined it from the few times he had helped her in and out of carriages. Not that she had wondered regularly about what holding his hand would be like, only once or twice.

"Will you excuse us?" Ian asked his mother. "We won't be long."

"Oh, go on," Lady Kellen said. "It's a beautiful day, and you both should be out enjoying it. Your father has some correspondence to finish, and I saw a good book in your library that I haven't read for an age. We will be perfectly content, so you must ride as long as you'd like."

Amie glanced at Lord Kellen to see what he thought of this new arrangement. His mouth drew into a grim line, but he did not look up from his newspaper.

Ian squeezed her hand. "Very well, we will be off." He led her out of the room and did not release her hand until they were in front of their bedchamber, where they could change into their riding clothes. "I might not be the most perceptive," he said, "but I could tell you desired an escape."

She grimaced. "I didn't mean to be obvious. I hope your mother is not offended."

Ian opened the door for her. "Did you see how excited she became when I said we were riding? Her smile was like a child at Twelfth Night. I warned you that she is the queen of matchmakers. Apparently, her enthusiasm extends to after weddings too."

"But your father—"

"Don't worry about him. I just remembered something though. Go right ahead and call for Edna and change into your riding habit while I take care of it."

She had been wondering what excuse he would give her to allow her privacy. "An excellent plan. Should we meet at the stables?"

Ian took several backward steps. "Yes. The stables in a half hour."

She grinned and let herself into her room. Thirty minutes later, almost on the dot, she approached the stables. Dressed in her new forest-green riding habit and fashionable hat with a feathered plume in the back, courtesy of her aunt, she searched for any sign of Ian. She

must have beat him there. As soon as she'd finished the thought, the
stable doors opened, and Ian came out leading his large gelding. A
groom followed behind him with a smaller roan-colored mare.

She watched Ian's eyes appraise her habit. The smallest smile appeared at the corners of his mouth. She took it as a sign of his approval.

"Are you ready?" he asked.

She bit her bottom lip. "I forgot to tell you, I haven't had much
experience riding."

Ian grinned. "I daresay this was even more inspired than I
thought." He handed his reins to the groom and exchanged them for
that of the mare. Then he led the mare to the mounting block and
waved Amie over. She obeyed, but her steps were tentative. The horse
was beautiful from a distance but rather large up close. It had been
some years since she had ridden, and sudden nerves fluttered in her
middle.

Ian held his hand out to her once more. "Don't be shy." His smile
was broader than usual, his mood completely reversed now that he
was away from his father. The carefree grin enhanced his already handsome features.

"Shy of whom? You or the horse?" She accepted his hand before
he could answer.

He chuckled, squeezing her hand again. "The horse. It is never a
bad idea to be wary of me. Though with kicks as strong as yours, perhaps I should be the one who is worried."

She stole her hand from his and swatted his shoulder. The action
was far more playful than she ought to have allowed, and she quickly
turned her attention to the mare. "Is this where you help me mount
this great beast?"

"Correction, Lady Reynolds, this is where I help you mount this
docile animal."

She barely suppressed her laugh. She liked this version of Ian. And
it did not go without notice that he had finally said her new title with
ease.

With a little help from him, she managed to safely ascend into the sidesaddle. Glancing down, she grimaced. Had the ground always been that far away from atop a horse? The animal shifted, and she pulled up hard on the reins, making the mare back up.

"Whoa there." Ian put his arm around the mare's neck, and his other hand came up to catch Amie's hold on the leather reins. "Gentle now. Her name is Claire, and she will do right by you if you do right by her."

Amie frowned warily. "It might take a moment to remember all the particulars."

"How about I take the lead rope, and we do a few circles around the pasture until you're comfortable again?"

"Could we?" she asked.

It took a moment to arrange the lead rope, but then, with a tug, they were off.

"How is that?" he asked.

"Not very frightening after all. She is a beautiful animal."

He grinned up at her. "She is beautiful." His eyes, however, never left hers, sending an unbidden thrill through her. He seemed to realize it and looked away, pulling the mare into a walk. It gave Amie the freedom to smile without his seeing. He couldn't have meant his words about her. She wasn't a real beauty. But perhaps she wasn't *unattractive* to him either.

And even more importantly, this morning they felt like friends. The progress filled her with contentment. Perhaps the cadence of the mare's steps and the charming scenery played a part in it too. The layers of green around her seemed brighter with every passing day as spring reached for summer. She was excited to see more of what this place had in store for her future.

"Where do you normally ride?" she asked. The hunting box itself was small and close to the road, but she did not know how far the estate extended behind it. The untamed land stretched as far as her eye could see.

"I prefer variety and following my mood," Ian answered, pointing to the west. "There's a rise not far from here that has a breathtaking view just above the trees."

"Is it a difficult ride?"

"Not terribly." He looked at her over his shoulder. "I know neither us slept well, so if you aren't up to it today, perhaps I can show you another time."

"I should like that."

"When was the last time you rode?"

She thought for a moment. "Just before my father died, so I suppose I was a few months shy of thirteen."

"And did you care for it then?"

"I was fearless as a youth. For my twelfth birthday, I was gifted a pretty buckskin mare I named Pegasus."

"Ah, the flying mythological horse. A very romantic choice."

She laughed lightly. "She was no white stallion, but she soared when she ran. To my great dismay, Papa did not allow me to give her her head often, saying my form had to improve first. I grumbled a great deal about it."

"So you grumbled about someone other than me? I like this story more and more. What happened to Pegasus?"

Amie glanced wistfully at the countryside. "As much as I loved Peg, we had to sell her after Papa died. I refused to cry. I cared more that I would not ride with Papa anymore."

"I'm sorry for that little girl. She lost a great deal."

"Riding was one of the few activities we did together, as you can imagine. A man does not often have time to visit the nursery."

"My father certainly did not, so I can understand." Ian spoke toward the trees, but she wished she could see his expression and know exactly what that memory did to him.

"Did you ever ride together?" she asked.

"I do recall a few rides with him over the years that I had forgotten about until now."

"Did you get along then?"

He shrugged once, his athletic form standing beside her horse. "I suppose we did. He was always an intimidating man, and I was quick to do as he said. I fear I resented him for his imperious attitude from a young age, but I also craved whatever attention he gave me."

She fingered the smooth leather reins. "You sound like a normal youth."

He chuckled. "If there is such a thing, then I suppose I was. There is too much buried in the past for me to want to dig it up."

There he went again, telling her just enough to answer a question but barely scratching the surface. There was clearly more in his past concerning his father, but it appeared to be a carefully guarded secret. Or maybe *secret* wasn't the word. A carefully guarded hurt, perhaps? Reaching forward to run her hand down the mare's mane, she asked the next question on the tip of her tongue, one he could answer with greater ease. "When you're not saving the world, what sort of pastimes do you enjoy? Is riding your favorite?"

He glanced back at her. "Ah, more prying questions. I do enjoy a good ride, but I also like swimming, fishing, archery, fencing, chess, and, generally, whatever my friends rope me into. What about you? Besides bringing broth to sick neighbors and tending to convalescing maids in our upstairs room."

Our. He said *our* upstairs room. Like when he had said her title, it felt like progress. Toward what, she couldn't say. But surely it meant something that he had finally admitted to following her and watching her charity visits.

"I like reading and sewing, though I do neither very well, but I suppose what I like the most is to listen." She felt brave confessing this much about herself, but she wanted to tell him. Wanted someone to know her. Wanted *him* to know her. "I like when people tell me their troubles. It makes me feel valued and useful."

"Are you hinting at something?"

She cast her gaze to the blue sky rippled with frothy white. "Is it working?"

He shook his head. "You already know far more about me than I ever intended you to learn. Listening, though, is a good quality, Amie. I wish more had such a unique talent."

Her cheeks warmed with pleasure. Did he really think so? "I've never thought of it as a talent."

"You don't just listen though; you act. Together, those are powerful tools that can change the world."

Her? Change the world? Not likely. "It's not like anything you do, but if a friend who is sad or lonely can smile again, I feel as if I have achieved something worthwhile."

Ian brought her horse to a stop as they finished their second loop around the pasture. "It is a great thing, Amie. God doesn't sit back in His throne in heaven, measuring our acts of kindness. He celebrates each one, because even the smallest spark can dissipate the darkness in another's life."

Amie swallowed, not expecting the sudden passion in Ian's voice. She gave a small nod of understanding.

"Forgive me." Ian shook his head. "I suddenly find Miles's sermons coming out of my mouth."

She smiled. "Your vicar friend sounds wise."

He nodded. "He's quite good with words and actually lives what he preaches."

"I should like to hear one of his sermons someday." She said it lightly, not meaning anything by it, but Ian's expression suddenly closed off, and he turned away from her.

"The day is still young," he said, with no response to her previous comment. "Are you ready to ride unassisted? You did come here to be an independent woman. Riding can help you with that."

She tightened her hands on the reins with the sudden reminder. "I'm ready." The words sounded false on her lips but maybe because she wasn't thinking about riding.

A few minutes later, Ian had mounted his own horse, and together they trotted toward the tree line, the curls framing her face blowing in the breeze.

"Is this pace agreeable?" he asked.

"It's bumpier than I remember," she said with a laugh, "but I love it."

He grinned at her. "You are braver than you made yourself out to be."

"And you are more diverting than you made yourself out to be," she quipped.

He laughed, a full, loud laugh that carried to her and warmed her through. "Your Lord Grumpy enjoys diversions now and then, same as anyone else."

Her Lord Grumpy? She liked that. She raised a playful brow. "Diversions are well enough, but *how* diverting can you be? That's what separates the bores from the rest of the world." She gave him a challenging look.

"A bore?" He drew his horse nearer and reached to grab her reins. "Never."

She swatted at his hands. "Prove it." She could not ever remember bantering with someone like this, and it made her excessively happy.

"There's a meadow not far from here," Ian said. "Let's see if you remember how to run a horse."

A thrill went through her. "Oh, I would love that. Do you think I'm ready?"

"Slow the moment you feel at all out of control. I will stay close and follow your lead."

"Let's try it." Her grin must've been contagious because Ian returned it.

She kicked her heel back, and Claire shot forward. Amie squealed with pleasure, and Ian laughed from just behind her.

Once they reached the meadow, she challenged him to a race, which she royally lost. Ian cheered her up with some Shrewsbury cakes he had hidden in his saddlebags. He had pilfered them from the kitchen when he had stopped to greet Tiny on his way to the stables. Though he had carefully wrapped them in his handkerchief, the delicate biscuits were broken. He and Amie laughed and ate the pieces, their hands touching as they shared back and forth atop their horses.

All Amie's worries fled from her mind. She couldn't remember ever feeling this light. This was the freedom and happiness she had longed for. It was the ride, the warm sunshine on her back, and the song of the skylarks in the gorse bushes and the treetops. But it was also Ian. She tried to tell herself it wasn't him, but her heart knew every lie her mind told.

CHAPTER 25

"YOU DID WELL, AMIE." IAN handed his reins to the groom and moved to her horse to help her dismount.

"It was Claire who performed well." She ran her hand down her mare's neck. "Good girl, Claire."

"You won't take any credit? Cantering takes bravery for a woman who previously needed to walk around the pasture." He held his arms up to her waist.

"Remember, my father only cared about my form." She set her hands on his shoulders and fell into his hold.

"Your form," he said, setting her down in front of him, "is perfect." The last word hung on his lips, lasting an extra beat.

Their eyes met, and he forgot what he was doing. Her form truly was impressive, but it wasn't her position on a horse he was thinking about right now. He was thinking of the form between his hands— the soft curves he'd tried not to notice but couldn't help but do so when he was holding them.

"Thank you," she whispered.

"You're welcome," he whispered back. Speaking louder than that would chase him back into the reality he had forced them both into, and he was not eager to return there just yet. He wanted to stay in this exact moment, his intrigue heightened and his senses wide awake. It was easy to forget about the rest of the world with Amie so near him.

They stood that way for several long beats, sharing each other's breath and gazing into each other's eyes. It wasn't exactly an embrace but a line they straddled between safety and unknown possibilities. He fingered her smooth habit between his fingers, barely resisting the powerful urge to tug her closer.

She was a breath of fresh air—a tonic for his nerves and a distraction from his problems. She threw herself into messes often enough, but those moments made him forget to be so serious all the time. Being with her helped him see life in a new way—the way she saw it—at a slower pace, where learning was still exciting and people were inherently good. She was genuine and humble. And beautiful. So beautiful.

His heart pounded, and his eyes dropped to admire the curve of her lips. She lifted her chin, waiting for him. He wanted to appease her. To tell her how beautiful she was in that one motion. Hesitation battled desire. Kissing her would mean crossing the line he'd drawn so carefully between them. A line drawn with clear purpose for their own good.

He traced her every feature with his gaze: the slight upturn of her nose, the sprinkle of freckles on her cheeks, and the pull of the small scar above her left brow. When he reached her exquisite eyes, he knew his answer. He let go of her, taking a slow but deliberate step out of her arms. Pretending he could like her for a moment might be acceptable, but that was all he could indulge. He had an entire life he'd set for himself and promises to keep. Promises that protected Amie from him.

His tone came out deep and husky. "Shall we return inside?"

She visibly swallowed, a shy smile touching her lips. "Yes, I'm ready."

The groom took her horse, and they walked side by side to the house. They said not a word, but a current pulled between them that was difficult to ignore. They made their way up the steps and just before he opened the front door for her, he said, "I will see to my parents while you change."

Her eyes sparkled in the sun when she turned to answer him. "Thank you."

Once inside, he walked her to the bottom of the stairs and watched her ascend. He hadn't noticed he was staring until she turned the corner at the top and left his view. Turning away, he moved toward the drawing room, his footfalls unhurried and methodical. He'd needed that outing with Amie. It reminded him of being with his friends, only far better. It was the kind of enjoyment that only two could share. The fatigue that had weighed on him earlier had dissipated. He felt lighter and easier about every aspect of his life.

His smile came unbidden at the thought of her in his arms, the empty corridor as his witness. He could be attracted to a friend, could he not? Because every part of her intrigued him. He couldn't study her enough. Not to mention the way his hands fit perfectly around her waist. Wasn't such a quality deserving of note?

He wouldn't put himself in a position to be tempted again, but for now, he was choosing to appreciate the wife he'd been blessed with. Content as he had not been in some time, he pushed into the drawing room. A quick view of the room was all it took to have much of his peace of mind flee. Father paced by the window, and Ian's unflappable mother looked close to tears.

"What is it?" Ian asked, striding into the room.

His father stopped in his tracks. "Are you alone?"

"Yes, Amie is changing."

"Shut the door behind you. We need to talk."

Ian returned to the door and closed it, his brow lowering. "Is something wrong?"

Father spoke to the window, his words punctuating like wheels on gravel. "Yes, something is wrong. It's your wife."

Mother, strong and confident always, held a handkerchief to her nose.

"Amie?" A sick sensation rushed through him. Was it her mother? Amie would be devastated if anything had happened to her. His mind jumped to that day at the graveyard and Amie's heartfelt conversation with her father, and Ian's heart sank further. "Tell me straightaway."

"I won't mince words, Ian." His father folded his arms across his chest and faced him straight on. "I want you to leave her."

CHAPTER 26

A COMMOTION SOUNDED FROM SOMEWHERE in the house. What was that noise? Had Tiny escaped the kitchen? Amie could well imagine his chewing on Lord Kellen's boot and the outrage that would follow. Edna stuck another pin in her hair, but Amie was already twisting to look at the door, as if she could see beyond it.

"Just finished, miss," Edna said.

"Thank you." Amie did not even check her appearance in the mirror before hurrying from her bedchamber to investigate. The noise increased in the corridor, and she could distinguish it now as voices—yelling voices.

No doubt Ian and Lord Kellen. She had never heard Ian yell before. He could be stern, but there was a collected manner about him that seemed to come from someone who valued self-control. She wondered what had happened to provoke him so.

Should she hide in her room until their tempers had cooled? She looked to the stairs and back to her room. Kneading her hands together, she finally proceeded forward. If there was anything she could do to help, she had to try. At the bottom of the stairs, the sound of her own name jarred her to a stop.

She swallowed, her heart pounding, then drew closer and closer to the closed drawing room door until each word was clear and accented with sharpness.

"If you wanted influence for your idealist projects, you shouldn't have married so far beneath you."

Shame coursed through her. Ian had been right. Their wedding had done nothing to change Lord Kellen's opinion of her. In truth, she could not blame the man. She herself had thought Miss Foster a far more complementary fit for Ian.

"I never asked for your help," Ian growled. "And I would thank you to keep my wife out of this."

"You might not ask for it," Lord Kellen said, "but you need it. I know you fancy yourself capable of changing our centuries' old criminal law, but you cannot conceive of doing it without my backing and that of my associates."

Ian laughed, but it was an angry sound that worried Amie. "Don't flatter yourself, Father. Just because you have been spying on me doesn't give you a right to involve yourself. I have connections of my own, so you need not concern yourself."

"Why do you have to be so dashed prideful? For years, you have been disrespectful and sour, and I know you did this to spite me. You can still annul the marriage," Lord Kellen said. "We could work together."

Ian huffed. "How can you invite yourself here, on my wedding trip no less, and say that to me?"

"Darling, really," Lady Kellen pleaded. "Lower your voice, I beg you."

"You have made excuses for him for long enough," Lord Kellen snapped, making Amie jump. "This is between your son and me."

"Then, say your piece and be done," Ian commanded.

"Very well. I came here to persuade you to see reason, because I know you, and I know the truth. This marriage is a farce. It was a scapegoat to avoid marrying Miss Foster, and we both know it." Lord Kellen paused, and Amie leaned closer to the door. "I—I will consider a different arrangement."

Ian's response was low but still laced with anger. "It was never your choice to begin with. I have made my choice and will stand by it."

Amie shivered at the words. They were powerfully spoken . . . but would he live to regret them?

"You're a stubborn fool." Lord Kellen's voice pitched. "How can you throw your future away on some useless, pathetic, penniless woman?"

Amie lurched back, her every weakness suddenly stripped and laid bare. Moments ago, her heart had soared as Ian had held her, caressed her with his gaze, and smiled down at her. Her emotional pendulum now swung in reverse, and all she could see was how worthless she was. She did not deserve this title, this home, this security. She did not deserve Ian.

She had never felt so small.

Ian's voice followed a moment later. "That *useless* woman is my wife and deserves your respect."

His words came without comfort. She did not believe him. She tasted the tears on her tongue before she even knew she was crying. Her feet, however, would not move though she longed to run, and run far.

"Ha!" Lord Kellen's laugh was devilishly high. "When I see a grandchild, I will give her the respect she has *earned*."

Amie cast her watery eyes to the ceiling. That would never happen. She would forever be an outcast—less wife and more charity case—while acting a dual role as an anvil holding down Ian's career. She wasn't supposed to care—it wasn't part of their arrangement—but the sensation of worthlessness nearly overcame her. It wasn't a new sensation, as she had been cast from relatives' homes too many times to pretend otherwise, but this somehow hit deeper.

"I think you should leave," Ian said, his voice ringing with finality. "I don't want to see you *ever* again."

The words stunned Amie, if possible, more than any of the disparaging comments against her. Ian couldn't mean it. *She* was nothing to him. His father was his family!

The door swung open before she could move. Lord Kellen, with his austere expression and hard eyes, took in her tear-stained glory and did not have to say anything; she could feel his loathing. He brushed by her and strode to the door.

Lady Kellen hurried after him but stopped as soon as she saw Amie. "Oh, dearest. Please tell me you did not hear any of this." Her gaze was frantic and concerned. The perfectly collected countess Amie had come to know was completely unraveled.

Amie opened her mouth to say something, but the words she had overheard were compounding inside her with such force that she could not think to deny hearing them.

Lady Kellen took her hand. "My husband can be a difficult man to understand, but he acts out of love for his son. We must go, but I will write to you." Her hurried words, though sincere, flitted just above Amie's head but did not sink in. "Goodbye for now," Lady Kellen added, squeezing Amie's hand and dropping it.

Amie stood there for several minutes, torn between a sense of duty as hostess to see that Lord and Lady Kellen had everything they needed for their trip home, a fear to approach Lord Kellen at all, and a yearning to speak with Ian. There was so much that had to be said and no courage to go with any of it.

In the end, she could bring herself to do nothing. She made her way to the servants' entrance and sneaked outside, breathing deeply the liberating air.

She suddenly wished she had never come here.

CHAPTER 27

THE HUNTING BOX WAS IAN'S property, not his father's. How could Father invite himself here and make his selfish demands as if everyone were pawns to be moved at his will? The man aggravated Ian to no end. Ian collapsed back on a sofa, his arm going up over his eyes. He sat that way for what felt like an hour, the same conversation circling in his mind, torturing him.

At least now that Ian was married, his father would not disinherit him. Ian was sure about that. The grandchild comment had given him away, insensitive as it was. But his father was still his father, and the cut of his words ran deep.

A knock sounded on the open drawing room door. Ian dragged his arm down and turned to look over his shoulder. "Amie." Her name was all he could bring himself to say. He didn't want to speak to her but didn't know how to politely send her away either. This was her house too.

Standing in the threshold, she lowered her head and spoke to the floor. "Your parents are gone."

He turned his head forward again, away from her. "Good."

A moment passed before her soft voice carried to him. "Can we speak?"

He sighed. He had heard his mother conversing with her, so he assumed Amie had heard the argument. She'd given him nearly an hour to himself already, and he wouldn't be able to put this off much longer. He leaned forward, propping his elbows on his thighs. "Come in."

Her quiet steps and faint swish of her skirts brought her farther into the room. He expected her to sit on the opposite sofa or maybe even stand, but she sat directly beside him, bringing with her the tantalizing smell of vanilla. Her small hand came up to rest on the middle of his back, and his muscles tightened at the unexpected touch. Gentle pats of her hand left a slow circle of warmth behind. The wild, racing thoughts fled one by one, and the tension in his body eased as a comforting wave engulfed him. He could think of nothing now but that rhythmic pressure and Amie beside him.

Neither of them said anything for a long time. He didn't know what to say to reassure her. He had done exactly what his father had accused him of and not even given Amie the independence she'd desired. He was always trying to fix things, but he was the most broken of all. He could not even comfort the beautiful woman beside him. Instead, she was comforting him.

A crooked smile crept onto his face. "You really are terrible at keeping rule number one." The hand on his back that had gone from pats to smoothing the lines of his jacket froze. He hadn't meant to scare her. He shifted his head to look at her, and she quickly withdrew her hand altogether. He missed it already, but it didn't seem fair to make her wait on him any longer.

"What did you want to speak to me about?"

She inhaled sharply and blurted, "I think I should go."

His brow furrowed. "What?"

"I think . . ." she said cautiously, her eyes glossing with sudden moisture, "I think we should annul this marriage."

The sensation of cold water rushed over him. "Amie?"

"Ian," she pleaded.

He shook his head. "Don't let him get to you. He doesn't have that right over us."

She shrugged. "You don't need to do this for me. I'm no one to you. He's your father."

A sudden memory of a conversation he'd overheard in the card-room at a ball played in his mind. The distinguished men had bragged about their disgusting conquests, revering Ian's father as their role model of discretionary debauchery. "Amie, he's my father in blood alone. I will never do as he says."

She stood and stared down at him. "Lord Kellen is right. I'm your wife in name only. All your hopes of changing the world should not hinge on this decision. You should listen to him."

He stood too. "I won't listen."

"But you must." She stepped closer to him. "Don't you see? Lives depend upon it."

"I refuse to believe that. I am not so weak that I must stay in my father's shadow." His words didn't seem to take purchase. He'd never heard such desperation in Amie's voice, and he didn't care for it. Not when it concerned his father.

"Ian, see reason. I don't want you to regret this."

He shook his head again. "I'm sorry if my temper scared you. I should not have been so easily provoked. But I stand by my words. I won't give you the annulment, Amie. I swore to never marry, but I have, and I won't turn my back on another commitment I've made." He would never cast her aside to fend for herself. Did she really think him capable of that?

Her wide brown eyes welled with tears, gutting him. He valued open communication, but no good would come in continuing this argument. He was too tired, too frustrated, too hurt, and he'd already lost control once and wouldn't do it again. She deserved better. "I'm going for another ride, Amie. Please, put this from your mind, and don't let my father's words poison you. You'll always have a place here. Always."

He strode from the room and through the narrow corridors, his clipped steps echoing against the tile. The warm evening air greeted him and curled its wispy fingers through his hair. He pressed his eyes closed. Must he lose his father and his wife in one day?

Amie wasn't *no one* to him. She was his. So what if they didn't love each other as man and wife? He couldn't abandon her. He wouldn't. He had made vows to her, endured sleepless nights with her, and shared his private plans with her. He cared too much about her to simply walk away.

His eyes widened.

He . . . he cared for her.

Blast!

CHAPTER 28

FOR THREE DAYS, AMIE AND Ian lived like strangers in the same house. It was worse than when they'd first arrived at Oak End, because they had grown closer while Ian's parents had been there. With them gone, there was no need to pretend to be madly in love, no reason for Ian to hide in the library with her or for them to sleep in the same room.

She returned to her long walks, visits to the neighbors, reading to Gwen, whose leg was not healing well, and putting the finishing touches on Mama's room. The door had been painted just that morning and would require drying time, which meant their extra room would be completed on the morrow. Not certain what project would occupy her time next, she picked up her sewing again, plucking at threads while her mind wandered to Ian.

If he was not riding, he was squirreling away in his office with Tiny as his companion of choice. She refused to be jealous of a dog—a dog he wouldn't even have if she hadn't rescued the creature. But not once had Ian asked for her to act as his scribe, though she had offered at least twice. He anxiously awaited his letter from Sir James, and she expected him to whisk away to London the moment it arrived. They were back to their original plan, one where they lived separate lives. She never brought up the annulment again. With Ian so set against his father, she knew it would come to naught.

Loneliness like she'd never known settled over her. After a taste of Ian's time and attention, she craved more of it. She never knew it possible to ache for the company of someone who was only a room away. But she had learned to be happy on her own before and would discipline herself to do so again.

She rubbed her eyes, tired of the sewing project she'd started. She needed a fictional solution from the library. She set aside her sewing, thinking of what she should read. Something completely immersive. Books were meant for people who had problems and were smart enough to want to escape them. She might not be intelligent enough to not overthink a marriage of convenience, but she knew her limits otherwise.

She glanced at the closed door of Ian's study on her way to the library, wondering if he had gleaned any new information that could aid his efforts to change their criminal law. Or was his sole objective to hide from her? Was there nothing in her company that enticed him to leave his work for even a minute?

Likely not. After all, she was useless, pathetic, penniless . . . Lord Kellen's words came easily to mind, as they had over and over since he'd departed.

For heaven's sake, someone give her a book! With a quick tug on the handle, she thrust the door open into the library. It stuck halfway, coming to an abrupt halt.

"Oof."

Amie sucked in her breath at the sound of the very human noise and peered cautiously around the door. Ian stood on the other side, holding his nose.

"Ian?" She ducked into the room. "Fiddlesticks. I didn't see you."

"That much is obvious." He pulled a handkerchief from his waistcoat pocket and dabbed at his red nose. The cloth came away with a small smear of blood.

"Good heavens. I'm dreadfully sorry." She grabbed his arm. "Come sit down before you get blood everywhere." He let her pull him to the sofa, and they took a seat together. "Does it hurt much? I feel terrible."

"It was an accident, Amie. It's not like I haven't bloodied my nose before. My friend Tom has a fist like a rock. The door was nothing in comparison."

"That's hardly comforting." Sunlight filtered through the window and gave her a good look at Ian. "Your nose appears straight. I don't think it's broken."

"We have hard heads in our family, literally and figuratively."

"It's no excuse for barging into the library like I did."

He raised his brows. "I underestimated your passion for books."

"No one should stand between us," she quipped.

He chuckled, the sound dancing in her ears like music. Maybe it had been worth bruising his nose for a moment of friendly banter.

He shifted and tipped his head back. "So what will you read today, then?"

"Something riveting."

"Oh? Are you feeling restless?"

"You have no idea."

He tilted his head and eyed her. "What's bothering you?"

It was her turn to raise her brows. "I thought we weren't talking about anything but the weather."

"Yes, I suppose you're right," he said playfully. "So you grew so bored, you tried to kill me?"

She shrugged. "That seems to be the summation of it."

He stared at her for a long moment. "I'm sorry. I've had a lot on my mind. I shouldn't have ignored you."

Amie looked down at her hands. "You're busy."

He checked the handkerchief, and when there was no blood, he removed it from his face. "Not so busy that I have permission to be rude."

His apology eased some of the ache inside her. "You can ease your guilt by telling me about your work. What have you learned?" She was stalling. She wanted to continue to sit by his side. She didn't care what they spoke about as long as they were talking again.

"What have I learned?" He sighed. "Not enough. Mail is slow, and I've read through the materials I have a dozen times or more. I've listed all the names of constituents whom I hope to persuade and have started penning more letters."

"Without the help of your secretary? For shame." She already knew the answer but couldn't resist.

"I thought you might appreciate some space from me. I keep promising your independence, then encroaching on it."

Independence was the last thing on her mind these days. Her hand itched from its spot on the sofa beside him. What she really wanted was for Ian to reach over and take it in his, to reassure her with his touch. She felt like a sparrow hunting for another spare crumb of his attention. Or was it his *affection* she was hungering for?

She purposefully moved her hand to her lap, burying her silly, indulgent thoughts as she did. "I don't mind your presence, Ian," she admitted, but then she hurried to reassure him that she wasn't expecting anything from it. "But I know your work is important. I admire your efforts."

He didn't seem to dwell on her admission. "When lives are at stake, I do feel an urgency to act. I'm eager to get to London, but I haven't wanted to return too early and alert my father. I don't want to fuel his anger."

The dreaded but inevitable talk of leaving. "When will you go?"

His mouth formed a grim line. "I planned to tell you at dinner, Amie. I plan to leave in the morning."

She had survived his departure before, and she would do so again, but her stomach knotted all the same. "Will you write to me and tell me the outcome? As secluded as I am here, it will take time for news to reach me naturally."

He looked like he wanted to say something else but stopped himself. "My hand is not as fine as yours, but I will write."

A smile touched her lips. "I should like that. Thank you."

Someone cleared their throat behind them. It was the butler.

"What is it, Mr. Hamburg?" Ian said.

"Mrs. Tyler has arrived, asking to see her daughter, Lady Reynolds."

Amie's gaze whipped to Ian's. "My mother is here?"

His brow furrowed. "Did you send for her?"

"No, did you?"

"No." He turned to the butler. "Please, show her into the drawing room." He shoved his handkerchief into a pocket inside his jacket and stood. "Am I presentable enough for your mother?"

Amie stood too. "Your nose is a little red, but I doubt she will notice. I can't imagine why she has come."

"I suppose we will find out." He held his arm out to her. "Shall we, then? We bumbled our act on one set of parents, but perhaps we can convince your mother."

"Do they have books on the subject?" She cast her gaze to the shelves. "Perhaps we should study up."

He yanked back his arm. "Did you forget rule number three?"

She bit back a laugh. "I did, didn't I?" She crossed her hand over her heart. "Absolutely no studying romance."

"That's the spirit." He extended his arm again. "Ready?"

She accepted his arm, extended only out of good manners, but didn't know how ready she was. Pretending to be in love with Ian was feeling far more real with every passing day. Frankly, that knowledge scared her.

CHAPTER 29

IAN STOOD BACK WHILE AMIE greeted Mrs. Tyler in a tight embrace. The women were about the same size, but Amie put her head on her mother's shoulder while her mother stroked her hair just above her ear, where it was pulled tight back into a chignon. They clung to each other for a time, each whispering whatever it was a close mother and daughter said after being parted for a few weeks. They had been everything to each other for a long time, and he would not rush them.

He clasped his hands behind his back just inside the drawing room door. This surprise visit meant rethinking his plans. Again. He wasn't used to always considering someone else before acting, and it would take some getting used to.

"Let me see this husband of yours," Mrs. Tyler announced, releasing Amie and coming toward him.

Something about the word *husband* seemed more regal a title than lord, and he straightened. "How do you do, Mrs. Tyler?" He dipped his head. "We are pleased to have you with us."

"You must think us silly for being so happy to see one another after such a short time."

"I do not think it silly at all."

Mrs. Tyler smoothed her wrinkled travel gown, though it was the tired lines in her face that concerned him. "I did not get a proper goodbye with her, you know. You missed the wedding breakfast."

Guilt settled on his shoulders. "Forgive me. I was anxious to get on the road." What had seemed like a necessary escape at the time now felt extremely selfish. His apology was as sincere as could be.

Mrs. Tyler gave him a comforting smile. "Don't think on it again. It does not matter now that we are together."

"Thank you for understanding. Please, take a seat and rest." He motioned to the sofa closest to her.

Amie took her mother's arm. "Tea should be here any moment. You need some refreshment after your long journey."

Ian took a seat across from them. There would be no hiding from Amie today. He must face her head on while also facing whatever strange, obsessive feelings he'd tried his utmost to avoid for the past several days.

A maid arrived with a tea tray, and Amie began to serve everyone. She handed her mother the first cup. "I told you in my last letter that Lord Reynolds would send a carriage for you in a month or so. How did you manage to come on your own?"

Mrs. Tyler took a delicate sip. "Oh, it wasn't any trouble. Lady Kellen arranged it."

Ian sat forward in his seat. "My mother?"

Amie came over and handed him a cup fixed just the way he liked it, but his mind was caught up in why his mother would interfere. There was no doubt she had ulterior motives and sent Mrs. Tyler on purpose. He loved his mother, but she was as conniving as she was sweet. When would she learn that her interference had the capacity to wound people deeply? He and Amie weren't dolls to be forced together at her whim.

He didn't want that for Amie.

Looking up from his tea, he observed her asking her mother about the inn she had stayed at the night before. There was nothing shiny about Amie's apparel or appearance, but something about her sparkled all the same. He yearned to be near her and run his hand down her silky cheek.

He cared for her. He had accepted that much. But he'd made a commitment to them both, and he would not let himself fall any deeper. Silky cheek or not.

After tea, Amie sent her mother to her room to rest. Ian was retreating to his study when Amie called to him.

"Ian, may I have a word?"

"By all means." He might have been the smallest bit excited to spend another minute in her company. He opened the study door and followed her inside. She took a seat opposite his desk. Instead of circling around, he leaned against the front of it. He realized too late that he was closer to her than need be. This particular study was more like a glorified closet. He cleared his throat, hoping to push down the awkwardness of their proximity that only his thoughts were creating. "What is on your mind?"

"Your nose is looking better."

He reached up to touch it. "It feels better. But I don't think that's what you desired to speak to me about."

"No, it isn't." She made a face as if bracing herself for his reaction. "It's about my mother's room."

Ah, this must be a question about money. "I saw it is finished. If there is anything that you would like to add for her comfort, please do not think twice about the cost."

She bit the side of her bottom lip, her hands coming together tightly in front of her. "It isn't exactly finished. I had the servants paint the door this morning. It cannot be shut until tomorrow, or it will stick."

She was joking. One hand went to his hip. "And our convalescing maid?"

"The doctor saw her yesterday. She is to remain in bed for another week before she can be moved."

He groaned. "So your mother is resting in your room?"

She nodded.

There had to be another answer besides them being together again. "Can you not stay with her tonight?"

Amie looked at her lap. "She would not expect it."

He bit hard on his tongue. The blasted agreement about making this marriage believable was coming back to haunt him. "Say no more. You may stay with me tonight."

"Thank you." There was not an ounce of excitement in her eyes. Was he such a bear that she feared the arrangement? And why did he feel disappointed that she was dreading being near him? He was the one who should be dreading it. Not only did she kick and disturb his sleep, but he had boundaries to maintain as well.

"My mother did this on purpose," he grumbled.

Amie answered without guile. "I am the one who arranged for the door to be painted."

"No, she sent your mother here because that is exactly the kind of person she is."

Amie's brow knitted together. "Because she is kind?"

Amie saw the best in people, but she needed to know what they were dealing with. "Because she is playing matchmaker. They knew I left you to travel to London, and my father learned why I was there. My mother must have caught on. Which means she knows I want to return as quickly as possible. This is her way of keeping us together."

Amie's expression softened into one of amusement. "Surely you're jumping to conclusions."

He pushed his palms into the wood on either side of him. "I'm making an educated conjecture based on years of experience watching my mother rearrange other people's lives. Every friend you met at my wedding has my mother to thank for their marriage."

She wrinkled her nose. "Even that winking man, Mr. Harwood, who complained about the kiss at his wedding? He seemed far too flirtatious with his wife to want to remain single for long."

"Even Teasing Tom was against marriage before my mother got to him."

"And the vicar? I cannot imagine it. Every last one of them seemed deeply affectionate toward their spouse."

He shuddered. "*Deeply* is the right word for it. I've been suffocated by the mere sight of them. She has all the matrons in Brookeside as her little helpers. My mother is very good at what she does. She never fails to make her match."

Amie's hand flew to her mouth, barely smothering her gasp.

He straightened. "What is it?"

"Your mother was at the graveyard the day my mother created the lie about our engagement. You don't think . . ."

Ian gritted his teeth and fell back against the desk once more. "She was the one to tell me about the rumors circulating about us. She was likely the one who created them."

Amie shook her head. "Surely not. Your mother is one of the kindest, more sincere people I have ever met."

"My mother has the very best of intentions. The Matchmaking Mamas' mantra is simple: 'A match is not a match unless the couple falls madly in love.' Unfortunately, that is where they will fail with us since you and I will not fall victim to their schemes."

Amie stared at him. "You sound confident for a man whose friends could not withstand the same pressures."

"I have the advantage of being me," he said with a measure of self-loathing. "Lord Grumpy, remember? No, I am nothing like my friends. Where their hearts are soft, mine is hard. Where they are kind, I am short-tempered."

She pushed away from her seat, standing before he could finish listing his final and greatest reason. Her gown billowed over his feet, her stance nearly eliminating the space between them. With him sitting on the edge of his desk, their heads were nearly the same height, giving him an excellent, and rather heart-stopping, view of his favorite pair of brown eyes.

"Why do you disparage yourself?" she asked. "No one cares so utterly and completely for the livelihood of others as you do. You're giving up all your time and every ounce of your energy, and why? Not because anyone asked you, but because of the goodness of your conscience. You deserve to love, Ian, and to be loved. There is no reason you could give me that could make me believe otherwise."

For a moment, he had lost himself in her passion of words and in the depth of her eyes that reflected her very generous soul. Only his tight grip on his desk kept him from pulling her to him and breaking all his promises. "I have a good reason," he finally said. "Even if you cannot see it."

She shook her head. "Then, it is by choice and not because you are not capable. It is your own fault that you chose me when you could have had anyone."

He didn't like where this was going. "What do you mean by that?"

She gave the smallest, almost imperceivable shrug. "I'm not a fool. You chose me because I was the last person you could love."

Her words were like a sucker punch to his gut. She couldn't actually believe that. "Amie—"

"I shoved mint leaves in your mouth and told you off, remember?" She cut him off. "I pulled my hair out because of Cousin Robert and looked like a mad woman. You saw a charity case, not a wife. I know what I am to you, so there is no use pretending otherwise. The point is you are still free to consider what your father said. We could still end this contract and annul the marriage."

Did she really think he saw her this way? "Amie—"

"No, Ian. I am much too beneath you; we both know it. You will have opportunities beyond what you have now with the right woman by your side."

Each statement out of her mouth made his blood boil. And she thought he had disparaged himself, where she was being completely cruel in her self-estimation.

"I heard you agree with your father that I am useless, and it's true. Listen to him," she begged, the plea in her gaze undoing him, "and give yourself a chance at living a full life equal to what you deserve. One with a woman who deserves you in return. This isn't—"

He put his hands on her waist and pulled her to him, cutting her off, and she stared at him, their faces inches from each other. He could feel her chest heaving with surprise against his own.

In a low and husky tone, he mustered the words he had to say, "There is nothing useless about you, and you are not, nor will you ever be a charity case to me." And he would prove it to her. He did what he'd been resisting since their wedding and set his mouth against the smooth flesh of hers and kissed her. She would know what he really thought of her with every slow, deliberate move. He let himself explore the shape of her lips, one hand curling around her delicate neck and the other bringing her tight against him.

This kiss, even though it was a release of a yearning he'd struggled against, wasn't for him.

Every touch, pressure, and emotion it elicited was strictly for her. He wanted—needed—for her to know that she was far above what he deserved—she was everything to him. Her quiet beauty was devastating, so much so that after years of resisting passing attractions, he wasn't capable of resisting her. Her heart was too good, too perfect.

Her hands found his neck, and she started to return his kiss. He sighed inwardly with pleasure, hoping she felt the same. She was warm and soft, and her vanilla scent filled all his senses. She was the right woman by his side—the only one he would allow; she had to know it.

She pulled back enough to breathe his name. "Ian?"

"Hmm?" he said, kissing her again.

"You're breaking rule number one," she whispered before meeting his touch again.

He didn't want to stop, but her reminder was timely. With every ounce of self-control left that he possessed, he pulled back. His hands came up to cup her face, indulging himself in stroking that milky smooth skin he'd missed. "Amie, my reasons for resisting love have nothing to do with you. Trust me when I say, it would not take any effort at all for me to fall madly in love with you." She blinked, her brown eyes rich in color. "Can you understand that, Amie?"

She nodded beneath his gentle hold, though he could see that she did not quite understand at all. But he didn't want to spell out a lifetime of goals and commitments or his father's transgressions and his grandfather's too. There was no need to ruin the moment completely. This would be their memory alone. Something to live by in the lonely years to come.

"Good." He stripped his hands away from her and forced them to his side. He straightened and squeezed past her, moving a few steps to the door and to safety, his heart pounding dangerously in his chest. He turned back when he reached the edge of the room, taking in her flushed cheeks and swollen lips. "I won't kiss you again. Not even if you grow confused. So you mustn't forget what I've told you. It will be a few days until I leave for London, but you *will* have your independence. I might have broken my own rule, but I won't break my promise about your future. I'll give you what you've always wanted."

CHAPTER 30

AMIE FLOATED THROUGH THE REST of the day, her emotions suspended by Ian's kiss. It had lasted a few short minutes, but she had lived a lifetime in them. She wasn't the same girl her father had abandoned in death, homeless and begging to be cared for. Nor was she the wallflower unnoticed and forgotten.

She had been wanted. And that—despite what she had told Ian before their wedding—was what she truly wanted.

Those strong arms had cherished her, those lips caressed her.

There would be no satisfaction in life now. She had felt the best of it.

At dinner, she tried to school her attention from Ian at the other end of the table and focus on Mama. Increased awareness of him ruined her efforts. She could sense his hands on her waist, back, and cheek. With a subtle lift of her shoulder, she brushed her face against it, hoping the sensation of the memory would fade.

"Amie? Amie!"

She blinked and looked at her mama. "Yes?"

"That's the third time I've asked you to pass the french salad."

Her brow rose. "Oh, forgive me." She passed the cold meat strips heavily garnished with shallot, anchovies, and parsley to Mama.

"I do not think you've heard anything I've said tonight. Are you well?"

Her gaze flicked to Ian's. His curious expression held hers for a moment, and heat flooded her cheeks.

He would never kiss her again.

She tore her gaze away and fumbled for her fork. "I am well, Mama. I was lost in thought."

"If you're sure." Then Mama raised her voice as if Ian were in another room. "My Amie has an excellent constitution. It's all the walking she does. Indeed, I cannot recall the last time she had a cold. And she only overeats when distressed, so she rarely ever has an upset stomach."

A pity Amie hadn't missed hearing this particular comment. "Mama, Lord Reynolds does not need to know such unimportant details about me."

"On the contrary," Ian said. "I am happy to know my wife has good health."

Reluctantly, she met his gaze again. His expression was perfectly sincere and seemed to repeat, "*You are not a charity case. . . It would not take any effort at all for me to fall madly in love with you.*"

But he hadn't repeated those words. They were a beautiful echo in her mind. Her stomach fluttered at the recent memory, knowing that he cared. Even if he never acted on it again, at least she knew that much.

Mama spoke again, breaking the thin string of connection between Amie and Ian. "You two have been wed for such a short time, I should think you would like to know such details. But don't ever give her warm milk. I used to do that when she couldn't sleep as a child, but it always gave her stomach pains and nightmares."

Amie's cheeks flushed with embarrassment.

A low rumble sounded from the other end of the table, and it sounded suspiciously like a subdued laugh. Ian quickly cleared his throat. "Warm milk, you say? These nightmares don't make her thrash around, do they?"

Mama put a hand to her chest. "Oh, something terrible. Her bed-sheets would always be in a knot come morning."

More low rumbles. "I shall endeavor to remember that."

"I haven't given it to her for years," Mama said. "There is a chance she has grown out of it. I wouldn't worry, for as I said, Amie is a healthy woman."

"Just the same," Ian said. "Absolutely no warm milk."

Amie would gladly trade places with the peas in her soup over discussing her humiliating nighttime habits and food sensitivities. She forced herself to give Ian an apologetic look across the table, and she was surprised when he met it with a reassuring smile that warmed her all the way to her toes.

After dinner, Ian excused himself to work. Part of her was disappointed, but the other part was relieved. Now she could focus on Mama's words, and there would be no need for repeated sentences.

Mama took a seat in the drawing room beside Amie. "Robert cannot be at peace with your wedding. He is depressed and despondent."

"He will move on soon enough," Amie said, hugging a throw pillow to her chest.

"I do hope you are right. He really did care for you." Mama spent the next hour telling her all about the news from town. "Everyone asks about your wedding, and I have never had so many visitors before. It's like before your father died, but I do not have the energy for it like I used to."

She hoped her mother hadn't said or done anything untoward. After the way she'd spread the news of her own daughter's false engagement, it did make Amie wonder.

Mama stifled a yawn. "Oh, dear me. I should retire to bed before your husband thinks I have no manners at all."

"He wouldn't think that." Amie took her arm, and they walked together through the house and up the stairs. It was nice having Mama by her side again. She really had missed her. Amie entered the bedchamber long enough to yank the bellpull for Edna and to fetch her night things. "Sleep well, Mama."

"Good night, dear."

Amie wasn't worried about interrupting Ian when she opened his door. Knowing him, he would work in his office until his candle all but disappeared. She cast her gaze about the empty room. His large, four-poster bed dwarfed the rest of the room. The mahogany wood scrolled at the ends and gleamed from polish even in the low light. Dark-blue drapes hung from the top, and a matching quilt covered the bed.

She breathed in Ian's scent: a masculine musk with a hint of amber. If she closed her eyes, she could almost imagine him standing right in front of her. He had said it correctly when he declared her sentimental. She shook her head and waited for Edna to finish with Mama.

The maid hurried in a few minutes later, long enough to help Amie out of her dress and into her nightgown before Mama called for Edna again. She gave a flustered huff.

Amie handed Edna her evening gown to take with her. "Go ahead, I can brush and braid my own hair." Not as well as Edna could, but Amie did have years of practice seeing to her own toilet. "Then see yourself to bed. I expect to be up early." It would do no good for her to linger in this room.

Edna gave a grateful smile. "Thank you, milady."

Laying her robe on the back of Ian's chair, Amie sat and picked up her brush. Mindlessly, she worked the tangles from her hair. When she finished, she set her brush down on the dressing table beside Ian's shaving supplies. Her fingers trailed down the handle of his razor.

The door opened behind her, and her hand stilled. Through the reflection in the mirror, she saw Ian hesitate on the threshold.

"Is it all right if I come in?" he asked.

"Yes, of course." She reached for her robe and hurriedly put her arms into it.

"I saw Edna on the stairs. Do you need another minute?"

"Not at all." She stood and tied the strings by her neck. "I'll turn down the counterpane. Which side do you prefer? I haven't had any warm milk; you needn't worry about that."

Ian smiled, as she'd hoped he would, and shut the door behind him. "I'm planning on staying until your mother is asleep. I will spend the night in the library."

"The library?" Her hands went to her middle.

"Amie," Ian came farther into the room, stopping at the end of his bed. "After this morning, you know why I cannot stay here tonight."

She understood. He wanted to maintain boundaries. "Will you take a pillow and blanket?"

"I'll find something downstairs." He sat on the edge of the bed. "Are you happy to have your mother here?"

"I think so. I didn't realize how much I missed her. We've been by each other's side for so long."

He clasped his hands lightly in his lap. "After my father's visit, I hope she will be a great comfort to you."

Amie played with the ribbon on her robe. "I hope that is the case. I would have liked to have more time to establish myself with the staff before her arrival. Mama can be . . . unpredictable." Amie came and perched on the bed, too, leaving several feet between them.

"Who does that remind me of?" Ian teased.

She scowled. "Don't make me throw a pillow at you."

He chuckled. "I meant it in the best of ways." He looked over at the wall between his room and hers. "How long does your mother take to fall asleep?"

"It depends. She has sleepless nights when she misses Papa. She seemed tired after dinner though."

Ian pulled out his pocket watch. "I will stay a quarter hour and hope she is asleep by then."

"Thank you."

He nodded. "Since you ask all the questions and I tell all the stories, perhaps it should be the opposite tonight. You mentioned you weren't out in Society much before I came along. Did a man catch your fancy and try to court you?"

She shook her head, a little embarrassed to speak of such things in front of Ian. "Mama always said something outrageous, and no matron would let her son near me. We made quite the reputation for ourselves everywhere we went."

Ian scrunched his brow. "She seems so docile to me."

"It's usually when she's flustered. She was raised well-off, and she can act above her current station. People do not appreciate such airs from a penniless widow."

"I see. So, no courtships? Just an infatuated cousin?"

"Not an official courtship, but I did have a business suitor. He had a fancy title, but I always preferred Lord Grumpy."

Ian chuckled. "Aw, I have heard of him. Handsome fellow."

"Some might think so," she teased. "He proved himself to be thoughtful too. He drove me to the orchard and accompanied me to the musical and the theater."

"Don't forget the lively family dinner party, where he became your besotted swain."

"You mean the night I thought your father would have an apoplexy from your brazen behavior, and Lord Halbert would request a duel to protect his daughter's honor?"

"I'm a good shot, you know."

She drew back. "What does that mean?"

"I would have won."

She snatched up a pillow. "I reserve the right to use this if you make any more idiotic statements like that one. Honestly, duels are not a joking matter."

Ian leaned across the bed, propping his elbow up on it. "Very well, no more talk of duels. What were you like as a child? Sweet with a gentle disposition? I can imagine two braids, darker freckles, and a toothless grin."

She hugged the pillow. "I don't know about sweet, but I was shy. I didn't care for large groups. I had one good friend I would spend hours playing with. We did our fair share of exploring outside, playing pirates and lost damsels in distress. She is two years older than I and is married now with a few children. We write occasionally at Christmas and Easter, but we have grown apart. Our lives—our stations—are very different from each other."

"Even now that you are a viscountess?"

She laughed. "I forgot about that title. I suppose there is not such a vast rift between us now."

Ian smiled. "So you were a shy little thing. What made you start visiting your neighbors, then?"

"Neighbor visits were nonnegotiable. From as young as I can remember, I was taught happiness was spelled *s-e-r-v-i-c-e* because service is the key to true joy." She said it robotically from years of repetition.

Ian grinned. "I remember the way you spoke to your father's headstone, as if he were someone you truly admired. Did he teach you this principle? Is that why you value it so much?"

"No, actually. It was my mother."

Ian's brow rose. "Truly?"

She ran a hand down the silk pillowcase. "The full estimation of a person cannot be made when they are at their lowest. Mama has been stuck in her grief for many years now; sometimes even I forget who she used to be. She spent years giving and created many friendships along the way. When Papa died, the few who held fast to Mama, she pushed away. She had never learned to receive charity, only give it. Now that she lives on charity, she deeply resents it. I believe that's the real reason she offended our family and we had to move so often. You know, I never saw it before until this minute."

Ian sat up a little. "I will endeavor to see this view of her when I am with her next and try harder to understand her. I have a great respect for people who put others before themselves. It's not a natural inclination for most of us."

"Practice helps," she said.

He eyed her. "You have a Rebel spirit."

"Do I?" That seemed the greatest compliment coming from Ian.

"I am the unofficial leader of the Rebels, so I would know."

"What is the nickname that they called you?" She had been dying to ask about it since Tom had mentioned the name at their wedding.

His brow lowered. "Favorite Friend, probably."

Seeing his predictable reaction, she couldn't help her mocking tone as she took hold of her pillow. "Oh? I thought it was *Mother Hen.*"

Ian glowered, then dove to grab a pillow of his own. She didn't wait for him to throw it at her but swung hers at his head. He gave a half-laugh, half-growl before swinging his own toward her back. She dodged it and hurled herself off the bed. Ian rolled toward the end and jumped to his feet. She squealed and sprinted around the bed with him chasing after her. When he slung an arm around her waist, she tried to hit him with the pillow from around her shoulder. Their laughter mixed together, and somehow, she managed to turn in his arms and get him good in the face.

He took her arm and pinned it to her side, his head coming down until—

It stopped a mere centimeter from hers. His eyes dropped to her mouth, and his breath tickled her lips. Would he kiss her? She wanted him to with everything in her.

He abruptly let her go, his chest heaving. "I should go."

She took a step back, hugging the pillow again. She'd have preferred to hold something else—him—but the pillow seemed the only thing she had permission to hold. She swallowed and gave him a slow nod.

He stared at her for a moment, an apology written on his face, and disappeared through the door. Amie reached for her heart, willing for it to cease pounding. He had made her a promise, and she admired him for doing right by her. But weren't some promises meant to be broken? She would gladly relinquish him from this one if he'd let her. She doubted her consent would change anything. He seemed quite determined to follow a course he'd set long before he'd met her.

CHAPTER 31

IAN HAD MADE A GRAVE mistake. One he couldn't seem to undo. Collapsing onto the library sofa did not help either. A recent memory of Amie sitting beside him on this very sofa flooded over him. Even then, he'd tried not to notice her soft voice and gentle touch as she'd worried over his injury. He groaned. Every time he closed his eyes, there she was: her penetrating gaze and vanilla scent. He flipped to his other side, tucking a hand under his head, waiting for sleep to overcome him. Amie's playful smile danced behind his eyelids. Her shriek of laughter replayed in his mind, and the playful way she'd hit him with her pillow. His own lips crept into a smile in the dark.

She was lovely.

Her eyes had competition, for he had recently developed an obsession with her lips. Before he could stop himself, he replayed their kiss from that morning. Not once but easily a dozen times. No amount of tossing and turning could keep her from his mind. When the early hours of dawn began to lighten the room, he discovered that Tiny had come and fallen asleep on his leg.

What a great future he had before him—spending long nights with his dog and his miserable self. He shifted Tiny off his leg, and the dog looked up sleepily at him before nestling back into the blanket. Then Ian rose from the sofa and stretched his tight muscles—penance for his irritating lack of self-control.

Growling under his breath, he swore to himself that today he would be a better man. But no matter how committed he was to keeping Amie at bay and devoting himself to his work, he couldn't do it while being near her. She was a chink in his armor—a soft spot that grew more magnified with every interaction until it felt more like a heady intoxication instead of a weakness. It meant one thing: he had to leave.

He no longer trusted himself.

What excuse could he give for abandoning Amie and her mother? He had promised to put on an act to convince Mrs. Tyler—though the act was becoming more real by the minute. He rubbed his thumb across the cleft in his chin. What could he do?

He stepped out into the corridor just as his butler came toward him with a silver platter in his hand. Atop it was a letter.

"This was delivered by way of the servants' entrance," Mr. Hamburg said.

"Thank you." Ian picked up the folded note and stared curiously at the unrecognizable seal. "I'll find you if a response is needed."

Mr. Hamburg nodded and left him.

Was this what he hoped it was? Ripping into it, he scanned the contents. Sir James wanted to meet right away. He had plans to present to parliament soon and begged for Ian's immediate response.

Energy coursed through Ian's veins. This was what he needed to convince Mrs. Tyler of the need for his quick departure. And Amie . . . It would put the necessary distance between them and allow him to return to his senses. He would ask her feelings first, but he knew she would understand. She understood far more about him than most who had known him his entire life.

Watching through the drawing room window, Amie followed Ian with her eyes until he and his horse disappeared behind the tree line along the road. Their goodbye had been stilted, forced—affectionless.

The clouds formed a gray shade over her view, and a heaviness settled inside her. He was gone. Just as planned.

Mama came up behind her and set a hand on her arm. "It is usual for men to have business they must see to. You cannot depend for them to always be about. It wouldn't be good for a marriage anyway. You would start to irritate each other." Mama sighed, glancing out the same window. "Though he was rather vague about when he would return."

Amie forced a smile. "I am used to entertaining myself. He should be gone as long as he likes. I won't pine for him, I assure you."

"Good girl," Mama patted her arm. "It feels like a fresh start here. I rather like it."

Amie studied her mother. She seemed much refreshed after her night's rest. Her words, though, were what captured Amie's attention. They were filled with hope and promise, and they were just what Amie needed herself. She covered Mama's hand with her own. "We will have a good life here, Mama. We'll be happy again."

Mama smiled. "I am already. The day you married Lord Reynolds, my grief shed like an old skin. Living with your uncle and aunt, though, did not encourage me toward any amount of joy. But here I can breathe again."

"It is not too small for you?"

Mama hated cramped spaces.

"Not at all. This room is a decent size." Mama moved to the sofa and smoothed her hand over the wood frame. "We ought to redecorate though. Get it up to snuff. A viscountess cannot entertain with these dated fabrics and rugs."

She had forgotten that Mama had a good eye for decor. Amie should have waited until her arrival to do over her bedchamber. Ian had left plenty of money to see to other rooms too. "Shall it be our first project together?"

Mama grinned—a full ear-to-ear grin. "Let's ride into town to get a swatch of fabrics."

Amie couldn't remember seeing her mother so enthused. She nodded, and they hurried to gather their bonnets and reticules. The distraction was needed. Surely, after suppressing the gnawing ache in her chest for a few days more, it would fade completely.

❧

A week passed, and Amie hadn't heard anything from Ian. She had hoped by now a letter would come. Mama asked every morning over breakfast, and every morning, Amie disappointed her. It rained off and on all week, but no thunder or lightning accompanied it. Every once in a while, an anxious thought would creep into Amie's mind. What if Ian hadn't made it to London? What if he'd been thrown from his horse? It was nonsense brought on from the paranoia of her father's death. Ian was fine.

He simply had no reason to write to her.

In time, he would remember his promise and send her word out of obligation. She could manage until then. Couldn't she?

Amie decided to bring Mama on her walk to introduce her to the neighbors and tenant farmers. Mama had not wanted to do this sort of thing for ages but seemed to truly enjoy it today. When they returned home, Mama shed her shawl and called for tea, departing into the drawing room to rest. Amie removed her bonnet and unbuttoned her spencer at a slower pace, nagging thoughts of Ian distracting her.

Mrs. Hamburg approached her with hesitation on her face.

Amie set down her spencer on a chair in the vestibule. "What is it, Mrs. Hamburg?"

"I hate to trouble you, but I have a conundrum I would like your advice on."

Her advice? It felt like an important moment, being trusted and recognized as the lady of the house. "I am happy to help if I can."

"A missive came for His Lordship. It carries Lord Kellen's seal. The rider said it was urgent."

Urgent? Normally, they would have all Ian's mail forwarded on to him, but she knew why she hesitated now. The servants couldn't have missed Ian's declaration to never speak to his father again. Would he want the letter, or would he toss it in the fire before reading it?

"I will take it for now and decide what is to be done," Amie said.

"Yes, Your Ladyship." Mrs. Hamburg extended the letter.

Amie took it and studied the seal with the eagle head, waiting until Mrs. Hamburg had left her. If there was something truly urgent, she needed to know to what extent before she made her decision on how to act. With a fortifying breath, she broke the seal with her finger. She unfolded the letter and noticed right away the hand was feminine. It was from Lady Kellen, not her husband. Two sentences in, Amie's jaw dropped. "Good heavens."

Lord Kellen had suddenly taken ill, and the doctors thought he did not have long to live. Lady Kellen begged her son to come straightaway. Amie's hand fell to her side, the paper crinkling against her skirt. They must not know that Ian was in London.

Her mind whirled. Ian needed to be with his father. If his father died before they reconciled, the guilt could weigh on Ian for a lifetime. Lord Kellen had known when Ian had returned to London mere weeks ago. He probably had a connection with one of the servants. Why had he not discovered it this time around?

Unless . . . unless Ian wasn't staying at his townhome. That was the only answer that made any sense. Ian could be staying with Sir James. It would take time to find where he resided. Would Sir James have left a forwarding address with his letter?

Without another thought, she raced to Ian's office. She yanked the drapes open, and daylight poured into the empty room. She turned to find the desk clear of any papers. It was a small chance he had left the letter anyway, but if he had, she must find it. Pulling the top drawer open, she discovered a stack of financial record books. The second contained some loose papers. She picked up the first one and sucked in her breath. This was it. And at the bottom was Sir James's address. It was a miracle. A sign . . .

Mama burst into the office. "There you are. The tea has arrived, and a maid thought she saw you coming this way."

Amie set her hand on the desk. "Mama, can you spare me?"

"What?"

"I just received a missive, and Lord Kellen is very ill."

"Oh, mercy." Mama waved her hand in front of her face like she might faint. They were too acquainted with death to take such news lightly. "You must go to him."

"I think I must."

Ian wouldn't want her to come, but someone had to force him to see his father. She didn't know if she was capable, but she would certainly try.

Within the hour, all was prepared. Amie was going to London. Mama miraculously agreed to stay behind, understanding that death was a private family affair, and promised to send her ideas for the drawing room before any changes were made.

Amie couldn't care less about decorating now. It seemed so trite when Ian's father was suffering.

Mama walked her out to the carriage. The footman held the door open for Amie, and she turned and embraced Mama in parting. "Will you look in on Tiny? He is quite attached to Ian, so he will need attention."

"I will see that he has daily exercise." Mama pulled back. "Where will you sleep tonight? Have you instructed the driver properly?"

Amie nodded. "We will change horses at the inn we stayed at previously, but we will ride through the night. Time is of the essence."

Mama's lips pulled tight. Neither one of them preferred to travel at night after what had happened to Papa. "Travel safe, dear."

"Don't worry for me. All will be well." As she stepped toward the carriage to join Edna, who was already ensconced inside, she felt a few drops of rain graze her cheek. She cast her eyes upward to the thick, ominous, gray clouds.

Her courage wavered.

"Not now," she whispered.

CHAPTER 32

IAN STRETCHED HIS LEGS, HIS body tired from sitting for so many hours in Sir James's library. The committee had finished for the day, but Paul had arrived an hour ago. Ian had found the other men tolerable enough, but no one was a better sounding board than his good friend.

"Your committee carries a misconception that it is the elite ruling the Bloody Code." Paul leaned over the long table that fit snugly in the narrow room, his voice even and sensible.

Ian frowned. "The elite thrive off tradition. Of course, *we* must change before anyone else can."

Paul dug his hand into his dark, russet-colored hair, a noticeable sign that he was growing impatient. "Ian, you must not overlook that the people have been groomed for nearly a century and a half to believe death is the only way. They want consequences to control the madness."

Ian leaned over the table as well, frustrated that his friend was being so blasted logical. He didn't want to hear about tradition again. "Then, we must inform the people. Change their mindsets."

Paul sank back in his seat. "Such an endeavor could take years. And what of the judges? They are the ones who mete out the rulings. They will not change their ways so easily."

Ian hated how much sense Paul made, but it did not change Ian's optimism for progress. He was too stubborn for that. "God-fearing men will see that justice cannot be served without mercy.

Consequences are a natural part of life, but they should be appropriate for the crime. We don't live in the time of Moses, where we pluck out eyes and cut off hands. We have prisons for lesser sentences."

"Prisons in dire need of reform," Paul continued. "Do you remember the workhouses? These are far worse."

Ian rubbed his chin with an irritated hand. "Are you on my side, or aren't you?"

"I will always be on your side, Ian. Not just me but all the Rebels too. Tom arranged for a man at Oxford to hold a few lectures to discreetly rally public support. Miles sent letters to his associates in the church. Even Bentley has reached out to his connections. But I must caution you to lower your expectations. I'm not certain I see a clear path to the change you seek. This could take a lifetime to fight."

Ian's frustration waned. He couldn't ask for better friends. "I thank you for your sincerity. I know you mean well, but it's already been decided. We're going to put it to vote next week."

"Next week!" Paul shook his head. "Tell me you're joking. Do you even have a convincing plan?"

"The committee has been working night and day for much longer than I have been involved," Ian said. "Though even I have exhausted my strength these last weeks both at home and here in London." He did not add that he'd needed every minute of distraction this week to keep him from thinking of home—of Amie. Even London had not been far enough to rid his mind of her. "I've put a little weight on key people, and it'll be close, but we have to strike before either side has time to talk themselves out of it."

"It's rash, Ian."

He nodded and tapped a set of folders in front of him. "There's enough stories of cruelty here to make your skin crawl. A few family members came and shared their painful stories with us. It's a fight I cannot walk away from. Just yesterday, a boy not older than thirteen was killed. Thirteen!"

"I heard. He pleaded self-defense but did not have the witnesses to support his case."

"This could propel changes in the prisons too." A cause he knew Paul was passionate about.

"You don't have to convince me," Paul said. "You have to convince Parliament."

"We will." Ian rubbed his eyes, trying to fight off the worry nagging in the back of his mind.

Paul sighed. "How can I help?"

"Pray."

Paul raised his brow but said nothing. Ian wasn't the most religious man, but some matters were too big for men to fix. If ever he needed faith, it was now.

Paul gave a succinct nod and released a sigh. "Enough of this heavy talk. How is Lady Reynolds?"

"Amie?" Ian reflexively tensed.

"Yes, your *wife*?"

Ian straightened the folders in front of him, suddenly needing to do something with his hands. "She is entertaining her mother at Oak End."

"Will she come to London afterward?"

Ian shook his head. "She has no plans to come here at present. She is content to remain in the country."

Paul eyed him strangely. "I see."

Annoyed, Ian furrowed his brow. "What do you mean, 'I see'?"

"I see you are still fooling yourself."

Only a Rebel would be idiotic enough to challenge Ian on a personal matter. He glowered at Paul. "We have an arrangement," he hissed. "And you are fully aware of it. She doesn't want to see me, and I don't want to see her."

He didn't know why the mere mention of Amie had his hackles up. He was far too sensitive where she was concerned. His tendre for her would fade, and he would forget her soon enough. Maybe by then his friends would learn to keep their ideas to themselves.

A knock sounded on the door, and Sir James's butler stuck his gray-haired head inside. "There is a caller for you, Lord Reynolds. She says she is your wife."

Ian nearly jumped out of his seat, his eyes flicking to Paul.

Paul had an annoying smile growing on his face. "She doesn't want to see you, does she?"

Paul's response did not irk him this time. All his thoughts were for Amie. Thoughts full of concern. He hurried to the door. Something had to be wrong for her to come to him.

"Where is she?" he asked the butler.

"In the entrance hall, my lord."

He pushed past the older man and jogged toward the entrance hall. Amie was facing away from him when he saw her. His chest caught, hungry for the sight of her. "Amie?"

She turned at the sound of her name. Her face was drawn and her skin pale. Too pale. "Oh, thank heavens," she breathed, stepping toward him.

He closed the distance between them and started to reach for her, just stopping himself. He would not undo the progress he had made in one thoughtless moment. "Why are you here?"

His voice came out gruffer than intended, and she hesitated. "I—I have news."

"Is it your mother? Is she ill?"

She shook her head before reaching a hand up to rub her tired eyes. She looked poor indeed. He fisted his hand to resist the innate need to steady her.

"It is not Mama. I received a letter while you were gone from your mother with urgent news. It's your father who is ill. I traveled through the night, and I hope I'm not too late with the news."

He stepped back. "My father is ill?"

"Lady Kellen says that they are not sure if he will live the week. Ian, you must go to him with all haste." She dug into her reticule and handed him the creased parchment.

He took it and read it through. Dropping the letter to his side, his eyes went to the long windows beside the door, glazing over. "It's a trick."

"What do you mean?"

"My mother. She wants us to be together. This is just like her. She has this sixth sense about my motivations. First, she interfered with us and now with Father. I am needed here and cannot go."

"Ian, you're not thinking straight." Amie drew closer, her brown eyes wide and imploring. "Your father could die. If you cannot be there for him, you must be there for your mother. Please. You could regret this for the rest of your life."

He shook his head. "My father cannot be that ill. We saw him mere weeks ago and in perfect health." It was not denial. He just did not believe it.

Amie put her hand on his arm, making him tense. Reminding her of rule number one likely wouldn't remove her purposeful grip. "I'm sorry, Ian."

Reality seemed to sink into his understanding. He was not so naïve as to believe that life couldn't change in an instant. Mother had never lied so outrightly before. He couldn't see her joking about something so serious. "I suppose . . . I suppose I could look into it."

"Don't waste a moment," she begged. "I would have given anything to see my father once more before he died."

It couldn't be so dire. Ian refused to believe it. That deuced man didn't have it in him to show any weakness to anyone. But the worry in Amie's eyes was Ian's undoing. He didn't have to see his father to visit the house. He would speak to his mother and ascertain the circumstances. Finally, he nodded.

Amie sighed, relief evident on her worn features. Why hadn't she sent someone to deliver the news for her?

"I told them to keep the carriage ready," she said. "I hope we find him better when we get there." She pulled away and turned to the door.

He caught her hand without thinking twice. "We?"

Amie raised a brow, glancing at their hands and then up at him. "I'm not trying to force myself on you. I thought you might burden your mother further if you left me behind."

She was exhausted and didn't need to be around his volatile family again. Not after the way she had been treated last time.

"I will have Sir James put you up for the night and make arrangements for you to return home in the morning."

Someone cleared their throat.

Ian turned his head to see Paul step into the entryway. His eyes went to Ian's hand holding Amie's, making Ian immediately drop it.

Amusement flickered in his friend's gaze. "May I greet Lady Reynolds?" Paul asked, stepping forward without any consent from Ian.

Paul took Amie's hand, the one Ian had just dropped, and bowed over it. "It is a pleasure to see you again, my lady."

Pleasure? Ian ground his teeth. Why did Paul get to take pleasure from seeing Amie again when Ian had to keep all his confusing feelings locked up tight? Nothing was right anymore. Nothing.

"Your journey was long," Paul continued. "You must take a seat and have some refreshment. Sir James is nearly finished with his business, and I am sure he would like to meet the new Lady Reynolds." Paul suddenly reached forward and steadied Amie's arm. Ian's friend didn't care to touch anyone but his wife, so his gesture did not go unnoticed. It was then that Ian realized Amie had begun shaking. It was all he could do to keep from taking up her other arm, but it seemed Paul's arm was sufficient for her.

"I am well enough, thank you," she said. "I must be going."

"So soon?" Paul frowned and sent a chastising gaze Ian's way.

Ian folded his arms across his chest, ignoring Paul's glare and sending one of his own toward his wife. "You are resting here, and I am going."

"I won't be in the way," she said. "I'll stay in the drawing room or wherever the family is not."

Paul's frown deepened. "Why would you need to stay hidden away? What is this, Ian?"

"My father is ill," Ian explained. "And Amie clearly needs rest."

Surprise lit Paul's face. "I came straight here after my recent trip. I hadn't heard any news or opened any correspondence after reading your invitation to come here. How serious is it?"

"Very," Amie said.

"Mother sent a letter." Ian didn't have any specifics to offer him.

Amie smiled up at Paul. "It was good to see you again, Mr. Sheldon, but we really must go."

"Amie," Ian sighed.

Paul released his hold on Amie. "I will explain everything to Sir James, Ian. Send me word when you arrive. I want to know how he fares. I will let you two alone to discuss the particulars." Before he left, Paul leaned toward Ian's ear and hissed, "Take her arm. She looks like she is going to collapse."

Thoroughly chastened, Ian moved to Amie's side and put his arm around her back, his voice full of apology. "Come, you need to sit down."

She immediately relaxed against him. "I'm well enough. My nerves are a little taut from a pesky little storm on the way over."

"A storm?" They'd had rain here but not thunder or lightning. His stomach clenched at the thought of her suffering alone. "I'm sorry for what you had to endure."

"It was mostly rain, and Edna's constant chatter was distracting. I can rest in the carriage."

He met her gaze, the proximity making the effect far more lethal to his heart than before. Her genuine concern for his father's welfare and his mother's comfort touched him. "This wasn't part of our agreement, Amie, you having to race through the night, in a storm no less, to give me this news yourself."

"I wanted to," she whispered. "But I will stay here if the only way you will go is alone."

His jaw tightened. He didn't want to leave her here, where he was unsure if she would take ill herself. He knew it made her feel of worth to help others, and that was why she had come all this way and risked her own mental faculties, but it didn't make his decision any easier. He swallowed. "I don't wish to go alone. Would you please accompany me?"

A tired smile crossed her face, not one of rejoicing for getting her way but one full of genuine care. "Whatever you need, Ian. I want to be your friend, come what may."

Friend? He wanted to scoff at the word. It didn't come close to defining the wave of comfort her nearness gave him, or really anything he felt for her anymore. But if his father were truly ill, Ian suddenly knew she was who he would need most of all.

CHAPTER 33

AMIE HADN'T EXPECTED IAN TO rejoice at seeing her again, but his abrupt greeting played over and over in her mind. She had no right to long for him, though she kept fooling herself that she did. Even now, in the carriage, sitting across from him and beside Edna, she could not help but wish to be beside him. His arms rested on his thighs, with his head bent forward, keeping her from reading his mood.

How selfish she was. His father was dying, and she wanted him to comfort her. If she couldn't be near him, she wanted to at least hear his voice. Heaven knew, they both needed the distraction. "Did you make any progress with Sir James?"

Ian lifted his head and looked at her, his face blank and emotionless. "Time will tell."

The answer seemed to apply to her unspoken questions too—about her and about his father. Time was a relentless soldier, always marching steadily on. Sometimes it gave generously, and sometimes it proved to be the enemy. She wondered what sword it would wield today—for better or worse—and whose side it would be on. Would Lord Kellen die? Would she live out the lonely, independent life she had so long sought for? Would Ian ever let himself return to her?

His voice startled her from her thoughts. "Are you feeling any better?"

Even with the tension and unanswered questions hovering between them, she still felt easier in his company than not. "I think so."

They had been in the carriage for a half hour, and sleep had evaded her. Though Edna had not suffered from the same problem. A soft snore sang from the seat beside her.

Ian leaned back and studied Amie, making her shift with self-consciousness. "I wish we would have waited for tea. You could have used some."

Did she look so poorly? She hadn't wanted to waste a moment, but an entire night in a carriage must've left her appearance wanting. Perhaps his reaction to her would have been different if she had arrived looking as pretty as Miss Foster.

There she went, thinking selfish thoughts again. "Please don't worry about me," she said. "Not when it is your father who deserves your attention."

Ian shook his head. "My father gave me his attention when it was to benefit himself, so I spare him the same decency I would any other person on this earth."

It was said so matter-of-factly that Amie could only frown in response.

"Judge me as you may," he said. "I can imagine you think me quite spoiled and ungrateful."

"I think you do not know what it is like to lose a father." The words spilled out before she could hold them back. "I hope you never have to learn what I have."

Ian's face softened. "I'm sorry. I did not mean to offend."

"You didn't," she said. "I'm worried for you. I know you don't want me to be, but considering my own experiences, you must know I cannot help it."

Ian's mouth pursed, and he nodded.

A moment later, the carriage pulled to a stop in front of the same townhome they had dined at a month previously. Ian helped her down, and he took her arm, leading her inside.

A strange silence filled the house. She noticed it the moment they entered through the front door.

The butler attended to them, whispering back and forth with Ian. Amie braced herself as she watched them. Was he telling Ian that his father had died? Ian's eyes went to the staircase, following it to the top, where she assumed his parents' bedchamber was located.

Ian turned to her, his voice low. "My father is resting, and my mother is with him. You were right to hurry me here."

She couldn't release her breath in relief that he was alive because the news still sounded dire. "I can wait in the drawing room. Take as long as you need."

He hesitated, his eyes trailing back to the stairs. She had never seen Ian nervous before, but she swore she saw a glimpse of it now. He, no doubt, had many conflicting feelings warring inside him. How she wished she could tell him to forget any hatred he bore. It wasn't worth carrying. Not now.

"Mr. Derrik," Ian said to the butler behind him. "See that a meal is prepared for Lady Reynolds, and prepare a guest room in case she cares to rest."

Again, he was worrying about her when he shouldn't be. The butler nodded and stepped away to do Ian's bidding.

Ian led her to the drawing room door. "I'm not certain how long I'll be."

She frowned at him to show her disapproval of his misplaced concern. "Stop fussing. I'm in no hurry."

He nodded, his eyes solemn, but there was no mistaking the silent thank-you. He pulled away from her, his shoulders weighed down by an invisible burden as his long legs strode to the stairs. She watched him for a moment before slipping into the dining room.

She was supposed to be his wife in name only, but the way her heart ached for him and his family made her feel like far more than a mere partner in some convenient arrangement. But she had to remember that not everyone believed she belonged here. If his family had accepted her, she might have accompanied Ian to see his father. Even so, she regretted staying behind, afraid Ian was about to upset a dying man.

CHAPTER 34

Ian's father lay asleep in his bed, his coloring ashen. His arms rested over the counterpane tucked neatly around him. Vials of medicine lined the bedside table. Mama sat in a chair by his side, a handkerchief balled in her hands. When Ian entered the bedchamber, she lifted her tear-stained cheeks, her eyes reaching his. They were raw with worry and pain.

She said nothing but stood and came to him. Her arms circled his neck the moment she met him. His mother always tried to be strong for everyone else, but there was no hiding her weakness this time.

His teeth clenched until pain crawled up his jaw. She shouldn't be crying alone for his father. How dare that man break his mother's heart again. But even in Ian's frustration, it wasn't easy seeing his father knocked down like this. It unsettled him in the worst way.

Mama pulled back. "Thank you for coming so quickly."

He wouldn't have without Amie's interference. "What happened?"

"He became worked up about something and collapsed."

Ian tried to think of what bills in Parliament his father was working on, but he tried not to pay too much attention to his father, so he was not certain. "What could have upset him so much?"

Mama looked at her hands. "You might as well know. Lord Halbert came over. They argued for a long time. Lord Halbert said he was engaging his daughter to another and wasn't waiting for an annulment that wasn't certain to happen. After he left, your father was in quite a rage before his sudden collapse. The doctor said it's his heart. Your father is still with us, but no one knows for how long."

Ian smothered a wave of guilt and shock. "What is being done for him?"

"There isn't much that can be done besides laudanum for the pain. He has mostly slept but isn't showing any signs of improvement." She brought her handkerchief up to her mouth, but no new tears formed in her eyes.

He put his arms around her again. She didn't have to hide her emotions from him. "There, there. I'm here now, and I will do all that I can to help."

"Oh, Ian. I know this cannot be easy for you."

She had no idea. "Amie is downstairs. It would be good for you to leave this sick room and eat with us tonight."

Her eyes brightened. "You brought Amie?"

More or less, but there was no use going into details. "Why don't you rest first while I sit with Father."

"Would you?"

"Well, he cannot argue with me if he's asleep, now can he?"

"But if he wakes up, you might upset him."

He gave a halfhearted shrug. "Maybe fighting me will give him a reason to live."

Mama swatted his shoulder. "Don't tease at a time like this." Amusement flicked in her expression, even as she chided him.

"I won't tease. I'll sit obediently in the same chair you were in and be as solemn as a church mouse."

"Good." She sighed and looked at Father once more. "I could use a moment to myself. Thank you, Ian."

He nodded and led her to the door. Taking up his mother's vigil, he sat in the chair and stared at his father. He noted Father's mussed hair—gray at the temples and dark on top—and the rumpled state of his dressing gown around his impressive upper body. Was this what a dying man looked like? Minutes passed and then an hour. No change.

"You brought this upon yourself, you know," he muttered aloud. "You couldn't just let me live the life I chose. It might shock you, but I don't want to live your life. I'm chartering a course that doesn't involve breaking anyone's heart in the process."

He thought of his mother, no doubt crying in her bed, afraid to lose her husband, and for some reason, it made Ian think of Amie the night of the storm. She'd been terrified. Had it been the same on her carriage ride here? He wasn't like his father, immoral and unfaithful, but in a way, he was very much like him. He still wasn't a good husband.

He leaned forward and covered his face in his hands.

Ian brought Amie to his townhome to sleep before returning to stay with his parents, should his mother need him. He paced the corridors most of the night, frustrated with himself and with his father, remorse giving way to growing frustration and then guilt winning over once more. He finally fell asleep in his old room as the sun was rising, filling his window with dark orange mixed with hues of pink. Somehow, the light comforted his mind enough to allow him to finally rest.

When he woke, his view through the window was a dull gray-blue, with the sun peeking through the cloud cover directly overhead. After dressing, Ian left his bedchamber and went in search of Mama. He hadn't expected to find Father's door open or for Amie's voice to filter through it. When had she come over? Ducking his head into the room, to his greater surprise, he discovered her reading to Father while he slept.

The words were familiar to Ian, but it still took a moment to register what story they derived from. Was that *Robinson Crusoe*? Oh, Father would be groaning in his sleep if he knew. He detested reading anything but the news. The image almost made Ian laugh. Sweet Amie with her good intentions. He would bet a guinea that she was spelling Mama so she might rest.

He half feared Father would wake and say something mean to her, but Ian could not bring himself to interrupt. His view was so perfect and her reading voice so lively, he was quite enthralled. He did not know how long he stood there, but eventually, the growling of his stomach made him pull away. He would leave her long enough to find some toast or some small fare to satiate his needs before he rescued her and took a turn of his own.

CHAPTER 35

AMIE ENJOYED READING ALOUD, THOUGH she seldom had the opportunity to do so. She never thought the moment would come while sitting beside Lord Kellen's bedside. Reading to him had been her idea to get Lady Kellen to rest after what had appeared to be a sleepless night, but now it seemed to be for her own sake. Amie hoped the words of a story would soothe Lord Kellen as much as they were soothing her. Doctors ought to prescribe more books to their patients—if only to distract their caretakers.

Robinson Crusoe had not been long captured by pirates when a gravelly voice interrupted her.

"What are you doing here?"

She jumped, and her eyes flew to meet Lord Kellen's narrowed pair, her heart on the verge of some sort of attack. "You're awake." She stated the obvious, for nothing else came to mind. She set her book on the table beside his bed. "Let me get your water." Taking up the glass, she brought it to Lord Kellen's mouth. Only a little dribbled onto his pillow, which she quickly wiped with a nearby handkerchief.

As soon as she set the glass down again, she was met by another of his glares. "Did my son bring you here to finish me off?"

She awkwardly smoothed her skirt. Avoiding responding to his threat might be the ideal approach. The last thing she desired was to upset him further. "Your family is resting. Can I send for any food? Or perhaps the doctor?" She took hold of the bellpull and gave it a hasty yank. Even if he did not desire food or help, she was going to request it. Anything to keep her hands busy.

He grunted. "I don't want food or laudanum. What I want is for my son to annul his marriage."

"I see."

Lord Kellen's grouchy words sounded less authoritative and a great deal more petulant when given from a prostrate position in bed. It was one thing for *her* to ask Ian to annul their marriage, but Lord Kellen's demand felt entirely wrong coming out of his mouth. She wanted to tell him that she would never, ever end her marriage for him. This wasn't the time to speak her opinion though. She'd encountered a few cantankerous individuals before on her dozens of neighbor visits over the years. He couldn't hurt her with anything more than his words, and for some reason, that gave her an absurd burst of courage. "Shall I read until a tray is brought up for you?"

He drew his eyes away from her. "I'm not a child to be tended to, nor do I care for your presence. Leave me, and tell my wife I'm awake."

Perhaps Amie's offer hadn't been the most attractive to him, but she *had* meant well. If she upset Lord Kellen and caused a relapse, she might not be able to forgive herself. And yet Lady Kellen had looked ready to collapse this morning.

Amie chewed on her lip, determined to do right by them both. "Your wife has kept a faithful vigil by your side, and she very much needs her rest. I daresay she is on the verge of illness herself." Amie took up the book and sat again. "After another chapter, I wouldn't be surprised if she wakes on her own."

Lord Kellen groaned, his eyes pressed closed. "Of all the impertinence. I'm a sick man. Do you want me to grow worse yet?"

Her brow furrowed. "Why would I wish that? Your wife and son are beside themselves. I want nothing more than for you to recover straightaway."

Lord Kellen tipped his head back and stared at the ceiling. "My wife, I would believe, but my son would worry more for my recovery than my illness. And you . . . you have no reason to wish for my health, I assure you."

She should leave; she really should. Instead, she opened the book and started reading again. Not ten minutes later, she observed Lord Kellen's heavy breathing and relaxed features. He was asleep again. Shoulders drooping, she sank back in her chair. Good. She hadn't killed him.

Yet.

After a maid set a tray with broth and drink in the room, Ian stepped inside. He took in Amie and then the tray. "Broth? Did my father awake?"

"He did." She reached for her hair to make certain her appearance was in order.

"Did he speak?"

"A little."

"What did he say?"

"He was not ready for food or more medicine, but he did mention that he was happy you were here and that your mother was resting." Never had Amie told a more blatant lie. But this was a delicate situation, and no one needed another reason to be angry with each other. She perfectly remembered Ian's response the last time they'd tried to discuss an annulment. This was the time for peacemaking.

Ian's brow rose. "Really? Perhaps his illness has humbled him." He looked at his father, and his face actually softened. It wasn't much, but it was a step in the right direction. "I see you have been reading to him. A kind . . . and brave deed."

He had no idea how brave.

"Have you been reading for long?" he asked.

"A few hours. I had nothing to do at your townhome, so I came over to see if anyone could make use of me. Your mother did not appear as if she had slept at all, so I took her place."

A gentle smile touched Ian's mouth. "That was kind of you. Why don't you take some exercise while I sit here for a spell."

She was all too eager to put distance between herself and this room but worried about Ian and his father arguing again. However, peace was not something one could force upon another. If Ian wanted to sit by his father, she had to let him. "I could use a walk about the neighborhood." She set her book down and moved around her chair to leave.

Ian caught her hand as she passed. She looked up at him, curious about what he wanted. His warm gaze quickly made her forget whatever thoughts she had.

"Thank you, Amie," he said. "You were right to bring me here."

She could barely form words. "You're welcome."

His hand tightened, as if to keep her from pulling away. But she would never think to do that. "And thank you for sparing Mama. That means a great deal to me." His thumb caressed the back of her hand, trailing a line of heat.

Her mouth curved into a small smile, and she nodded. The tenderest of smiles graced his own lips. Finally, he released her and eased into the chair she had vacated.

She stepped into the corridor and curled her hands around her arms. He had touched her again after swearing not to do so. She loved when he broke his own rules.

Slowly descending the stairs, she had one thought that persisted. Ian couldn't listen to his father and annul their marriage. She was tired of feeling beneath him. For she was quite certain that when she and Ian touched, she was his equal. She had spent years fighting for a roof over her head, and now she wanted to fight for something far greater—for them.

In those few seconds with her hand in his, she had known her heart. She was in love with him. She had likely been so for some time and had not openly admitted it to herself. She gripped the banister tighter, a second realization dawning on her. Lord Kellen was responsible for her sudden determination. His words inspired her to hold on to her love and never let go.

How she had tried to ignore her feelings, telling herself that she would grow used to life without Ian. She knew now, without a shred of doubt, that her heart would always belong to him. No fear accompanied this realization, only peace and happiness. She wanted to protect this new, growing emotion inside her. She couldn't alter her past or her connections, as Lord Kellen wanted, but she would do everything in her power to support Ian in his passions. After seeing the glimmer of Ian's smile as she'd left his side, she was nearly convinced that she could make him happy too.

She took another step down and froze again. One question could not be ignored: Would Ian ever let her love him? There was the matter of their contract and his deep-seated reasons for wanting to uphold it. Drat Lord Grumpy and his stubbornness. Could she persuade him to give their marriage a real chance before his father did otherwise?

If they stayed married, she had a lifetime to convince Ian to love her. But for some reason, she felt a clock ticking somewhere in her head and a sliver of fear telling her to convince him soon, or their future apart would be sealed.

CHAPTER 36

IAN CRUMPLED THE LETTER IN his hand. He dragged his gaze to his father's bedchamber door, as if he could will him to be better, then looked down again at the ball of paper in his hand. Sir James was panicking. Their committee had been tallying vote predictions, and they weren't even close to the majority. They had mere days to persuade the people. If they delayed, more lives would be unjustly lost—possibly for decades more.

Ian dragged his free hand over his jaw. He couldn't abandon his family, but nor could he ignore this plight. He already had two men he employed copying the records from the Old Bailey, and the papers were piling up at his house.

He shook his head. It would have to be enough for now. He couldn't leave when there was a doctor upstairs with his father, determining who knows what.

A doctor who had been up there long enough to make a proper diagnosis.

Taking the stairs two at a time, Ian hurried to his father's bedchamber, anxious for news. He reached the doorway but did not cross the threshold. The doctor leaned over his father and checked his eyes, tested the use of his arms, and glanced down his throat. Father had woken a few short times yesterday but never when Ian was present.

That particular coincidence might have been divinely arranged.

Finally, the doctor rose to his full height, which did not even reach Ian's shoulder. His expression, though, was as commanding as any Ian had met. "It's a miracle you're alive, Lord Kellen. Your heart is weak, but your will must be stronger. I'm giving you strict orders to stay in bed. You must continue to rest, or your health will easily succumb to the worst outcome imaginable."

"I haven't spent more than a day of my life in bed," Father grumbled. His voice did not carry the same power it usually did, and his pallor matched the white of the pitcher on his bedside table.

The doctor chuckled. "This will take some getting used to, I imagine. Heed my advice all the same, Your Lordship. I must be off, as there is nothing more I can do. No need to see me out, Your Ladyship. I know the way."

Ian's father's eyes set on him as the doctor passed by him in the doorway. Ian found himself holding his breath once more.

"What are you doing here?" Surprise laced every one of his father's words.

Ian came into the room. "Visiting the sick."

His father huffed. "Unless you're here to announce your annulment, I don't care to see you."

"You don't mean that," Lady Kellen said, taking her husband's hand.

"I do mean it."

Mama shook her head. "You mustn't upset yourself, dear."

"It's all right," Ian interjected. "I will excuse myself for now. Maybe some rest will help him see things more clearly." He likely should have kept that last part to himself and left before his father could stage a counterargument.

As soon as Ian rounded the corner, he sank against the wall. Relief spread through him. Father was alive. Seeing his eyes open and hearing his voice released a weight off Ian's chest. The near-death experience hadn't changed his father—no, that had been wishful thinking—but he was awake and that had to mean something. It felt oddly like a glimmer of a second chance, but Ian didn't know if he could trust it. It would require him to see his father in a different light, and he wasn't certain it was possible.

The good news was that it would allow him to help Sir James. Ian retired to his old bedchamber and spent the rest of his day reading and writing correspondence to the committee and wishing he were there to help. But even in these desires, he was easily distracted. He wished for the weight of Tiny on his lap and the sound of Amie moving about Oak End. He almost always knew what room she was in or, by her lingering scent, where she had just been. That he did not know her exact location now bothered him. She had written a note saying she would spend the day at his townhome and join them for dinner. Shouldn't that suffice? Instead, he found it odd that she would not come sooner.

Ink pooled on his letter. "Dash it all." He quickly blotted the paper. He wasn't used to his mind wandering. He had important matters to see to. Time was running out. His maddening lack of self-discipline had to stop.

When the dinner hour came, he began to anticipate seeing Amie. Shaking his head and blowing out heavy breaths did not help. Despite all his self-talks, when she entered the drawing room, he was there eagerly waiting for her.

She looked very much the same. He'd seen her gown of choice several times, and her hair was styled similarly to other times. So why did his heart react like he was in a foot race? He went to her and thoughtlessly reached for her hand. Warmth traveled up his arm, but he didn't let go. It was just a hand, and it wouldn't hurt anything to hold it.

"Good, you're here," he muttered, when inside he was shouting it.

"Is your father any better?" she asked.

He gave a nod. "He is waking more and more, and the doctor thinks he has a chance to pull through." He hadn't realized he'd been waiting all day to tell her this.

"I am pleased to hear it."

His feet moved nearer to her of their own accord. People who were having a private conversation generally stood close to each other, so it seemed perfectly justified. "I thought I would see you sooner."

"I apologize if I was missed."

"I never said I missed you," he said quickly, inching ever closer to catch her vanilla perfume. "But it is true that you were missed."

She blinked as if she did not understand him. Confound it, he didn't understand himself. "But you're here now, and that is what matters."

"Oh? Perhaps I should stay away more often."

He scowled. "Why would you do that?"

The beginnings of a smile touched her lips. "So you hurry to my side when you see me again."

He took stock of his position, practically hovering over her, and swallowed. How had he let himself get so close to her? He cleared his throat and stepped back, affording her a bit more space. "How was your day?"

Her smile faltered. "Oh, uh, it was unexpected."

His brow knitted together. "What do you mean?"

"I received a—"

His mother waltzed into the room, cutting Amie off. "Oh, Amie, you are here, and just the person I was hoping to find."

Amie smiled, but he noticed it was forced. "Thank you for having me for dinner."

"Why wouldn't we have you?" Lady Kellen frowned. "You are family. I simply meant that I am in need of a favor from you."

"I'm happy to help in any way I can," Amie replied.

"My husband is awake again and is asking for you to read to him again."

Ian felt as shocked as Amie looked.

Her hand went to her chest. "He asked for me? I mean, certainly. I will go to him now."

Ian tugged on her hand before she went more than a step. Need she go this very minute? "You must eat first." Besides, this idea sounded suspicious. Even if Father had not been openly mean to Amie and reserved the majority of his rudeness for Ian, it didn't sit well.

Amie's smiled turned more genuine at his concern. "I had a late lunch, and I'm not very hungry."

"You're sure?"

"You know how I enjoy reading."

He did. He dropped his hand with great reluctance. "Very well. I will have a plate sent up in case you change your mind."

"Thank you, Amie," Lady Kellen said. "I have a good feeling about this. I think he's warming to you."

Ian wouldn't have gone as far as that. His father likely desired a distraction while also wanting his wife to have a break from his side.

Amie looked up at Ian. "Will you find me before I leave tonight? I did hope to speak to you about something."

Did it have to do with her unexpected day? He couldn't help but wonder. "Certainly."

She thanked him and disappeared from the room. At least he finally knew right where she was, and that alone was satisfying.

"Ian?"

Ian blinked and turned to his mother. "Yes?"

"I spoke to you just now, and you didn't even hear me."

She sounded more like herself, but there were still tired lines pressed around her eyes. "Forgive me, I was thinking about someone—I mean, something."

Mama laughed. "Of course you were. Let's eat our dinner so you will be free to join her later."

He didn't bother correcting his mother. She was happier believing that he was in love with Amie. And heaven knew that his mother deserved more happiness than ever. Despite all his fuss and obstinance against the subject, deep down, he knew love was exactly what he felt. The only thing holding him back was his lack of trust in himself. He was his father's son, and hurting Amie was out of the question. He'd already been doing it without even intending to. It was hard to imagine himself capable of anything else.

CHAPTER 37

"You came." Lord Kellen sounded genuinely impressed. She had not thought he would ever be impressed by anything she did.

"I am happy to help." She moved around the bed and picked up the book she had left on his bedside table the day before, noting that he had more color in his cheeks than the last time she had been in here. "Would you like me to start where we left off yesterday?" She took the seat beside him, all the while feeling his stare on her face.

"You are rather daring for a penniless widow's daughter."

She swallowed. "I would not call myself daring at all."

"Did it not take bravery for you to face me again?"

It took a great deal of courage. Every step ascending the stairs had been like a fateful walk to meet Madame Guillotine. "Perhaps I wondered why you would request that I read to you when you clearly did not appreciate it before."

"Ah, curiosity is an interesting quality. It is both good and bad, but in this case, I will still reward you with a point for coming here."

"Is this a competition of sorts?"

He pursed his lips. "More of a test. For starters, why did you choose that particular story to read to me? Did my wife select it for you?"

She shook her head. "I found it in the library on my own."

His brow rose. "Is that the truth?"

Confused, she nodded.

"I believe you." He did not say anything for a moment. Was that her cue to begin reading? She started to open the book when he spoke again. "I read that same story to Ian when he was a boy." Of all the things, she hadn't expected him to say this. "Ian likely doesn't remember. He chooses to see me as the villain in his life. I've not spoiled him with affection, that much is true, but what good I have done is erased from his mind."

She tightened her grip on the book, unsure of what to say. It turned out, she didn't have to say anything. Lord Kellen wasn't finished.

"There are a few things in life a father can do for his son that truly matter. Setting him up with a secure future is perhaps the greatest of them all. When I die, Ian will have my title, my lands, my seat in Parliament. A man could thrive on this alone. But without the right companion, he could curse it too. I wanted to give him the perfect wife—a woman equal to him. A gift that he would someday look back on and truly thank me for."

Her earlier convictions about fighting for her marriage began to wane. Had she not imagined for a small moment that she was Ian's equal? Clearly, Lord Kellen could not even imagine the possibility. Her day had contained so much turmoil that she couldn't capture the same feelings of confidence she'd found yesterday.

"But then you came along," he added. "I wasn't prepared for you. Your pretty face and strange manners swayed him. Now my son will forever be against me."

"You are generous to give me the blame for this, but I cannot accept it. Your relationship suffered before I ever met my *husband*." She hadn't meant to put emphasis on the word *husband*, but it did add a nice touch to her statement.

To her surprise, Lord Kellen chuckled. "You *are* brave."

She looked down at the book in her hands.

"But are you brave enough? Do me a favor and prove your worth."

Her gaze flew upward. "What?"

"You heard me. Prove to me that you are meant to be my son's wife. Tell me why my son despises me."

That would require far more bravery than she possessed. "And if I give you your answer?"

"I will let the state of your marriage fall to the two of you. It's obvious you love him."

Her eyes widened. Did her face betray her innermost feelings?

He chuckled again. "Read to me now, and think about it. I'm growing tired, and you know where to find me when you're ready."

This had been a most confusing day. She picked up the book and thumbed to the right page. Her voice started shaky, but she persevered through each sentence, refusing to show how much Lord Kellen intimidated her. Her attention, however, was not on the words but on Lord Kellen's challenge. Even if she were to ask Ian about his father, she didn't know if he would tell her. But she had a feeling that whatever it was was the same reason that he had written their rules and sworn her to their contract.

CHAPTER 38

IAN SET HIS HAND ON Amie's shoulder, and she stopped reading. He smiled down at her and pointed to his sleeping father. He put his finger to his lips and motioned to the door with his hand. They did not stop in the corridor but continued to the stairs. They walked side by side as they descended. She really wished he would offer his arm. After the day she'd had, she wanted to lean on him.

"Thank you for reading to my father," Ian said. "We can speak in the library, if you'd like."

"Thank you." The library sounded perfectly private, which she needed for what she was about to tell him.

"How did the reading go? Was my father on his best behavior?"

"He wasn't on his worst behavior," she ventured.

Ian halted on the stairs. "Blast. I knew he was up to something. What did he say to you?"

His voice was loud enough to wake his father. "Nothing new."

"What does that mean?"

She continued down the stairs without him. "It means he does not dote on his only daughter-in-law, but on a positive note, we know that my reading voice bores him to sleep."

Ian shook his head and caught up with her, his long legs making short work of the distance. "You are not to see him again unless I am with you."

"He is all bluster and no harm."

"He is a monster."

At the base of the stairs, it was Amie's turn to stop. Her voice low, she asked, "Why do you say that? I know he disapproves of me, but that isn't the most monstrous attribute. I have plenty of relatives who have disliked Mama and me."

Ian's hand went to his hip. "That doesn't make me feel any better."

"But you have to a good reason for despising him as you do."

"It's a long story."

She hesitated long enough to muster her courage. "Will you tell me?"

Ian stared at her for a moment, indecision flashing behind his eyes. He dropped his shoulders, sighed, and motioned her to the library. Silently, she followed him, wondering if this was the end of their conversation. Rosewood shelves lined the room, teeming with books. It was cozier than she'd hoped. A large Bible stood on display on a pedestal in the corner, and a family portrait hung above the mantel. A small fire flickered behind a decorative grate, with a sofa and stout sofa table with thick legs placed before it.

Ian motioned her to sit but did not take a seat himself. He folded his hands across his chest and, without preamble, said, "My father is a philanderer."

She raised her brow but said nothing.

He reached back and scratched his head. "It is a common, accepted sin amongst most of the *ton*, but they have not watched my mother suffer for years because of it."

"I had no idea."

"I first learned of it while away at school. One the boys at Eton had heard the rumors about my father and thought to harass me about it. I wanted to defend my father, but the clues of his behavior became apparent to my innocent mind in a way I had not seen before. I lost all respect for him that night and could never look at him the same again. You might not deem him a beast for such, but his cold, unfeeling nature does not lend me to think otherwise."

The cozy room suddenly grew quite chilly. So this was why Ian hated his father. "Oh, Ian. I'm sorry."

"Now you know why I cannot abide him and why I will not let him say anything against you. You must promise me that you will heed my warning and not visit his room without my presence."

She nodded without hesitation. As a woman, it was easy for her to have compassion for Lady Kellen. Both genders committed adultery, but when the woman was the victim, she had little right to do anything about it.

Ian sat on the stout sofa table and rested his arms on his legs. "Now, what is it you wanted to speak to me about?"

She'd dreaded this moment all day, but it had to be done. She fingered the thick ribbon of her dress just below her ribcage, pulling out the hidden folded paper she'd concealed there. "I received this just before breakfast. I thought I could come up with a solution on my own, but I admit defeat and must humbly apologize." She extended it to him. She knew telling him would be impossible, so he would have to read it himself.

"How cryptic." Ian accepted the paper and unfolded it.

She put her hands together and brought the steepled fingers to her lips. She wasn't praying, but perhaps she should be. Yes, she definitely should be.

Ian began reading aloud, "My dearest Amie." He paused and looked up at her. "Are you trying to make me jealous?"

She almost smiled, but this was not an amusing matter. "Can you not tell it's in a woman's hand? It's from my mother."

Ian grinned. "I could. Perhaps my humor was ill-timed. I can see whatever is contained here has you worried. Forgive me." He cleared his throat and began again.

"I hope you've arrived in London safely. You must find time to rest, as I know you will sacrifice yourself to care for everyone around you. You have never been very good at setting limits on yourself, and your haggard look is not your best."

"You can skip that paragraph," Amie said. She'd forgotten about the introduction. "Read further down."

Ian chuckled and picked up on the next paragraph.

"I do hope Lord Kellen did not die. What terrible timing so soon after the wedding to have to wear black. Bad luck, indeed."

"Skip that part too," Amie said quickly. She leaned forward and found the correct starting place and pointed to it. He looked up, their faces much too close. She sat back down and swallowed. "The third paragraph, if you please."

He nodded.

"You had done such a marvelous job making over my bedchamber that I thought to surprise you and make some improvements to yours."

"Is this the right part?" he asked.

She brought her fingers back to her mouth. "I'm afraid so."

He began again in his deep reading voice.

"It was a simpler project than the drawing room and one I was sure you would trust me to do without your help. But when having the furniture moved so the room could be painted, I stumbled across your diary."

Ian lifted his eyes to meet hers. "Your diary?"

She gave a solemn nod. "Keep reading."

"Are you sure you want me to?"

"I must insist."

He bent back over the letter. She squeezed her eyes shut, anticipating what was coming next.

"You have always hidden your diary under the mattress, so I was not at all surprised. I admit to reading it a time or two, but as you are not a regular writer, I gave up long ago. This time, however, what I read was purely accidental, so please, do not be angry with me. A paper fell to the ground, and on it was a sort of oath of conduct. It was written in a male hand and signed by you."

She opened her eyes in time to witness Ian's deep swallow.

"The oath contained three alarming details that quite shocked me and are not at all in order with a typical marital arrangement. I have

raised you to be innocent and naive, so it is hard for me to say this, but I must be frank. Amie, dear, I do believe that your marriage is a hoax.

"I have already written to your uncle, begging him to employ a lawyer and hasten an annulment. Fear not, my child, I will be on the next coach to London. Together we will see this right."

Ian lowered the letter to his lap and stared at her. "So this is why you did not come over today?"

She pursed her lips and nodded.

His tongue created a temporary bulge in the side of his cheek. "I see. And instead of telling me straightaway, you read a book to my father?"

She nodded again. It seemed all that she was capable of doing.

"I've never met another woman like you, Amie. Trouble seems to follow you about, wherever you go."

She lowered her eyes to her hands now knotted together. "Indeed."

"You are fortunate that I am your husband."

She lifted her gaze. "I am?"

"You are. I will take responsibility for this. We will simply tell your mother and uncle, if need be, that the letter is a joke. I did not sign it, and there were no witnesses, so nothing will come of it."

"But what if I say something by mistake? They will know it's a lie."

Ian tipped his head back and groaned. "It's no matter. This is because of my foolishness, not yours. There was never meant to be a written document, and it was because of my own weakness that I put it to writing to begin with."

His weakness? What did he mean by that? "But it is my fault that we are found out. If your father hears about it . . ." She could not finish.

"He won't. He is currently confined to his bed, and Mama is not ready for him to have visitors. The only news he will receive is what we bring him."

She had been so afraid to bring this matter to Ian's attention and had stalled all day without any answers. Instead of yelling at her, he assumed full responsibility, like some heroic knight. This rather awkward trial hadn't pushed them farther apart, as she feared, but had made her care all the more for him. "You are too kind, Ian, but I still do not see how we will sort this."

"It will call for a little Rebel acting, I believe. We will have to disperse with the rules, so they know there is no truth to the paper. You didn't add any other recent accounts to your diary, did you?"

She shook her head. "I haven't written a single line since last Christmas."

He frowned. "I would have thought there were some significant events you might have wanted to remember."

He almost sounded hurt. She supposed there was their wedding and all their kissing, but right now, that seemed an impossible memory to ever forget. But that he cared about what she put in her diary at all entertained her. A small smile crept out, but she quickly covered it with a cough.

"Did *you* write anything down?" she asked.

"Me?" Ian blinked. "No, I don't keep a journal."

Amie smiled. "Then, I suppose our children will never have anything to remember us by."

Ian's eyes widened.

Hers widened, too, when she realized what she'd said. "Which won't be a problem," she said hurriedly, "because of the rules."

He lowered his gaze and laughed under his breath. "We're forgetting the rules, remember? They've been pretty useless from the beginning."

She didn't think he meant to forget them forever, but this was certainly a step in the right direction. "Thank you, Ian."

"For disposing of the rules? I thought you liked them."

"No, I hate the rules. The *thank-you* is for not getting mad about my mother."

"Oh, I'm mad about it, but not mad at you. You didn't do anything wrong." He paused for a moment. "Wait, you hate the rules?"

She had said that, hadn't she? She stood suddenly, her courage for the night fleeing. "It's getting late. I really should return home and get some sleep."

He stood too. "You're avoiding my question."

"Am I? Yes, I suppose I am." A sliver of a smile formed on her lips—one she had not thought possible a half hour ago. "Good night, Ian."

"Wait, I will see you to the door."

There was a look in his eyes that she couldn't quite place. It wasn't an expression she had seen on him before. Should she be nervous? "Very well."

He held out his arm to her, and she took it. A second later, he put his other hand on hers. She glanced at it and then up at him.

"For practice," he said. "So we are ready when your mother comes."

Is that what this was? Well, she wouldn't complain. "We *are* out of practice. We might need a lot of it."

He nodded, the blue of his eyes darkening and softening all at once. "My thoughts exactly."

When they reached the front door, Ian called for the carriage to be prepared. "Now that my father is turning a corner, I will likely return to the townhouse to sleep. I have a few things I want to finish here, so do not wait up for me."

"After the long day I've had, I don't think I could if I tried." Though the thought of him staying nearer brought another wave of comfort to her.

"Good," he said. "I hope to spend some time in the morning reviewing records from the Old Bailey before I return here. We need to find as many unjust cases as we can to use as evidence to convince the representatives. We have a few days left to sway at least a dozen key people. I could use the help of a secretary." He raised an expectant brow.

Did he really want to spend time with her? "What did you do with Lord Grumpy?"

Ian chuckled. "I don't think you should be alone after today. If your mother or your uncle shows up, I should be there. I imagine your mother won't be far behind her letter."

Amie sighed inwardly. So he didn't want to just be with her. "Since I make an excellent secretary, I will gladly accept. And I will be most grateful if I am not alone when my relatives arrive. I can handle Mama, but . . ." Her voice waned, fatigue settling over her just thinking about her uncle and cousin.

"I understand. I have met them, remember? They're partially to blame for our marriage, you know. I couldn't bear leaving you with them."

The way he looked at her and the emphasis on his last words sent a wave of pleasure through her limbs. "Despite all your fuss to the contrary, you're a good man, Lord Reynolds."

"I do try, Lady Reynolds."

She smiled at his flirtatious tone. "It shows."

"Does it?" He grinned. "I generally try to hide my halo. I would hate to appear a braggart."

She laughed. "I said you were good, but an angel?" Her brows lifted in question.

Ian shrugged. "Not all of them look this good in a cravat."

She bit her lip but couldn't hold back her escaping grin. "You certainly fooled me."

He leaned impossibly close. "My secret is out, and the lady did not even swoon."

She pushed lightly on his chest. "Hardly. It takes more than an angel to tempt me." She didn't know where those words came from or how they dared escape her mouth.

Ian's lips twitched. "Is that so? You have a taste for wicked men?"

She cleared her throat. "I wouldn't say *wicked*. I prefer mostly good with the occasional dark mood to keep things interesting." Warmth bathed her cheeks as she heard herself speak. She was turning into her mother and blurting all sorts of ridiculous pronouncements. Her ramblings seemed to amuse Ian all the more. The familiar sparks lit between them as his gaze heated. He didn't pull away, as he usually did. She sensed he lingered by her side for the same reason she wanted him to.

It was hard to remember the obstacles between them when the moment felt so perfectly right.

He felt perfectly right.

If he asked her again what she wanted in life, she was certain she would not hesitate this time. Being with him was what she wanted most in the world.

CHAPTER 39

SPRAWLED OUT ON HIS OFFICE floor, Ian had a pillow under his head and a stack of papers hovering over his face as he read through another record from the Old Bailey. Moving his papers to the side an inch, he stole a glance at Amie. She sat above him on the two-seated sofa with a knitted blanket on her lap and her legs curled up beneath her. She had the tip of her finger between her teeth and her own stack of papers in hand.

"This one is a terribly sad case," she murmured, reaching over him to set the paper on his desk, where they had compiled the worst cases to show the other members of Parliament.

"Excellent," he said, finishing his own case and tossing it into a haphazard pile of unusable documents on the floor behind his head. Each time they found something, it gave him an ounce of hope, but it also brought an equal feeling of dread. If they did not make changes, the old system would perpetuate the same heartless results it had for more than a century. Amie's help had been a godsend, keeping up his spirits and cutting down on his workload.

He started his next case, but his thoughts wandered to Amie.

After hours of being tucked away in his office, she hadn't complained once. Not even after getting up early, a nearly unheard of event among the *ton* during the Season. Something about that alone made him smile. Any other lady would have complained that such reading material was shocking to their sensibilities. Amie devoured the records as if they were as important to her as they were to him. If ever there were a key to his heart, this sacrifice might be it.

He squeezed his eyes shut, chastising himself for his lack of focus. He quickly adjusted the papers to hide his view of her completely. If he couldn't concentrate on his work, the least he could do was come up with a solid plan of how to handle Amie's mother and uncle when they arrived. Paul had been right to caution him about the contract. It all seemed rather immature and stupid now. But after watching all his friends swear off marriage and then succumb one by one to the Matchmaking Mamas, he had needed to proceed with the utmost caution.

With the slightest effort, he shifted his papers to the side to glance at Amie again. She grew more beautiful to him every time he looked at her. He loathed thinking of her facing her relatives and any form of embarrassment.

"Is there something on my face?" Amie's eyes flicked over to meet his. "Ink perhaps? You keep staring at me."

He'd been caught. He lowered his papers to his lap. "Staring? Me?"

"I keep feeling your gaze."

He shrugged one shoulder. "Perhaps you are imagining it?"

"Hardly. Did I not catch you just now?"

He pushed up on his elbow. There was no use denying the obvious at this point. If she were less beautiful or interesting, he wouldn't be staring at all. "I am making certain you're doing your work," he teased. "You know I only have three more days until the committee presents to the House." She did not appear as if she believed him. *He* wouldn't believe him either.

She gave him a dry look. "You've mentioned it a half a dozen times already this morning."

"Have I?" He grinned. He'd not expected her to be so fun to banter with when he'd first met her, but he'd come to value her hidden wit.

"Yes, but it seems *you* are the one who cannot concentrate on your work."

His grin receded as he tried and failed to summon a look of contrition. "I have my reasons." Reasons that he wouldn't voice aloud. What good would it do to tell her that she was far prettier than the papers in his hands? It was only reasonable that his eyes should prefer her face. Not to mention how her scent hovered about the room and had him thinking of too many times where she'd been in his arms.

Her brows rose, and she leaned her chin against the palm of her hand. "Reasons, you say. Do these reasons include my face?"

Was she reading his mind? "Perhaps it's because you put your feet up under you, and I'm waiting for you to kick me at any moment. My memory is too keen for me not to be on my guard."

She leaned forward, giving him a stare that reminded him of a mother berating her child. "You know perfectly well that it was because of the warm milk."

"Do I?" he teased. "I haven't been brave enough to sleep beside you again to be sure." His half smile froze on his lips. This conversation was taking a wild turn for the worse, and it was entirely his fault.

Instead of a look of shock at his flirtations, he got a glare. "Why not see if I kick better when I am awake than when I'm asleep?" She started to untangle her feet from beneath her.

He sat up in one smooth motion. "On that note, I think I'll move to the seat beside you."

She laughed. "We'll see if it improves your concentration."

Likely not. He'd been avoiding that seat to help him focus. It had worked for a few hours.

As soon as he was settled, the butler stuck his head through the door. "Pardon my interruption, My Lordship. A Mrs. Tyler, a Mr. Nelson, a Mr. Robert Nelson, and a Mr. Withers are here to see you."

A small hand suddenly gripped his. He met Amie's terrified gaze. "Mr. Withers is the Nelsons' solicitor. What is he doing here?"

"Relax, we have a plan, remember?" With his free hand, he gathered their papers and set them to the side while he addressed his butler. "See the guests to the drawing room and send for some refreshment."

"Very good, my lord." His butler dipped his head and retreated.

"What was the plan again?" Amie's voice heightened. She normally hid her ruffled feelings far better than this. He turned his hand so his fingers wrapped around hers and held their hands up to emphasize them. "This. This is the plan."

A plan that would surely be his undoing. Warmth already spread up his arm, and he was thinking about holding more than just her hand. Before he could act on any impulses, he stood, tugging her gently to her feet.

"Are you certain you can handle it?" she asked.

"I can restrain myself," he said, his voice suddenly rough as he looked down at her. "Though I admit it won't be easy for me." His will was waning rapidly.

She blushed pink. "I meant handle the situation."

He chuckled. "There will be no restraint there." He winked, a very Tom thing to do. Ian's friend was the flirt, not him. Amie brought out a strange, foreign side of him. "Are you ready?"

She took a fortifying breath and nodded.

He squeezed her fingers. "Do you need a minute?"

"Yes—er, no. I can manage." She gave him a tentative smile. "The sooner we see to this, the fewer rumors will get out. We've had enough of that already."

He agreed, and he was glad he did not need to remind her. With her permission, he led her out of his office toward the entrance hall, their hands clasped tight between them. An ounce of worry niggled inside him. He had managed to resolve many situations over the years with a little cleverness, but what about the problems of his own making?

They entered the drawing room, and their company rose to their feet.

Mrs. Tyler rushed forward. "Oh, Amie." Her eyes were red and puffy. Her steps halted well before she reached them, her eyes riveting on their intertwined hands. "I . . . I . . ."

Mr. Nelson and his son, who both teemed with anger, seemed to notice the same gesture a moment later.

"Is this a show?" Mr. Nelson stood. "I won't be taken in by a title and money. Not again."

Ian glowered at Amie's uncle. He had no respect for a man who kept his relatives at the end of a stick and only let them nearer when it benefited him. "Is what a show? Your temper? Do your niece and her husband not deserve a greeting when you storm into their home?"

"My lord," Robert whined. "You've had us all. We know about the contract. Aunt, show him."

Mrs. Tyler dug into her reticule and produced the folded parchment. "I have it here."

"Show me." Ian still did not know exactly what he would say once he saw it. Heaven help him.

Mrs. Tyler hurried to him and extended it.

Before he could take it, Robert spoke to Amie. "Dear cousin, we are here to help you. This is no fault of yours. You have not been well since the death of your father. There is a trail of stories that followed you from each of your relatives."

"Robert, what are you saying?" Amie shook her head.

Robert straightened as if he were about to say something more, something very brave and very hard. "Mr. Withers, I will testify in court if need be, but clearly, Miss Tyler had no idea what sort of an arrangement she was entering."

"*Lady Reynolds*, if you please," Ian said, correcting her name while accepting the contract from Mrs. Tyler.

"Lady Reynolds for now," Robert said. "We believe she is not sound of mind and was taken in by you."

Of all the ridiculous statements.

Mr. Withers was a wiry man with shrewd, boring eyes behind his spectacles. He clutched his satchel in a manner of self-importance. "There are grounds to annul a marriage if either party did not know what he or she was doing."

That word again. It dropped like a weight in Ian's stomach. How was it possible that both sides of the family were demanding an annulment? He knew marriage would be a complicated beast, but he had sorely underestimated the backlash from their families. Why had he not asked Paul to be here? His legal expertise would be useful about now.

"But both of us consented to this marriage," Amie said, stepping nearer to Ian until her shoulder touched his.

The action lent him a sense of unity.

"But if one of you is insane, that is different," Mr. Withers argued, addressing Ian and ignoring Amie. "The marriage between John Wallop, 3rd Earl of Portsmouth, to his solicitor's daughter, Mary Anne Hanson, was annulled after nearly twenty years of marriage once they proved the earl mad. Your Lordship, Mr. Nelson has a reasonable case against your wife."

Amie tensed next to him, and Ian's own temper flared. "You have a lot of nerve, Mr. Withers, coming in here and even hinting that my wife, a viscountess, is insane." There had to be a lot of money on the table to convince the solicitor to even make such threats.

Mr. Withers had the decency to give a look of chagrin. Ian had powerful friends, and there was no way Amie's relatives would seal their claim. Unfortunately, the rumors and gossip would do sufficient damage regardless.

Ian made a show of unfolding the paper in his hands, desperately racking his brain for a way out of this mess. He stared at his own frill-less handwriting and Amie's contrasting elegant signature. They had been two different souls from the beginning, but they had fit rather perfectly together ever since.

But that revelation did not accompany words to save them.

"Can you deny that this note was written by your hand, Your Lordship?" Mr. Withers asked.

Ian didn't want to answer, but withholding the truth when it could be proved otherwise was pointless. He shook his head.

Mr. Withers turned to Amie. "Can you deny that it was *signed* by your hand, Your Ladyship?"

"No." The simple answer was spoken without hesitation. The direct way she said it reminded him of the day she'd turned down his proposal, so certain no one could save her from her predicament. She'd been wrong then and was now too.

The right words came to him in that moment. "It is a private letter, but since it has been shared without our permission, let me put the matter to rest for you. You have discovered the rules from our engagement."

"Rules from your *engagement?*" Mrs. Tyler shrieked.

"Indeed. We did our best to keep a proper distance from each other, though I admit to some struggle on my behalf." He met Amie's gaze, her face still lined with worry, and the truth he'd been holding back slowly slid out. "Her beauty captured me, and I was taken with her from the start. She is like a diamond in a bed of river rocks. It is a wonder we could follow any rules at all." He stared into her wide, disbelieving eyes, losing himself in them as he often did. The sudden desire to tell her he loved her burned on his lips.

"You said this was a marriage contract," Mr. Nelson bellowed, his hot gaze skewering Mrs. Tyler.

The heated statement stopped Ian from uttering words to Amie he knew he would never be able to withdraw.

"Cousin?" Robert put his hands together and stalked toward Amie. "This cannot be true. You can be honest with us. You were taken in by this man and ill prepared for such a union. We are here to help you."

Ian's fist tightened. If Robert came a step closer to Amie, Ian would punch him in the nose.

Amie's words restrained him. "I knew exactly what I was doing when I married Lord Reynolds. We are happy together, and we do not appreciate your interference."

Happy, he repeated in his head. Yes, they were happy.

"Amie, dear," Mrs. Tyler said, "we want the best for you. If you plea madness, we can undo everything."

"Mama," Amie cried. "Listen to yourself."

Mrs. Tyler fidgeted with her hands. "I don't think you're truly mad, but your engagement was not made in the usual way. I have been beside myself worrying that I made a big mistake. After all, it was I who made the announcement."

Amie squeezed Ian's hand with more strength than he knew her capable of. He understood exactly what she was trying to communicate. Mrs. Tyler could not, under any circumstance, reveal how she had betrothed Amie to a dead man. Then they might have two cases of madness on their hands, and more evidence against their marriage.

"Mrs. Tyler," Ian begged. "That day in the graveyard when you met my mother was the most providential day of my life." He couldn't believe he was saying this, but it was no act. "I don't know if I have ever thanked you for your part in bringing Amie and me together. I can't imagine spending my life with anyone else."

The fervor in his voice surprised him. He had not known the depth of his feelings until it was cast from his mouth into the room like little seeds blossoming into full-grown truths. He might not have let himself love her or live with her, but no one else could ever be Lady Reynolds. Amie was the only one for him.

Mrs. Tyler's sad expression wilted away into a smile. "Oh, goodness. That is so romantic." She clutched the hem of her neckline. "I . . . I daresay I might have been . . . no, I am quite certain—I made a mistake."

He gave a firm nod. "Indeed, you were mistaken."

Amie reached for his arm. "You need not doubt again, Mama. We are happy together."

That word again. *Happy.*

How it rang in his mind.

"Truly, dear?" Mrs. Tyler asked. "Then, you do love each other?" Her smile bloomed ever wider, and Ian did not correct her. He couldn't. In the end, she did not give him the chance to say anything. "Oh, Mr. Nelson," Mrs. Tyler cried. "I let my emotions get away with me again. It was a contract from their *engagement*, don't you see? My daughter is finally happy."

"But she would be far happier with me," Robert cried, stomping his foot like a child. Ian half-expected tears from him at any moment.

"We will investigate this," Mr. Nelson said, though his forehead furrowed in confusion.

Mr. Withers clutched his satchel to his middle. "Without the mother's testimony, Mr. Nelson, we might not succeed."

"I warn you," Ian threatened, staring both the solicitor and Mr. Nelson down. "You will be the laughingstock of London if you try. Anyone who disparages my wife will see ruin." He switched which hand held hers and put his arm around her. He'd never felt more protective in his life, but no one wanted to know what sort of damage he was capable of with such emotion stirring through him.

All three men who came in full of indignation were suddenly reduced to scared little mice. Ruination was not a threat to take lightly, and Ian would follow through if they dared press him. They scurried from the room with their proverbial tails between their legs, leaving Mrs. Tyler alone with them.

Amie stepped out of his arms and hurried to her mother. "Oh, Mama!" The two of them embraced and cried together. He did not quite know what to make of it. He missed Amie's body pressed to his side, and the sound of her soft cries tore at him.

While he sensed the tears were of gratitude and relief, they still affected him. He wanted her to be *happy*. The same mantra he'd repeated over and over in his mind from the beginning only intensified the longer he knew her: He couldn't hurt her.

He clenched his hand to keep from reaching to comfort her himself.

He couldn't hurt her.

He wasn't his father or his grandfather.

He couldn't hurt her.

He would say this as many times as it took.

He wanted her to be happy. More than anything.

CHAPTER 40

IAN CARED FOR HER. AMIE had sensed it, hoped for it, but still could not believe it. She had seen the sincerity in his eyes as he'd proclaimed her beautiful and confessed to being taken with her from the start. How was that possible after the mint leaves, her wild unkempt hair, and the fact that her own mother had created an engagement between them?

A small laugh escaped, and she quickly covered her mouth with her hand.

"What's so amusing?" Ian asked from his position opposite her in the carriage. They were on their way to his parents' townhome. Tomorrow was the day his committee would present their proposal to change the criminal law to the House of Commons. As soon as they'd sent over the cases they'd compiled, Ian desired to check on his family. There would be another committee meeting by the day's end, but he had to reassure himself of their welfare first.

He was a good man.

Good enough that she had no reason to lie to him about why she had been laughing. "I was thinking of yesterday." The mere mention of it seemed to send a current of energy between them.

He rubbed his cleft chin as if honestly trying to recall what exciting thing had happened only a dozen hours ago. "Oh, when I admitted to being afraid you'd kick me in the face again?"

He was a good man, but his sense of humor still needed some work. "No, I did not find that part at all amusing."

He grinned, and she stared at it a mite longer than necessary before finishing her thought. "I was referring to how well your plan worked. You are an excellent rule breaker. No wonder you refer to yourself as a Rebel."

"As long as we convinced everyone, that is all that matters. By the cheerful way your mother hummed through breakfast, I think we are safe where she is concerned."

"Mr. Withers acted as though he needed her testimony to pursue anything."

"A relief, indeed. If anything more comes of it, I don't want you to be afraid to tell me. We'll face it together." He paused, his face taking on a serious demeanor. "I want you to know I don't normally break my own rules."

"Perhaps you have a talent for it that you have yet to discover." She wondered if he took her meaning. There was no reason for them to keep staying apart from each other.

"I hope not," he said, looking down at his hands. "I want to be a man of integrity."

The carriage pulled to a stop, and it was hard not to show her disappointment. She could see him building up walls between them again. They had come so far. She couldn't understand it. "I give you permission to hold my hand, then, so your integrity is not at risk. I rather liked the look on Robert's face when he saw us come into the drawing room yesterday."

Ian's lips pulled up on one side. "I suppose if the situation calls for it." He opened the door and climbed out, reaching back to help her out. "Like right now."

She grinned and took his hand. Sadly, he released her when her feet hit solid ground. "How very brave," she teased.

He chuckled and held his arm out to her. "It was quite the sacrifice, you understand. I think the driver saw, and I frown on public displays of affection." His words were playful, but she could read his underlying reservation. She knew she was pushing against his carefully made boundaries, but how else could she break them down?

Taking his strong, steady arm, she said, "You would think the leader of the Rebels would embrace such an opportunity to flout Society's social etiquette to everyone. Even carriage drivers."

Ian led her up the short path, and together they climbed the two steps to the door. He turned to her on the small porch, his gaze like velvet on her skin. "This particular Rebel is struggling at the moment, so please don't tempt me, Amie."

The blanket of clouds was too thick to blame the sun for the flush of heat on her face. She wanted to tempt him. She wanted a real marriage with love and laughter and children. But even more so, she wanted to know why he put up his walls. She wanted him to heal.

"Especially not in my father's house," he added quickly. "I'm trying to go easy on him for the sake of his health."

She could understand his reservation around his father. He seemed to be the key to Ian's reluctance. If she told Lord Kellen why Ian hated him, she doubted it would truly win his approval of their marriage. But she did wonder if it would be a catalyst of change for the two of them. Someone needed to soften. There were too many years of resentment for it to happen naturally. The logical solution was for her to create an opportunity for them to discuss the hurt that had caused a wedge in first place.

Ian had asked her not to speak to his father alone again, but she wasn't worried about what harm she would receive. With Lord Kellen bedridden, words were his only weapon. Her increased confidence in Ian's feelings would protect her from whatever unkindness his father threw at her. As for worsening the situation, the two were at such odds already that there was little chance of that. She was so filled with hope after yesterday that she couldn't dismiss the idea of helping Ian. He deserved to be as happy as he made her feel.

Ian knocked twice and held the door open for her until a footman rushed to take his place. "What does that look mean?" Ian asked.

"What look?" Amie tried to smooth her expression.

He stopped her in the middle of the entrance hall and studied her. "A sort of mischievousness passed over your eyes and mouth just now."

"Oh? What does such an expression look like?" Could he see the guilt on her face now?

He pointed to his own features. "Your eyes were happy and your mouth serious."

She tried to laugh it off. "Is that even possible?"

He eyed her again, his head tilted. "It does sound strange saying it aloud. I must have imagined it."

If he discovered her thoughts, she would fail before an opportunity even arose to speak to his father. It could take days or even weeks before the others were detained. It would have to be a long enough distraction for her to sneak into Lord Kellen's bedchamber and remove herself before she was discovered. The less Ian knew, the better.

Why did that sound like something one of Ian's fabled Matchmaking Mamas would scheme up? Love certainly gave one foolish ideas.

Lady Kellen came around the corner, carrying a few books in her hands. "I thought I heard your voices. Your timing is excellent. Ian, a man just arrived to see you—Sir James Mackintosh. I put him in your father's study."

"Sir James is here?" Ian's hand went to his hip. "I wonder that he did not come to see me at my home instead?"

Lady Kellen shrugged. "He said he came straight from there and found you gone."

"His horse beat our carriage."

"Do you mind if I slip out for a minute while you meet with him?" Lady Kellen asked. "I haven't left this house in weeks. Louisa Sheldon is approaching her time of confinement, and I want to make certain she is not in need of anything."

"That is your friend Paul's wife?" Amie asked. She remembered seeing her protruding stomach at the wedding.

Ian nodded.

Lady Kellen shifted the books to the crook of her arm. "Louisa is quite without a mother to help her. Mrs. Sheldon, Paul's mother, wrote a list of needs she hopes I might assist with. She dearly wants to be here but won't be able to come until after the baby is born."

"Do not worry about us," Amie said. "I am happy to help however I can."

Lady Kellen held the books out to her. "I merely require someone to be available if my husband has any dire needs, which I do not anticipate. He appeared much stronger this morning. The maid will find you if there is any concern at all."

"I can manage such a task," Amie said. This was the moment she had wished for.

"Thank you, dear. Would you take these up to Lord Kellen's room? He finished Robinson Crusoe and is ready for more."

Ian set his hand on the top book in the pile. "You may leave them at his door." The look that followed held a reminder of their earlier agreement.

She swallowed but did not nod. She didn't want to lie to him, but neither did she want to lose such a perfectly crafted opportunity.

"You can entertain yourself in the library until I finish," Ian said, "or until Mama returns."

Amie smiled at them. "Don't worry about me. Both of you go about your business, and I will tell the maid where to find me."

Lady Kellen disappeared to fetch her spencer, and Ian ventured off toward the study. Amie hugged the books to her chest. Could she be as brave as Lord Kellen believed her to be? Ian would undoubtedly be angry with her involvement. The very thought worried her. Could she sacrifice the strides they'd made in their relationship to help him with his father? She'd never been good with knowing someone was unwell and not doing something about it. These two were unwell in their hearts, and her feet itched until she directed them up the stairs to act on her plan.

Instead of leaving the books at the door for a maid to find, she rapped her knuckles against the white-painted wood.

A muffled voice filtered through the door. "Come in."

Amie turned the handle and let herself in. "Good morning, Lord Kellen."

"Oh, it is you again." His bored stare only encouraged her.

"I brought some books your wife selected." She forced herself not to cower by the door and strode to his bedside table to set them down. "You appear more alert today. Are you feeling better?"

"You should hope I am not. I have nothing against you, truly. But I still plan to separate you from my son when I am better."

"No hard feelings, Your Lordship."

His brow rose, and he chuckled. "Is that so?"

She nodded and motioned to sit in the chair beside his bed. "May I?"

"By all means. I could use some entertainment, and you do say the most surprising things."

She gingerly lowered herself into the chair, ignoring his jibe. Her nerves were stretching taunt, and she felt too much fear for annoyance to take purchase. Was she really going to break Ian's confidence? She prayed she was doing the right thing. "The last time we spoke, you asked me why Ian hated you."

Lord Kellen's amused demeanor fell. "I remember."

"I have discovered the reason."

"And?" He folded his arms across his chest, and for a moment, he looked very much like his son. Perhaps this wasn't her best idea.

"And," she began, her hands shaking, "he . . . he resents the way you treat his mother." She said the last part quickly, spitting the words out before they could get caught on her tongue.

"What?" Lord Kellen didn't believe her. She could tell by his incredulous expression.

She didn't care to go into detail, but it looked as if she would have to expound a little. "I cannot tell you much more, except that he disapproves of your mistresses."

What little color Lord Kellen had gained in the past few days drained from his face.

Good heavens. "Lord Kellen? Are you well?"

He did not answer her, his eyes swinging blankly to the end of the bed.

She jumped to her feet and hurriedly poured him a glass of water from the pitcher by his bed. What if she caused a relapse? What had she done?

"Drink this, please." She set it close to his mouth.

He pushed it away. "Sit down."

His voice did not shake or sound weak. That, at least, was something.

"Are you certain you do not need a drink? Or more medicine perhaps?" Should she call for the doctor?

Lord Kellen shook his head. "Please. Sit down."

The emphasis on the word *please* shocked her into listening. She sat with the glass of water still in her hand.

He stared at her for some time, but she knew not what he was searching for. Surely her revelation could not have surprised him into so much silence? Was he being racked with guilt or disappointment that his son cared so much about something he dismissed so easily?

"You must not care about my son if you eagerly betrayed him for my approval."

Her eyes widened, and her heart dropped into a pit in her stomach. "Pardon? I did not come to get your approval."

"Then, why did you tell me this?"

She huffed, suddenly exasperated. She had told herself that she wouldn't react to anything he said, but this was a terrible accusation. "Because your son suffers because of your behavior, my lord. The history between you is spilling over into other areas in his life."

"Perhaps the reason he was so against marriage?" he supplied.

She shifted to the edge of her seat. "Can you not tie the two together?"

"You did not come for my approval after all?"

She shook her head. "I know you will never give it. The only approval I seek is from God and my husband."

"Is that so? Ian will not take lightly to you speaking to me about this."

She dropped her gaze to her lap, pretending to study the tiny floral pattern of her skirts. "No, he will not. But if there is any way for the two of you to reconcile, I beg you to contemplate the matter."

Lord Kellen guffawed. "He will always see me how he wants to. He's been that way since he was a boy."

"You're wrong," she said, surprised at her own tenacity. "He is more open-minded than you might think. Oh, he is stubborn enough, but he is also compassionate. I cannot ask you to change your own habits, but I can ask you to consider the feelings of your wife and son." She ducked her head. "Forgive my impertinence. I must take my leave."

She shouldn't have come. Nothing she'd said had changed anything. She'd given stress to a sick man and betrayed Ian in the process. Regret lanced through her chest as she pushed to her feet.

She set the glass down and hurried to the door. Before she quite reached it, it swung open. Ian stood on the other side, his brows knitted together. "Why are you in here, Amie?"

She swallowed. "I was just leaving." She needed him to move his large form out of the way so she could run past him and flee the problems of her own making.

"What did you say to upset her, Father?" Ian glared at Lord Kellen, eyes filling with fire.

"I suppose I did upset her in the end, which is a shame, because I was just starting to like her."

Amie froze and turned her head to see if the man was as deranged as she thought.

Lord Kellen appeared perfectly sincere. "You have mettle, a quality I cannot disparage."

Ian reached for Amie's arm. "You don't get to care for her," he said. "Just stay away from her." He pulled Amie through the door, but before he could shut it behind them, his father spoke.

"We need to talk, Ian. Come see me this afternoon. It's about an important matter you cannot dismiss."

Ian didn't answer but shut the door, his chest heaving. He blinked a few times and looked at her. "To the library."

She gave a reluctant nod. It seemed they were going to have their own talk first. The library was the best location. There was a rather large Bible in there. It seemed almost sacrilegious to argue in front of sacred texts. Perhaps she would remind Ian of its presence before she told him any details about his father.

Dread kept pace with her all the way down the stairs. She had to confess what she'd done and beg for his forgiveness. Or maybe this was the opportune time to plead insanity. With her thoughts bouncing wildly in her head and Lord Kellen's strange declaration that he liked her, she was feeling quite mad indeed. Maybe Cousin Robert was on to something.

CHAPTER 41

"You what?" Ian couldn't believe it. Had Amie left her head at home this morning?

Amie put her hand on the oversized Bible on display in the corner of the library. It was a rather rare edition, with gleaming brown English leather and gold-leaf embossing, and it looked like it had *never* been touched. Yet she had fled directly to it when they'd entered the room. "I wanted to start a conversation between you and your father."

"By sharing something personal I told you?"

She inched closer to the Bible, almost using it as a shield. "I don't normally betray secrets, and I feel terrible about it, but I honestly hoped it would help."

He crossed his arms over his chest. "How? How would making my father angrier during his illness help anything?"

She grimaced "He didn't act terribly angry."

"Shock will do that to a person." He shoved his jacket back and set his hand on his hip. "I don't have time to speak with him about this. Sir James wants me to gather with them at a club in Town to go over his speech for tomorrow. I can understand your intentions, but my father doesn't deserve your compassion. He's not like the maid who broke her leg or the sick neighbors. He's a grown man who must reap the consequences of his actions."

Amie was almost behind the Bible now, the book solidly between them. "I didn't do it for him."

Ian ground his teeth together. "Then, why?"

She ran her finger along the Bible's lettering, avoiding his eye. "I did it for you, Ian. I don't want to see you hurting anymore."

He sighed. What could he say to that? "Come here."

"I prefer to stay here."

"Why?"

"So the Bible might remind you to forgive me."

He squeezed his eyes shut. "I will keep it in mind." He took her hand off the precious relic and carefully led her around it. "But please, don't try to fix things between my father and me. Nothing will ever change, trust me."

A wave of sadness passed over her eyes like a filmy cloud. "Never?"

"Never."

A sheepish smile tugged at her lips. "Then, I was a fool to believe I could ever be your wife in more than name only."

He dropped her hand like it was a hot coal. "What?"

She shrugged, her cheeks coloring. "I thought if you reconciled with your father, you could finally heal. Maybe whatever it is that keeps you from me would disappear."

Why did he feel as if someone had gut-punched him? His next breath tore from him. "I can't, Amie."

She blinked rapidly but not before he noticed the sheen of tears. "But why?"

He looked at the wall beyond her. "Because."

"Because why? Why can't you let me in? Just yesterday, you said that you couldn't imagine spending your life with anyone but me. I believed you."

Couldn't she leave things how they stood? They'd sorted matters with her mother and had developed a gratifying friendship—one in which he felt safe making a flirtatious comment or two and relishing every blush—but that was all this could be. He met her gaze head on though it killed him to do so. "I was putting on an act."

She shook her head. "You're lying."

How did she know him so well? "So what if I am? Speaking the truth won't make this any easier."

"Tell me anyway."

He threw his hands up in the air. "If you really want to know, it's because loving you means I'm one step closer to turning into a monster like my father."

His sharp words could have stabbed her for the pain that passed across her face. She looked away, her eyes not really settling on one thing. "I don't understand. Being with me would make you a monster?"

"No, Amie." He gritted his teeth. "You're twisting my words. I can't and won't love you because I do not want to perpetuate the life of my grandfather, father, uncle, and who knows what other relatives who were unfaithful to their wives. I won't break your heart as my father broke my mother's." He heaved a sigh, the words tearing from him. "I do care for you. I care enough that I can't let you get close to me again."

She swatted at a tear escaping. "Can't or won't?"

His voice lowered to a near whisper. "I don't trust myself."

He meant it. Those humbling, self-deprecating words. She should have stepped away. She should have let bygones be bygones. But she shifted closer, reaching for his hand. "But I trust you."

Her fingers grazed his, and he froze. She wouldn't let the matter go this time. How could she ask this of him? She'd known from the start where he stood. He couldn't give in. He couldn't hurt her. But despite his well-meaning intentions, he was already wounding her more than he ever dreamed.

Her touch was gentle and hesitant. She was being so brave, and he wanted to reward her efforts with his own and say all the reassuring things she deserved to hear. But what if he tried and failed? He wasn't like his friends. He'd always known that. He was gruff and surly and meant for arguing politics, not growing a family. One mistake and the innocence he loved about Amie would disappear forever.

Along with her beautiful smile.

He snatched his hand away from her, hating himself for causing the vivid pain to fill her eyes. This was who he was. A little hurt now would prevent far more later. It had to be done. Her trust wasn't enough to save him from himself. "I married you for one reason, Amie. For my inheritance. *Nothing* more."

He stepped away from her, slowly yet purposefully.

Her eyes begged him to come back to her, to want her, to love her. How he longed to do just that. But what she didn't know was that he *did* love her. And this was how he was proving it to them both.

CHAPTER 42

IAN SAT AT HIS FATHER'S desk, staring at a blank spot on the wall, lost in his thoughts. He couldn't bring himself to ride to the club in Town to meet Sir James. He couldn't bring himself to do anything. Not when he'd bungled everything with Amie.

Blast his temper. Blast his insecurities. Blast the deuced ache in his chest.

He'd done just what he'd sought to avoid—he'd hurt her. He had to fix the rift between them, but how could he when he didn't know how to fix himself?

He didn't know how long he'd sat there before Mother knocked on the door and peeked inside. "I brought you some refreshment. May I come in?"

He didn't answer her, but her skirts swished inside the room, where she set the tea tray on the desk between them. Without a word, she proceeded to fill a plate with some finger sandwiches, which she set before him.

"I'm not particularly hungry," he mumbled, pushing the plate back.

"I saw the carriage leaving when I returned home."

He nodded. "Amie's mother is in town. It is right that they spend time together."

"I thought I saw Amie crying through the window," Mama hedged.

He hated when she cried. "Leave it be, Mama."

"I tried to," she said, "but when I checked on your father, he told me what happened this morning."

Ian's stupor faded, and he glanced sharply at his mother. "He did?" That couldn't have been easy for her. Concern for her surpassed his feelings of self-loathing. "Are you all right?"

"Am I all right?" She gave a nervous laugh, and that was when he noticed her fingers shaking. "The question is, Are you?"

"I will be." If he could ever forgive himself for making Amie cry. All he'd wanted to do was avoid this, and yet staying away from her had hurt her anyway. Could he do nothing right? And now he couldn't even bring himself to aid Sir James.

"Your father would like to speak with you."

"I know."

"Eat a little, and then, please, talk with him."

"Must I?" He dreaded another confrontation, especially now when he was still reeling from his conversation with Amie.

Mama poured him some tea and set it beside his untouched plate. "It would mean a great deal to me if you would."

Why did she push so hard for him to get along with Father when she knew he couldn't respect the man? But that pleading look and the love he had for her won him over. "Very well. I will be up shortly."

A small smile appeared. "Thank you, Ian. You are the best son a mother could ask for."

He very much doubted that. He couldn't love his wife. He couldn't give his mother grandchildren. He couldn't even concentrate long enough to contribute to the preparations being made for the vote tomorrow. But upsetting Mama further was not worth the argument.

She left him alone with his tray of food and his turbulent thoughts. He stared at the tray for a good five minutes before downing his tea in three gulps and pushing away from the desk. There was no use procrastinating the inevitable.

A few moments later, he let himself into his father's room.

"Shut the door behind you," Father said, setting down a book beside him and adjusting the pillows that propped him into a sitting position.

Ian pushed the door closed and came to stand at the end of the bed, where he folded his arms across his chest. "I'm here. Tell me what pressing chastisements you want to lay at my feet this time."

Father's expression turned sheepish. "I have done you a disservice if our only talks are about your misbehavior."

What was this? An olive branch before the lecture? "No reason to mince words. I have business to attend to."

Father nodded. "So I have heard." Ian wasn't surprised. Father always had people watching his injudicious son. "You plan to vote on changing the criminal law tomorrow?"

"Yes."

"And your wife? Where is she now?"

Ian's temper flared. "Attending to her own affairs. She is free to do as she pleases."

Father nodded again. "I know you do not care to hear it, but she has grown on me. You have chosen better for yourself than I ever could."

Ian smirked. "You must be more unwell than I thought. Do you realize what you said?"

"I do." Father smoothed his covers. "Your young lady did a hard thing by speaking to me after all I did to frighten her away. I know you did not care for it, but I owe her a great deal for what she told me. She . . . she surprised me."

Ian wasn't sure where this was going, but he could at least agree with his father's assessment of Amie. "She is a good person."

"A good person who loves you very much."

The very emotion he'd tried so hard to prevent. "I know."

"And you love her."

Ian's jaw flinched.

His father nodded. "You don't have to admit anything to me. I can see it plainly. But because of me, you deny yourself the chance to tell her. I assume that is what she meant when she said my behavior was affecting you—the reason you swore off marriage for all those years."

Ian huffed. "I won't repeat the sins of you and your father."

"If what you're speaking of is the rumors of my mistresses, I want to correct you."

He shook his head. "There is nothing to correct."

Father clasped his hands together calmly. For once, Ian's words did not get his guard up. "I won't put down your mother, but there is something you must know about her that you aren't aware of. For the sake of salvaging a relationship with you and for the sake of your marriage, I feel compelled to explain."

"What does this have to do with Mama?" Ian frowned. "I know not what you speak of."

"For good reason. I have done my best to prevent anyone from knowing. But as you are our son, and this secret is keeping you from living a full life, you must know."

Ian braced himself, but Father's face only softened. "Your mother suffers from extreme anxiety in large social settings."

This was not what Ian had expected. "Mama?" He shook his head. "I have never seen proof of this." No one was more confident than his mother. She led an army of women in Brookeside and commanded attention everywhere with her regal presence and benevolent attitude.

"I am not wrong. Your mother does not come to London every Season, not because I am unfaithful but because of a terrible experience she suffered from during her coming-out Season. A man tried to take advantage of her, and though she was mostly unharmed, vicious rumors spread. It was enough that even after we married, she was paralyzed in fear at the thought of attending any party or ball.

"It became so severe that London was no longer a viable option for her. Brookeside became her safe haven. The women there eased their way into her life, putting their arms around her and coaxing her into their small society. She started healing, but even after some years away, we both knew that returning to London would not be wise.

"Since that time, your mother has managed a few short visits here and there, but no Society. That she is here now and handled the theater and musical with such strength attests to her years of healing and personal growth."

Ian couldn't wrap his head around this tale. He did not know what to make of it.

"So now," Father continued, "I must correct an untruth. Upon my honor, I have never been unfaithful to your mother. There are no mistresses and never have been. Like you, I swore I would never bear the sins of my father, and I am true to my word."

Ian needed to sit down. Mind reeling, he reached for the post at the end of the bed and leaned against it. No mistresses? But he'd heard the men talking in the clubs. He'd seen his father leave Mama behind year after year for his own pursuits. Why else would he abandon her in the country and come to Town alone? Mother was no wandering spirit who longed for adventure. She preferred her home because of its comforts. Did she not? "It cannot be true," he argued. "Any thought of your family is gone the moment you leave for Town. You cannot tell me you spared one thought for my mother all these months away."

"I do not blame you for your judgments, Ian. Everyone else thought our marriage was troubled, too, and I knew not how to correct them. I determined it was better for them to assume the worst in me than for them to think less of her. I miss your mother when we are apart. When you care for someone as deeply as I do, you are not meant to be separated. Your souls long to be together, as God intended. I was born to responsibilities that require a great deal of sacrifice, and thankfully, your mother supports me as I do her, but it wears on us both."

Ian had never heard his father discuss such vulnerable feelings openly. The words *care*, *miss*, *sacrifice*, and *support* were not vocabulary words that matched how Ian imagined his father. "Then, you *do* love her?"

"Of course I love her," Father snapped. "It's one thing to think I'm unfaithful, but how could you ever doubt my love for your mother?"

Ian stared, completely baffled. "Do they not go hand in hand?"

His father glowered. "I suppose one could think that, but it sounds very bad, indeed, coming from your mouth."

Ian ran his hand through his hair. "I'm at a loss. If I believe you, everything I've ever thought about you changes." Mother had argued Father's good qualities to Ian for years, but he had refused to believe her. When it came to Father, she was soft, besotted, ignorant. Ian rubbed his temple. Could her devotion be rightfully placed and Ian's opinion be the one in the wrong?

His father shifted against his pillow. "I admit, I have weaknesses enough. I can be obsessive with work, and I am not the most affectionate of men. My own father saved lives with his donations and public lectures, but he was not a family man. His strict mannerisms were all that were modeled for me, and I assumed your independent nature led you to resent my firm hand.

"I did not think I deserved your ire and long wondered why you loathed me so entirely. Having your wife come and confide in me your reason clarified years of hurt and confusions. Why I couldn't reach my son suddenly illuminated my mind. To know you thought I hurt your mother—the same way my father hurt my mother—deeply wounds me. I was younger than you when I decried the vileness of such a lifestyle.

"I loved your mother from the moment we wed, and I knew I had to cherish her and protect her with my whole soul. And when you were born, I committed to giving you every opportunity at life and goodness and opportunity. This is why I throw myself into my work, so you might have a legacy worth inheriting. Even as you grew and drew yourself away from me, I vowed to give you all a father should give his only son with the hope that someday you would see my efforts for what they were."

Father's chin quivered ever so slightly. "I am sorry you thought the worst of me. I should have recognized the reason sooner. Now perhaps you might think your old man a decent person."

It was not so much a request as a plea. Father had never asked him so earnestly for anything. He had only ever demanded it. Ian's gaze darted absently around the room before settling back on his father. "I don't know. I've never thought of you as decent."

Father sank back against his pillows. "Not a very encouraging start."

"But it is a start," Ian said quietly. A start that would require humility and forgiveness and letting go of past hurt. His feelings wouldn't just disappear in a moment, even with the truth dangling in front of him. The words were still sinking in, but Ian couldn't doubt his father's sincerity. He knew Father well enough to know there was no possible way he would fabricate such a tale.

The door opened, and Mama stood within the small gap. Her gaze darted between them, while she worried her bottom lip. "Is it done?"

"It's done," Father said, his shoulders drooping.

She sighed and let herself in. "Finally." Coming up beside Ian, Mama put her hand on his arm. "Oh, my son. If I'd known the reason you despised your father all this time, I would have told you myself. I thought it was merely your headstrong ways and differences of personality." Her eyes welled up with tears—tears he so rarely saw in his strong mother. "It is hard to admit to a weakness, especially when logically, my fears make little sense."

His own emotions were stretched thin, and he couldn't bear to see her struggling. "Mama, I—"

"Don't, Ian. I must own this trial," she said, cutting off his pleading. "I have caused this entire family to suffer because of my inadequacy."

"Not quite, dear," Father said, his voice softer than Ian had heard it in a long time. "We all have our struggles. You are no less than anyone else."

"It doesn't diminish the regret," she said.

Father sighed. "No, it does not. No one would understand how troubled I was to inherit so young after my father died. Everyone thought I should rejoice in my fortune. We cannot always choose the scars we bear." Father's eyes seemed to cradle his mother. "Some choose us and never let go. Just like that cruel day for you, dear, so many years ago. But while our scars affect us, they do not need to consume us. Not anymore. Let it be a lesson to us: We will never stop trying to rise above our circumstances."

The message struck a chord deep in Ian's chest. Ian's scars had been of his own choosing. All this time, his righteous indignation toward his father had felt perfectly justified, but his anger had been the real wedge in his family. His father was still obsessed with his work and a grumpy, controlling man, but then again, so was Ian. His father, however, was not guilty of the many sins Ian had laid at his feet. In fact, he had sacrificed much to support his wife, even bearing unfounded rumors for nearly thirty years. Suddenly, being so much like him didn't seem so disgusting to Ian.

And Amie . . . Never in his life had he considered that he could love someone—truly love someone. But his father had been a good husband, which meant there was hope that Ian could be one too. There was no reason to keep Amie suffering. There was nothing inherently wrong with him that would lead to a senseless lack of control once he truly bound himself to her. He would injure her from time to time with his stupidity, like today, and it would take discipline to put his family before his work. But like his father said, he would never stop trying to rise above his challenges to be better a husband to her. His previous commitment against marriage and against love was years and years in the making, but he would be brave like his father was being right now and start the wheels of change.

The sins of his paternal line no longer touched him as they once had.

Everything would be up to him now. It had likely always been that way, but sometimes, the past was a difficult coat to shed. He had let his cling to him, thinking it a source of protection. It lay at his feet now, freeing him to see hope for the first time.

If it weren't for Amie, he might not even want that hope. Now he was ready to run toward it.

His mother's sniffles caught his attention. Ian reached for her hand. "Don't cry another tear on the matter. You have our full support."

Mama blinked back the moisture accumulating in her eyes and set her hand on his. "I'm not worried about me. I'm worried about you."

He let himself perch on the edge of the bed, his mental energy spent. "There is a benefit to being born into a stubborn line of men. If we want to change something, we throw our energy into changing it. Today, we can begin anew, and when we misstep—an inevitable eventuality—we will try again tomorrow."

Father's mouth softened into a crooked smile, and Ian saw the hint of relief and hope there.

Mama gave a grateful smile of her own. "If you can find it in your heart to let go of the hurt we have caused you, we will want for nothing more." Her smile faltered. "Except . . . except for Amie. Don't let us come between the two of you. Since the moment I met her at the graveyard, I knew she had a heart as big as yours."

Ian couldn't help his amusement. "Is this your way of confessing to your involvement?"

Mama wiped at her tears. "I suppose I owe you an explanation for that too."

He nodded. "It's not a surprise if that helps."

"I didn't start out intending to find a stranger for you. All of us were feeling the strain and importance of your marrying, but I couldn't breathe well enough here to think clearly. London has always had that effect on me, and I had to escape it for a moment. When I arrived at the graveyard, I thought talking things over with your grandfather would help me make sense of the obligation you and your father carry to the family and the title. I didn't expect my nerves to follow me there. I was a splendid wreck, and I needed a friend desperately. No sooner had I wished for someone than Amie came right up to me and offered me a small bouquet of flowers."

"She never told me." Amie was always generous and thoughtful, but knowing she had served his mother touched him deeply.

A smile hovered on his mother's mouth. "Amie was an angel to me when I needed one. I had hoped something would come of that day, because our meeting felt orchestrated by heaven itself, but I must give Mrs. Tyler her share of the credit. I merely planted an idea, and she masterfully executed it."

"An idea?"

"I told her that the good name of Lord Reynolds would be at her disposal should she need it."

Ian sputtered a laugh and turned to his father. "Your wife is responsible for Amie and me being together. What do you say to that?"

He shrugged. "Your mother is a wise woman. She was smart not to tell me about it until I could see the truth for myself. It is clear she has far better taste than I, though I've often wondered what she sees in me."

Mama let go of Ian's hand and went to his father, pressing a kiss to his forehead. "I saw a good man intent on changing the world for the better, and the love of my life. I kept this little secret from you because I knew you were in one of your moods where you had a point to prove."

"I'm never in one of those moods," Father teased, reaching for Mama's hands.

As sweet as the turn in conversation was, it was too private for Ian's taste. He was still processing this new revelation and had a lot to work through. "On that note, I shall take my leave." He had something very important to do. A thrum of anticipation pulsed through him, urging him to act straightaway. "I need to find Amie."

"Please do," Mama said. "Kiss her for us."

He nodded and proceeded to the door.

"Son?"

The single word stopped him. Ian turned and faced his father. "Yes?"

"I've written to my colleagues about your criminal law proposal. I'm duly impressed by your ideas."

"Truly?" A letter from his father could go a long way, though Ian had sworn to never ask for it.

Father nodded. "Ian . . ." He hesitated. "I'm bumbling this, but I want you to know I've never been more proud of you. I should have told you a long time ago, but I've never been one to talk about feelings. When a man faces death, it makes him regret a few things. So I want to wish you luck with your work and new marriage. Something I should have done a long time ago."

The relief on his father's face was evident, as if each word had cost him but unburdened him. And the effort had been worth everything to Ian.

Ian's eyes stung, and he blinked furiously. "Thank you, Father. That means a lot." So much so that he suddenly felt taller, greater, and more capable. All because of the love of his father. A love he had not felt for as long as he could remember.

CHAPTER 43

AMIE HAD STOOD RIGIDLY STARING at the library door after Ian had left her. It had felt like Papa had died all over again. Lost and alone, she'd taken the carriage back to their townhome and found Mama in the drawing room, embroidering a coin purse, oblivious to the heartache staring at her from the doorway.

"Amie?" Mama finally set the coin purse aside and stood. "Amie, you do not look well at all."

"I'm returning to Oak End straightaway."

"Oh? Has something happened?"

Her throat constricted, and the careful words cut as they escaped. "My husband has duties he must attend to that do not concern me. It is better for me to be out of his way." There. It sounded reasonable and not with any traces of madness her mother might misconstrue.

"I will gather my things. We can leave first thing in the morning." Mama reached down and picked up her embroidery.

"I am leaving now, Mama," Amie explained, keeping her voice impossibly even. "You must stay here and travel with the trunks and Edna. We can meet at the inn. I'm certain Lord Reynolds will arrange everything. I must go on ahead before I do something foolish and try to stay behind." She couldn't travel with Mama. She wanted to have a good hard cry without her mother jumping to unnecessary conclusions. After yesterday, there was no taking any chances.

Before Mama could object, Amie backed out of the room and hurried to gather a small overnight bag. Soon, she would be away from here. Away from Ian. And then she could let her heart mourn and heal for good.

Not ten minutes later, she climbed down the front steps of Ian's townhouse with a parting glance at a place that had quickly become more than walls and a roof to her. Just as she tore her eyes from the three stories of off-white brick, the front door opened, and Edna stepped out.

"Excuse me, Your Ladyship." Edna hedged.

"What is it?"

Her usually talkative maid gnawed at her bottom lip before she blurted out her piece. "I haven't the courage to thank His Lordship again, so I ask ye please, if you would do it for me."

"Thank him?" Amie blinked in surprise.

The maid's eyes filled with tears. "Ever since he rescued me from the gallows and gave me a place 'ere, me sisters and I 'ave 'ad plenty to eat. Now, with me sisters working in the kitchens and all of us under the same roof, our 'appiness overwhelms me, and I 'ave to express it." A tear escaped, and she swiped at it, leaving a trace of flour on one cheek.

Amie's hand went to her mouth. "Forgive me for being so bold, but, Edna, are you the servant who was caught thieving?"

The maid dipped her head and shamefully nodded. "His Lordship told me not to tell anyone of my crimes or his service, but I cannot keep quiet any longer."

Amie kept her hand over her wide mouth. Ian seemed baffled by her own efforts to help her neighbors and the people around her, but he was the same—better even. He was so incredibly good and did not even realize it.

Amie took Edna's hand. "Thank you for having the courage to show your gratitude." Her voice wobbled, and she forced a quick goodbye. Somehow, the short conversation enlarged the ache inside her, the throbbing in her chest threatening to erupt.

Ian had saved this young lady, and he had saved Amie, but would he ever choose to rescue himself from his fears and hurt?

Amie would wait as many years as it took, but she wouldn't do it here. She couldn't endure it. She rushed to the waiting carriage and instructed the driver to not spare the horses.

Not an hour into her journey, her tears had already saturated her handkerchief. A thickness in the air permeated the open window, pulling her from her sorrow. She stuck her head out, seeing an angry storm brewing above her. Her heart sank. *Why now?* She remembered all too well the last storm she'd survived in a carriage, and the sky had not looked half so ominous then.

She took several long, steadying breaths. If they were lucky, they would outride it. If she were to be an independent woman, she had to learn to endure whatever weather came her way. Before the second hour passed, a dark cloud consumed Amie's carriage, pelting it with an angry staccato of rain. The storm was here. There would be no outriding it. Was it too much to hope that there wouldn't be any lightning or thun—

Before her thought was fully finished, a flash of light filled every inch of the inside of the carriage, and she choked on her scream before it ever left her mouth.

℘

Ian rode his horse as fast he dared through the crowded streets to his townhome, the rain growing in strength the farther he went. A footman took his horse's reins as he dove inside the house. He shed his jacket and took the stairs two at a time, eager to see Amie. He knocked once and burst into her room. Empty.

The library. She had to be in the library.

He ran down the stairs, whirled around the corner, and threw the door open. Empty.

Where was she? He jogged the short distance to the drawing room and froze at the door at the sight of Mrs. Tyler with her embroidery in her hands.

"Good day, Mrs. Tyler. Have you seen Amie?"

Mrs. Tyler nodded without looking up from her stitchery. "She's gone."

"On a walk?" his eyes flashed to the window, where the rivulets of rain trailed down the glass.

"In the carriage."

Perhaps his horse was not yet put away, and he could meet her at her destination. "To where?"

"To Oak End."

He clutched the door handle. "To Oak End! When did she leave? And why aren't you with her?"

Mrs. Tyler finally looked up from her sewing. "It's been nigh to two hours. I am to stay here with you."

"With me?"

She smiled. "That was Amie's plan."

Oh, joy. Was this her way of punishing him?

"She left a message with me for you."

"Where is it?"

"Right here," she said, tapping her head. "'Dear Lord Grumpy.' Now, I questioned the address, but she said it was an affectionate name you liked, and who was I to argue with a lover's nickname?"

Embarrassment singed his ears, and he waved his hands. "Proceed, please."

"If you insist. 'Dear Lord Grumpy, good luck with your business. Do not miss me too much, because I do not hope to see you until you have sorted matters with your father.'"

"And?"

"That is all she said, I'm afraid."

"Blast." He raked a hand down his face.

"Pardon?"

"Excuse my language." He backed away from the door. "The business she speaks of, it's time sensitive. I'll take my leave." He rubbed his temples and stumbled into the corridor and toward his office. In the long hours of research on the Bloody Code, had he learned nothing?

Not even the lesson to hold your dear ones close and do your best to live a good life?

He set his hands on his desk and leaned into them. Nothing blurred his vision, but his surroundings were mere shadows to his frenzied mind. The vote was tomorrow. If he left now to find Amie, he'd never make it. An entire nation depended on the outcome of the vote. Amie was just one person.

But she was also everything to him.

He groaned, wishing he could undo this morning and have a second chance to say all the right words. He thought of Edna and the fear in her eyes when she'd been caught thieving and then of all the people who would never have a second chance at life, let alone a chance to love. Could he abandon them?

A low rumble sounded in the distance.

Thunder.

His head jerked up.

Amie. He could still hear her quiet sobs in her closet on the night of that first storm they'd spent together.

Changing the world was his dream.

Loving Amie was something he'd never planned.

But there was no question now of what he had to do.

CHAPTER 44

THE CARRIAGE SLOWED ITS PROGRESS, nearly to a standstill. At least two hours passed with little progress in the relentless wind and rain, with Amie gripping the bench with white knuckles. She was alone and desperate. This was worse than losing Papa. Despite the ache in her chest, she knew he was in a better place. She'd held to that hope—clung to it.

But where was the hope for her marriage? The longing she could not suppress would be her undoing. Her emotions were already on the precipice of strangling her, the tumult of the storm pushing her over the edge. Lightning struck, and she crumpled to the floor of the carriage. Curling into a ball, she covered her ears and hummed to herself through her tears, praying the sound of the rocks beneath the wheels would drown out the sky and the moaning of her soul. Nothing, though, could shut out the sudden onslaught of memories, born from her anxiety. These were not of Ian but of a dark day from many years ago, flooding over her with vengeance.

She waited for the carriage to overturn like it had that night.

Waited to hear her father's moans.

Waited for the end to come.

A shout echoed in the distance. Must she relive every part of that horrible night? She squeezed her head tighter and hummed all the louder. The carriage rocked, and a jolt of light pierced past her tightly closed lids. She screamed.

A noise sounded beside her, and damp hands covered her shoulders.

"Amie!"

It was a dream. A nightmare. But those hands on her shoulders felt so real. "Papa," she whimpered.

"Amie, look at me." Someone pulled her hands down from her ears. "Amie, I'm here now. You're all right."

She slowly pulled her tightly squeezed eyelids apart, blinking into the darkness. That silhouette was so familiar. That voice. Lightning lit the carriage, and she saw him clearly.

"Ian!" The name tore from her throat, and she fell against him, weeping. There was no end. No one had died. Papa was already gone, and Ian would keep her safe.

"Shh, It's all right. You don't have to endure it alone any longer. I'm here." He reached over and shut the door, slapping the wall to get them moving again.

"Papa died in a storm like this," she whimpered. "I was with him when the carriage tipped over. There were flashes of light, and the ground rumbled, and it was so bitterly cold." She was rambling, but she couldn't stop herself.

He shed his wet jacket and tossed it onto the far bench. "I'm so sorry, Amie. I'm so sorry I chased you away." He tucked her close to his chest and smoothed her hair.

"I'm four and twenty, and I cannot manage my memories."

He pulled her into the seat beside him. "Some scars we cannot choose," he said. "But we will never stop trying to rise above our circumstances. My father told me that. This time, though, you won't have to work at it alone."

His eyes were too dark for her to discern their color or to see the sincerity of his expression, but she knew it by his voice. He'd come because of the storm, but it did not mean anything for their future. He said he would never change. She started to push him away. "But you shouldn't be here. You have the vote tomorrow."

"Hush, do not worry about the vote. Just breathe."

She pushed against him again. "You cannot keep holding me like this. You have to be there."

"Amie, darling . . ." He pulled back and set both his hands on either side of her face. "I can't change the world if I can't even change myself. You were right to speak to my father. It made all the difference. There were never any mistresses, and I was wrong—wrong about everything. My fears were illogical, but I couldn't see it." Guilt and sorrow lined his shadowed eyes and clung to his features.

"Coming from someone who is afraid of storms, I can understand perfectly." Her heart filled with an insensible amount of hope, drowning out the nightmare she had been reliving moments before. Had he really changed?

He stroked her hair again. "I regretted what I said in the library the minute I left you. It's time I start trusting myself because I do want a full marriage. I want it all—with you. The vote matters, but you are more important to me than all of England."

"I am?" His declaration left her dazed and in absolute wonder.

He pushed a lock of her matted hair behind her ear. "You shouldn't have to ask, because I should have already told you. I have done a poor job of making you feel secure in our relationship. All I've done is fight my feelings for you, causing us both an inordinate amount of suffering. I don't want to do that anymore. I *can't* do that anymore. Amie, I love you."

A flash of lightning filled the carriage, and she impulsively gripped his riding jacket and leaned into him.

He gave her a sympathetic smile. "Can I take that as an invitation?"

"For what?"

"For this." His arms circled more fully around her, and his head lowered until their mouths met. Their other kisses had been new and exciting, an introduction to each other, but this was everything she'd imagined a kiss between a married couple to be like, and better still.

Instead of the pressing darkness, she saw color. Instead of bitter coldness, she felt warmth. Instead of suffocating memories, she made a new one—the best one yet. He was pledging himself to her, and she finally had a home in him.

He pulled back just enough to lean his forehead against hers. "I love you, Amie."

She laughed softly. "You already said that."

"I plan to tell you over and over again. I have to make up for lost time." He dropped another kiss on her lips, smothering another laugh. "Is it all right if I come home with you?"

Home? She shook her head. "No! You must turn around. You could still make it before morning." She could endure the storm. The torture would be acute, but knowing he loved her would sustain her on the journey.

He stroked her jaw with his thumb. "I sent all my notes to the committee. They were working on this far before me and can handle the vote on their own. My father is graciously reaching out to his connections too. I've made my decision. I'm not leaving you again. Not if I can help it."

"Ever?" He would walk away from his most passionate project for her?

His eyes crinkled with vulnerability. "If you'll let me stay."

She stared at him. "It's *your* house, Ian."

"It's yours, Amie. I'll only come if you wish it. I promised you, remember?"

For the first time all day, she felt herself smile. "Hang your promise. Of course I wish it."

His thumb reached the corner of her mouth and slid toward the center. "And do you wish for me to kiss you again?"

"Must I beg?"

He chuckled. "Not at all, but I might." His finger stroked her jaw and neck, and she leaned back into the wall of the carriage. Again their kiss drowned out the noise of the night until all she heard was the beating of her heart and the feel of his pulse under her hand.

CHAPTER 45

A month and a half later.

IAN LOOKED AROUND THE DOME at the smiling faces of his Rebel friends, his hands covering Amie's eyes as he led her inside. The temple had been the Rebels' secret meeting spot since they were children, and he had been anxiously waiting for the day he could share it with Amie.

"Should we make her take the Rebel Oath?" Jemma asked from somewhere beside him.

"Next time," Paul said from the sofa. "Let her see what she is getting herself into first."

"Your hands are too big," Tom teased, his arm around Cassandra. "You're going to suffocate our Lady Brilliant before she even has a chance to learn to like us."

Lady Brilliant was Tom's new nickname for Amie. As soon as he'd heard Amie call Ian Lord Grumpy, he'd announced it utterly brilliant, which had quickly evolved into *Lady* Brilliant. Like all of Tom's odd names, it had stuck.

"You can breathe, can't you, darling?" Ian asked, leaning down and catching his favorite vanilla fragrance.

"I can breathe."

"Good. Just one more step." Ian directed her to where she would have the best view of the circular room. "Ready?"

"I've been ready since you told me about this place," Amie said.

Without further ado, he dropped his hands and let them rest on her arms as she took it all in.

"Well?" Miles asked, Tiny snuggled in his arms. Apparently, their little terrier liked tall men. "Is the Rebel lair like you imagined?"

"Not at all," she said, laughing. "It's bigger and smaller all at the same time."

"Give her the royal tour," Jemma insisted, looping her arm through Miles's, the wide skirt of her rather unique plum dress nearly surrounding her husband's legs.

"A tour?" Ian chuckled. "You can see everything by standing in one spot. There's only this one room."

"I'll do it," Tom released his hold on Cassandra, which was a notable feat. He had been hovering over her since he'd learned she was with child. He walked over to a set of wooden chairs. "Paul and Louisa generally sit here. Paul is the most rigid of us all, so he doesn't get any cushions."

Paul balked from his seat beside Louisa on the sofa. "So the only reason I get to sit here today is because Louisa just had a baby?"

Ian hadn't even seen their baby yet, as he and Amie had arrived the day before yesterday and Paul and Louisa the day before that. He was eager to remedy it.

"Of course that is the only reason," Tom said. "Louisa is supposed to be in confinement, so we gladly gave up our seats for her comfort. You're merely lucky to be attached to her."

Cassandra elbowed Tom. "Don't listen to him. He's jealous that you let Lisette hold the baby first. Babies are all he can think about from sun up to sun down."

Ian hadn't even noticed the small bundle of blankets in Lisette's arms. Lisette's soft, blonde curls on either side of her face swayed from side to side as she dropped her head to stare at the baby. He would have to get in line to hold the little thing after Tom.

"Never mind that," Tom said. "I can be patient for a moment longer. But only for a moment, mind you, Lisette."

Lisette laughed and leaned into her husband, Walter, to let him see the baby too. "We will share, I promise."

"Finish the tour," Ian prompted.

"The tour! Right. My wife and I usually sit where Paul is, and across from us sit Lisette and Walter and Miles and Jemma. The four of them can get quite cozy since Lisette and Jemma are inseparable and don't mind the crowding. But the crowning element of the tour is just here." Tom scurried to the head of the room—if there could be one in the circle, this was it.

Tom rested his hands on the green upholstered chair with the tall back. "This, Lady Brilliant, is our Mother Hen's throne of putrid."

Amie laughed. "Throne of what?"

"The name is self-explanatory, my lady," Miles said, and everyone laughed.

"You haven't finished," Jemma prompted. "There's one seat left."

Ian grinned. He'd been waiting for this part.

"Perhaps you recognize this," Tom said, moving to the chair directly beside Ian's throne.

Amie turned her head to look up at Ian. "It does look a great deal like the one in our townhome. The one you always like to sit in."

"It's the very same," Ian said with pride. "My Pocock original. I had it sent up just for you."

Tom cleared his throat to capture their attention again. "Instead of getting you a new, pretty chair with all his gobs of money, Lord Grumpy sent over his well-used favorite chair to be your new throne."

"It's sentimental," Lisette explained. "I think it's terribly romantic."

Ian slipped his hand down to find Amie's and wove their fingers together. "Well, Lady Brilliant? Care to be seated?"

She eyed him, laughing at his use of Tom's nickname. "I would be honored."

Ian led her through the middle of the room to her chair and held it out for her. She relaxed into it and sighed. "It's comfortable in all the right places."

"It's Moroccan leather. Wait until you put your feet up." He turned to Tom. "See? I knew she would love it."

Ian planted himself on his throne and captured Amie's hand again. He never liked to be parted from her for long if he could help it. He still couldn't believe what had possessed him to create rule number one all those months before. It was by far the most idiotic idea he'd had to date.

Ian used his free hand to motion to the room at large. "Everyone else, find a seat. I have an announcement to make."

"I do love announcements," Jemma said, pulling Miles toward the sofa.

When everyone was seated, Ian began. "This is not exactly how I imagined us all ending up—married."

Everyone chuckled. It was a far cry from the day not many years ago when they had all pledged to stay single against the threat of the Matchmaking Mamas.

"But we can all agree," he continued, "that we're all better for it."

Miles put his arm around Jemma, and Lisette's and Walter's arms were already entwined. Tom winked at his Cassandra, and Paul mirrored Louisa's ever-present smile and took her hand. There was a feeling about the room—a rightness Ian had never imagined possible. He believed Amie's hand in his had a great deal to do with it.

He reached inside his jacket and pulled out a folded piece of parchment. "The Rebels are twice as many as we started with, which means we have been able to make twice the difference in the world with our efforts. I received a letter just this morning that I have been anxious to read to you."

He unfolded the paper and found the section he desired. "This is from Sir James Mackintosh. I wanted you to be among the first to hear the good news:

"Our fight for progress, which has been more than a decade in the making, has passed from the House of Commons to the House of Lords and has been given the Royal Seal. The criminal law, as we know it, will no longer exist with the creation of what will be known as the Judgment

of Death Act. This, along with a few other acts, will lift the death penalty from over one hundred thirty crimes. In all but treason or murder, judges will now use personal discretion to execute a lesser sentence."

Gooseflesh rippled down his arms at the mere thought of the hundreds of thousands of lives that would be spared in the coming years. "Thank you for your help, Rebels. The part we played might have been small, but any effort for good is noteworthy and the effect immeasurable."

A humbled silence permeated the room. There would still be evil in the world and never enough of them to save everyone, but this felt good.

"Are you trying to make us cry?" Tom asked, wiping at one eye. There was no teasing in his voice this time. Cassandra leaned her head on his shoulder.

"If he is, it's working," Lisette said, mopping her face with her husband's handkerchief.

"Well done, Ian," Amie whispered from beside him. "You changed the world after all."

In his small way, he supposed he had. But what mattered more was that he had changed himself. "Thank you, Amie. For helping me."

It did not take long after Ian's announcement for all of them to shift their focus and crowd around Paul's baby, where Ian finally got his turn to hold her.

A girl.

And her name was Katherine Harriet, after both Paul's and Louisa's mothers. Fitting that the mothers should be honored since they really deserved a thank-you for all their effort in bearing children and then tricking them into marriage so that more children could be born.

Ian held Katie-Cat, as Tom had dubbed her, close to his chest, bringing up his large finger for her dainty hand to grasp.

"She's perfect," Amie said, standing on her toes to see the baby.

He lowered Katie so Amie could see better. "She is indeed."

"I haven't seen you hold a child before, but I can tell you have a fondness for them," she said.

Ian had to agree. "I never had younger siblings, but I rather like Tom's son, and I have a feeling that little Katie will be just as easy to love."

"Good."

He raised a brow. "What does that mean?"

"Well, our children might be a little *different*."

"Different?"

"Madness runs on both sides of the family. Do they have a chance?"

He chuckled. "I've always thought that those who are mad generally possess a higher capacity to feel. So yes, our children have a chance. They might even be happier than we are."

"Beautifully said, Ian." She grinned at him before reaching to run her hand over Katie's feather-soft brown hair.

"What project comes next?" Miles asked, coming to stand by them. "None of us can be without a purpose for long."

Miles had an entire congregation to care for, yet he always had more to give.

Ian hummed. "The prisons will soon be pushed past their capacity. With less hangings and more prisoners, we'll need prison reforms straightaway."

The room quieted at that moment, so all the other Rebels heard his response.

"Is that possible?" Louisa asked from the sofa.

Paul stretched his arm around his wife. "If the criminal law can be overturned, anything is possible."

Ian let Amie take the baby. "I've already written to Robert Peel and asked to join his committee."

"You know we will support you," Tom said. "Let me know if you need someone to sneak inside the prisons in disguise. I might know someone capable."

Cassandra grimaced. "If it's a last resort."

The visiting took up again, and Amie passed the baby to Jemma.

Ian leaned in and whispered, "Are you ready to return to the house?"

Amie's brow pulled in the middle. "You don't want to stay and talk longer with your friends?"

He grinned and curled an arm around her waist. "I'm ready to be alone with my wife again."

She leaned into him, molding to his side as if they were made to fit each other. "They will expect you to visit longer. I doubt you will be able to sneak past eight other people in such small quarters."

If he stared into those mesmerizing pools of brown much longer, he was certain those same eight people would throw him out and no sneaking would be necessary. "With all this talk of missions, I was reminded that my primary responsibility belongs to caring for you. I am not one to procrastinate my duty."

"Your duty?" She raised a critical brow.

"My honor," he quickly corrected, her smile instantly reappearing. That smile was everything to him. He couldn't resist and leaned down, capturing her soft mouth with his own. Marriage didn't have to be a man fighting against his desire to love and be loved in return. When done right, it was beautiful. In the month and a half that they had truly spent as man and wife, he had doubted his abilities in a lot of areas—including the way he bumbled his words. He wasn't perfect, and that much was painfully obvious, but he trusted himself with Amie in a way he had never thought possible. The protective instinct that he felt toward her in the beginning of their relationship was the same instinct that assured him of his unwavering loyalty to her. He would never give her reason to doubt him.

He loved this woman in his arms. She completed him. And because of her, he hoped to become a better man. Because progression would always start with him. Any sacrifice or effort was worth it to deserve her.

EPILOGUE

Three Weeks Later

AMIE SET DOWN HER BILLIARD'S cue stick. "You must never let Mama know that you taught me such a *vulgar* sport." She winked at him to show she was teasing. They'd been in Brookeside at Bellmont Manor for several weeks, and Ian had tried to teach her to swim in his pond, had given her archery lessons, and now this.

"As long you never tell my mother either," Ian said, wrapping his arms around her from behind.

Amie nestled back against him. "Have you received a response from Sir Robert Peel yet?"

He shook his head, his chin tickling her neck. "I expect one any day."

"You will need a secretary, you know."

"Undoubtedly."

"I happen to know someone I can recommend."

"Oh? My wife thinks she can stand working with me again? Does this mean I get a kiss after every letter you scribe?"

"Heavens no. *You* will kiss *me*. I don't work for free."

He turned her in his arms. "Can I pay in advance?"

A thrill stole through her, as it always did in anticipation of Ian's kisses. "You most certainly can." They spent nearly all their time together, never tiring of the other's company. Even while with company, they rarely left each other's side. Which was quite the feat considering they had met every tenant family and many in town, thanks to Miles's constant effort to deliver charity baskets to the poor in his parish and Amie's own desire to care for their neighbors.

For so long, she had been passed from house to house, never feeling wanted, never belonging. Those feelings were so distant now, she had nearly forgotten them. Ian hadn't been the only one to accept her, but all the Rebels and their spouses seemed eager to adopt her into their intimate society too.

Ian pressed his lips to hers, and she wrapped her arms around his neck. She relished the feel of his strong arms around her waist and back and grinned on the other side of his kiss. No sooner had this happened than they heard a commotion on the other side of the wall.

Amie quickly pulled back, anxious that someone would catch them in their passionate embrace.

Ian put a finger to her lips but did not fully release her.

Her brow furrowed, but she said nothing.

Voices sounded. Women's voices.

He motioned with his head toward the wall that separated them from the music room. Reluctantly, she followed his noiseless steps to the wall, where the voices became far clearer.

"The walls are thin in this room, so don't say anything you don't want overhead," Ian whispered in her ear before leaving a kiss on her lobe. The touch sent gooseflesh down her arms.

"I'm surprised we are still holding meetings," came a feminine voice through the wall.

"That's Miles's mother, Mrs. Jackson," Ian whispered.

"Indeed. It looks like our work here is done," came another voice.

"And that," he whispered, "is Lady Felcroft, Tom's mother."

Amie frowned. Why were all these women here, and why had no one invited her to join them? For a moment, the sense of being an outsider threatened to overwhelm her. Perhaps she should question her newfound feelings of belonging.

"Good heavens, ladies. Our work is far from done." Here was a voice she could identify. It was her mother-in-law, Lady Kellen.

"There are too many unwed, lonely souls in the world for us to put down Cupid's arrow now."

"So, we will continue our musical club?" a voice that sounded very much like Lisette asked.

"That's Mrs. Manning, Lisette's mother," Ian said a moment later. Amie was proud of herself for guessing so well.

Lady Kellen spoke again. "We meet Tuesday next, and I want everyone to come with a list of names to present. We will vote for our next project."

The women visited for a few moments longer before leaving, but no more was said about lonely souls or impending projects. Their voices slowly faded down the corridors until they were gone.

"What did we just overhear?" she asked Ian.

Ian seemed lost in thought but blinked a few times, then answered her. "That, my darling, was a secret meeting of the Matchmaking Mamas of Brookeside."

"They sounded serious."

He nodded long and slow. "Never underestimate a mother's intuition in discovering the perfect match for her child."

"Trust me," she said. "I won't."

They laughed together, and Ian pulled her toward one of the two chairs in the room. He sat first and tugged her onto his lap. "Before we started playing billiards, you mentioned you had something to speak to me about. What was it?"

"Yes, I did," she hedged.

"And? Are my mother's machinations scaring you?"

"Though I wonder who they will match next, this is something quite different."

"Go ahead."

She swallowed. "Remember how I teased you when you were holding baby Katie a few weeks ago?"

"Ah, yes. You were concerned that our future children would inherit some of our best family traits."

She giggled. "Well, I was merely testing the waters until I was certain."

"Certain of what?"

She stared into his sky-blue eyes brimming with love, and her smile wobbled. "Certain that I was with child."

Those same cerulean eyes widened considerably. "You're . . . you're with child?"

"It's still early, but when I went to Town yesterday with Cassandra, I stopped in and saw her doctor."

His arm tightened around her. "Are you well?"

"My symptoms are typical. He assured me that both the baby and I are healthy."

"The baby," he breathed, his hand falling to her middle with wonder. "I can hardly believe it."

"I know it's soon. Our marriage is so young, and our family is already growing." It was hard to explain her nerves . . . her anxiety to know if he approved. They had come so far, but each of them was still overcoming their past struggles.

He drew her ever closer. "It's going to be wonderful, Amie. You're a natural at taking care of everyone around you. I have no doubt you will be the best mother."

She had meant to reassure him, yet his words eased her. The sheer happiness in his expression and perfect assuredness in his voice brought a smile to her lips. Cupping his face in her hand, she said with equal fervor, "You have a way of making a person feel safe, protected, and cared for. You will be an ideal father."

Ian grinned, his eyes beaming. "Thank you, darling, for always believing in me. But you know it will be easier if he or she takes after you."

"I will be sure to pass that along."

He chuckled, reaching up and placing his hand behind her neck, his thumb gently caressing the skin there. "Just one more request. It is imperative that you join the town's musical club straightaway. I don't want our baby to get the last pickings for a spouse."

Her laugh was silenced with Ian's celebratory kiss. She relished every second in his arms. Moments like this were worth being engaged to a dead man or all the humiliatingly sleepless nights from warm milk. All that they had endured had brought them to this moment. They were growing a family now. Marriage to Ian had been a gift from heaven itself, and having his child would be the greatest privilege of her life. She had never been happier.

AUTHOR'S NOTE

MY CHARACTERS ARE NEVER PERFECT, but their growth and experiences inspire me. I have loved writing these Rebels, intent on making a difference in the world, and seeing them rise above their weaknesses to be better people. And while I know there are strong opinions about how much parents should meddle in the lives of their children, these fictional Matchmaking Mamas enchanted me from the beginning. I hope you felt the familial love come through the pages.

One of my favorite scenes of the book is Ian and Amie's wedding. Unfortunately, some of my research was contradicting. Traditionally, a father figure would walk the bride down the aisle, but in the Regency Era, the bride might have walked alone or beside her future husband. In the 1662, 1789, 1892 Book of Common Prayer, a ring is blessed and given to the bride, but other sources say that rings were not always part of the wedding ceremony in the early 1800s. This could be because of financial constraints or traditions based on the area. I took a few liberties to create my scene based on these varied conclusions, such as including kissing, which was not part of the Anglican ceremony but not unheard of either.

Many times while writing Ian and Amie's story, I thought, *How did I get here? Why am I writing about early-nineteenth-century criminal law? This isn't the stuff of cozy romances!* By the time I wrote the end, I had a different perspective. Real romance is about two characters supporting and lifting each other through the hard times and the good. It's about connection and hope. To fully understand the character growth that brought Ian and Amie together, we had to include what was happening in the backdrop of their lives.

There's a lot I don't know about this era, even after a bazillion hours of research. By definition, *bazillion* means "an exaggerated number," and it feels entirely accurate in this case. I did my best to represent what might have crossed the minds of those who were pushing for this vote and those who would have to receive the altered law. If anyone is interested, you can read the actual transcript in the House of Commons in which Sir James Mackintosh makes his case for change, and you can see the vote tally. Records of trials are also available at the Old Bailey, including a summary of the crimes and what the sentencings were.

I am a big proponent for not judging history too harshly, but I cannot sufficiently thank the men who spent years and years of their lives fighting for causes such as this one. It was an uphill battle, full of opposition, yet they persevered until they won the fight. We owe so much to these imperfect individuals whose sacrifice and diligence gave us a better world.

Ian first became impassioned to alter the criminal law when he rescued a young lady guilty of stealing. This is based off a record of a young woman who stole a large amount of pork and later hanged for it. I also mentioned the execution of a boy at the age of thirteen. This was not based on any one person, but there were children even younger than this who were executed during the extended period in which the Bloody Code reigned as England's criminal law. I don't encourage any sensitive souls to research it. Let my tears be enough for the both of us!

I hope you enjoyed this story and were reminded that each of us has the power to change ourselves and influence the world for good. God bless you in your efforts!

ACKNOWLEDGMENTS

EACH STORY IS A JOURNEY, and I'm so thankful for a loving Heavenly Father who led me through this one.

Readers, thank you for loving this series and begging for this last book! You motivated me to keep typing even when the sunshine was telling me to go out and play. A special thank you to my early readers: Sarah McConkie, Mandy Biesinger, Jill Warner, Rebecca Connolly, Heather Okeson, and Taylor Riddoch. As well as my awesome critique group: Sally Britton, Mindy Strunk, Laura Rollins, Laura Beers, and Heidi Kimball. I love you all!

To the incredible team at Shadow Mountain, thank you for polishing Ian and Amie's story and making it into something truly beautiful. I am honored to work with you!

I owe a debt of gratitude to my family for their unfailing support. They see all the sides to this publishing journey and keep cheering me on. Jonny, you're the hero in my story, and you and the children are my happily ever after. Love you always!